HELEN DUNMORE

Your Blue-eyed Boy

PENGUIN BOOKS

To Ollie

PENGUIN BOOKS

Published by the Penguin Group
Penguin Books Ltd, 80 Strand, London WC2R 0RL, England
Penguin Putnam Inc., 375 Hudson Street, New York, New York 10014, USA
Penguin Books Australia Ltd, 250 Camberwell Road, Camberwell, Victoria 3124, Australia
Penguin Books Canada Ltd, 10 Alcorn Avenue, Toronto, Ontario, Canada M4V 3B2
Penguin Books India (P) Ltd, 11 Community Centre, Panchsheel Park, New Delhi – 110 017, India
Penguin Books (NZ) Ltd, Cnr Rosedale and Airborne Roads, Albany, Auckland, New Zealand
Penguin Books (South Africa) (Pty) Ltd, 24 Sturdee Avenue, Rosebank 2196, South Africa

Penguin Books Ltd, Registered Offices: 80 Strand, London WC2R 0RL, England

www.penguin.com

First published by Viking 1998
Published in Penguin Books 1999
This special sales edition published 2003
1

Set in Monotype Garamond
Printed in England by Clays Ltd, St Ives plc

Prologue

There are things you should know about blackmail, in case it comes tapping at your door. There's what it does to you, and then there's what it makes you do. I used to think I knew what I could be made to do.

Blackmail doesn't work the way I always thought it would, if I ever gave it a thought. It doesn't smash through the clean pane of a life like a stone through a window. It's always an inside job, the most intimate of crimes. Somebody in the house has left that little window open, just a snick. The person who leaves the window open doesn't know why. Or else doesn't want to know. From outside a hand reaches up into the gap, and the window creaks wide. Cold air comes rushing in. I see that hand now, each time I shut my eyes to sleep. Sometimes it's heavy and alien, the hand of a stranger. I can count the hairs on the knuckles. But on other nights I feel the fingers move and I know they are my own.

You have to search for the person who left the window open, down all the alleys of yourself. In the end you'll get there. You'll learn how you betrayed yourself in the moment that seemed like any other moment.

When blackmail comes into your house you can learn to live with it, feeding it as little as you dare, trying to guess what it will take to make it go away before it gets too big. Then you begin to realize that it will never go away. The more you feed it, the stronger it grows. *Why should you feel guilty, unless you've got something to hide? Why should you be afraid? Watch me shake out your life in front of you. You know what's in there, don't you? See what comes.*

Some blackmailers just want money. That's frightening, but

at least you know where you are, and that a wad of used money is what you are talking about. I haven't got money.

The others put on pressure without letting you know what they want. They steer you where you don't want to go, but in a way that's so intimate you have to give in. They know more about you than you know about yourself. The pressure comes from what they don't say. They wait and wait until you can't wait any more, and you'll do anything to know why they've come. It begins to seem like freedom.

When blackmail comes tapping at the door, get up and open it. There'll be no one there. Just the yawn of a black night, with wind in it but no stars. Already there's wind hurrying through the house, licking the back of your knees as you stare out. Where's it coming from? That window at the back. Someone's round there already and through the slender gap like an eel. Already the curtains are whipping up, the doors are buckling, and the floorboards pitch and toss like the planks of a boat.

The wind blows harder and your house begins to move on a sea that was always there, beneath the crust of the land. And you're afraid, but you are beginning to move with it.

One

It's the end of the season now, and the summer visitors are gone, shaping up to their city lives. Some of them come to Annassett each year, and believe they're part of the place, but that's not so. As soon as they slam their car doors and drive away, they're forgotten. The sea closes over the splash they've made.

Now the most perfect days begin, so few that you can weigh each one of them in your hand like a new-laid egg. The nights are cool and the mornings misty, because the sea is warmer than the land. The mist carries a tang of autumn, until the sun strengthens and burns it away. The evenings are bluer now, the sun ripe and yellow as a pear. At the store there are no queues, and there's conversation again, lazy and convalescent. The days smell of dried seaweed and tar and anti-fouling paint and new sweet wood planed away in long shavings. There's the whine of a drill, the steady rasp of the plane. Simone sits back on her heels on the dock and watches Michael as he applies paint in long, supple strokes. He's repainting the cabin exterior on the Boesaks' cabin cruiser. The Boesaks are back in New York. Michael sweeps the brush, and Simone listens to the sound it makes, like the lick of a rough tongue. She shivers, though it is warm in the pool of sun where she sits. The boat, the heat, the smell of paint: it all belongs to them now. She squints and watches the muscles in Michael's forearm. He is precise. A fine workman; he has that reputation. He turns to look at her. Sunlight is getting onto the water now, making it dance. He shades his eyes with the hand that doesn't hold the brush. Does he smile? Maybe he smiles. He turns back to his work. She watches him. His hair has slipped forward round his face. If she was nearer she would smell the sun on him, his sweat and the T-shirt she brought in from the porch rail that morning, damp, but he put it on anyway. It smelled of night air.

Michael's got plenty of work lined up for the winter. People from the city ask him why he stays here in Annassett. It's beautiful and they love it, but a little place like this must be dead in winter. And most of the young people move away. Kids go to college and they don't come back. Michael looks up at them from whatever he's doing, though his hands don't stop their work.

'I already went away. That's why I'm back,' he says, and then usually they don't ask any more, because they know a bit of the story. It's their story too. They watch the way his hands move and they want Michael working on their boat, not anyone else.

The season's nearly over. There's time for the jobs that can't be done when the boats are out every day. The privately owned boats, and the fishing boats and tourist boats that have to be out all day long during the summer months, making the money to last the winter. In the mornings Simone's bare legs are cold as she runs down to the boathouse.

Everybody's going home, but not Simone. She'll stay on through the apple season and the pumpkin season, waiting until the rowing-boats are hauled up on shore and the boathouse is padlocked. She tucks her feet under her. She sighs. There is the dock with its pale, washed-out wood, the sea that scarcely moves but glistens like a great creature that has risen up to breathe. If she looks close she will see its flanks moving. It is full of fish, and whales that pass without stopping, far out to sea, going south. Is that true? She doesn't know what's true any more, only what Michael has told her.

*

4

The work is over. It's night, and they are in the boathouse, stretched out on the faded orange canvas cushions Michael's shoved together to make their bed. They couldn't walk as far as the cabin. He's stretched beside her, his long hair sliding down his face as he sleeps. His body jerks. One hand thumps on the cushion, and then goes still. A shudder runs through his flesh. It's like this every night. His face clenches and he cries out to people who aren't here or anywhere any more. She won't tell him about it in the morning, because he doesn't want to know. Sometimes he calls out names, but to Simone they are just words.

Simone leans over Michael. She sees the sheen on his face, caught by the thin moonlight that comes through the boathouse door. She catches the sharp, animal stink of his night sweat. She listens to the waves cluck against the stones outside in the dark. Tide's up. It'll be dawn soon. The wind is gathering, as it often does just before dawn. It pushes at the water, rocks the boats, sets up ringing in the masts, and a nervous slapping of water against the hulls.

She lies back. They stumbled in here last night. They knew they wouldn't get as far as the cabin. Her legs were shaking and she could barely stand. They'd drunk a jug of white wine but it wasn't that. They'd been standing down on the shore, on the edge of the water, watching the blackness of it before the moon came up. She felt the land prickling at her back, and thought that if she turned round there wouldn't be anything left that she knew. No dock, no boathouse, no clumps of light where the town was, no straggle of lights along the bay and around to the point. There would be nothing. The land would be furred by forest, and in the forest the ancient Indian towns would sleep with their crops around them, alive and breathing. The hugeness of the land crept up on her like grandmother's footsteps. She was cold, though they stood close together by the edge of the water, like one body.

*

Simone is cold now. She thinks of the heat of the night, the wet, slippery channels of their flesh, his cries. But sometimes in the morning he acts as if none of it ever happens. She sighs but doesn't move, because she'll do anything rather than wake him.

By noon it's warm. Michael has his hand on her thigh.

'C'mon, Simone,' he says. 'Don't be this way.'

The boathouse door is open, looking out onto a white square of sea and sky. Pasted across the square of light is the outline of a man's body, long lean legs, skinny torso, hands fondling a small black box. Calvin. He was meant to be in Boston the whole week, but he came back at ten o'clock that morning. He can't leave them alone. Like Michael, Calvin is ten years older than Simone. They graduated from high school together the same year. Bright boys, could have been college boys. They had everything it takes. But they went to Vietnam, and now they stay here through the summers and the dead winters, hiring themselves out to the city people and their boats.

Eight-year-old Simone watched them on TV. Or if not them, close enough to make no matter. She watched them run. Every night she saw the map that told the world where they were. She watched rows of kids surge at the camera on college campuses as they protested the draft. She always turned the TV up as loud as she dared. TV was a blanket, and she wrapped herself up in it while her mother's quick tread snapped the air in the background. Her mother walked fast from room to room, checking, switching the lights on then letting back the dark. She had to see the things in the rooms in order to believe they were still there. The TV blared and Simone crouched with her sister, colouring in homework maps of Britain in Roman times, not really watching.

Now Simone believes it is wrong to see so much and understand so little. But it's the way things are, since Vietnam. The world is scabbed with TV wars. Dimly she recalls kids with flowers, offering them to the barrels of guns. She does not like to say anything. It is Michael's war, and Calvin's, not hers. They went to war in front of the cameras. They could not make history in the dark. When they brought their story home people looked at them and said, *We already know*. And they didn't want to know any more.

'We didn't protest the war,' says Michael.

'No sir,' says Calvin. 'We registered for the draft.'

They look at Simone and smile.

'Why didn't we?' asks Calvin.

'There ain't no time to wonder why,' says Michael.

Often she thinks he's telling her something, but then she finds out he is only quoting a song she doesn't know. The thing about being ten years younger is that for her all the music is different. And them being Americans makes a difference too. She'll do anything to hide that difference. She's learned to listen, to smile and say nothing. She's their girl. They like it when she says in her English voice, 'Would you like some coffee?' then makes it and curls up quiet as a cat on the plank boathouse floor. They talk about music and grass and who Calvin would like to fuck. Once Simone saw them watching a girl walk across the beach. She wore a blue bikini and she had a sheet of shining black hair that caught the wind and flew straight out behind her. Simone cleared her throat and said, 'Hasn't she got lovely hair?'

'Oh yeah,' mimicked Calvin. '*Lovely hair*. Just what I was looking at. Ain't that just what you were looking at too, man?' And Michael laughed. He was always doing this to her when Calvin was around. As if the bond with Calvin was too tight to make room for Simone. He would look at Simone as if she was one of the visitors too and he was waiting for her to go away, leaving things here the way they'd always been. But it didn't matter, because when it was just the two of them together, Michael and Simone, he was back to himself.

He could have done anything he wanted. So could Calvin. But they stay here and they don't go to college, though they could run a fucking ring round most of those Ivy League kids. They say they're too old to leave Annassett now. They're twenty-eight years old.

'Why don't you go?' asks Simone, maternal. Calvin looks out at the sea and the bobbing boats and says, 'I like it here. It's pretty.' And he grins, but it is Michael he's looking at, not Simone.

Michael doesn't say he likes it here. When an owl cries, out of the wood, he tells Simone it's a barn owl. He shows her the tracery of Indian walls buried in milkweed and poison ivy. Once when they were fishing he pointed through the slumberous depths of the pond. She saw nothing.

'Come here. You're not getting it, that's the way the light bends.'

Suddenly she saw a great fish peel away from shadow and coast through the water.

'Trout. They grow big here.'

His hand was warm and tight on her shoulder, burning through the thin cotton of her T-shirt as she leant out to watch the fish slide back into its hole.

'Have you ever caught one that big?' she asked.

'Yeah.'

They watched the fish until it turned back into a shadow and disappeared. Michael began to talk, his voice light in her ear.

'I had a dream last night. I dreamed about this little kid.'

'Who?' she asked quickly, wanting him not to tell her. She was afraid of his dreams.

'There was this little kid used to hang around us while we played basketball. He was always there. Big eyes staring at everyone, never said anything. All the kids hated him. We passed the ball and it would always be way up over his head. He'd jump as high as he could but he'd never get to touch it. Somebody'd laugh, then we'd all be laughing at him, tipping the ball down low so he'd nearly get a touch then whipping it up in the air again. You should have seen that ball move. We never got ball control like that any other time, only when the kid was there. He never cried, just kept on jumping up.

'One day this big guy, Jimmie Walsh, finally got tired of it. He came to the game with a packing-case. None of us knew what it was for. After we'd been playing a while and the kid kept on jumping, Jimmie took the packing-case over to the basketball hoop. Then he grabbed the kid and swung him up in the air and climbed onto the packing-case, holding him. He stuffed the kid through the basketball hoop. He just about fit. You'd think his weight would tear the ring off the wall, but it didn't. "Come on, you guys," Jimmie said, and we all followed him. I looked back and the kid still wasn't crying. Just hanging there with those black eyes like bubbles staring after us. Jimmie didn't say a thing and none of the rest of us opened our mouths.'

'How old was he?'

'We were all about twelve, I guess.'

'I mean the little boy.'

I think he isn't going to answer, then he moistens his lips and says, 'Six. About six.'

'But it wasn't you who did it. It was Jimmie Walsh.'

'But I liked it. When Jimmie did those things, it gave me a warm feeling. A sexy feeling. That's why I hung around with him, because I knew he would do those things and give me those feelings. You don't work it out like that when you're a kid, but that was the way it was.'

They were both quiet. Sun splashed through thick leaves, onto the surface of the pond, making patterns that hid what was there in the water.

'Did you go back?' she asked suddenly.

He stooped, picked up a stone, let it fall in the deep water. The ripples rocked then seemed to swallow themselves, to make the pond still again.

'Yeah,' he said. 'He's still in the basketball hoop, right? Slipping down with his own weight and it's getting tight. And he's scared now, but I think he's trying not to make a noise in case we come back. Those big bug eyes staring at me. Even more scared now I'd come back. And I got up on the packing-case and I tried to lift him out of there but I couldn't. He was too heavy. And I wasn't as tall as Jimmie Walsh. I'd haul him up and he'd slip down and each time it would be harder to pull him up again, out of the hoop. Then he started making this little noise like he couldn't hold it in any more. I looked at his face and it was twisted up and there was stuff bubbling out of his nose. He didn't know why I was lifting him up. It was like he believed I wanted to – '

Michael paused.

'You were trying to help him, but he didn't know it,' said Simone.

'Yeah, well,' said Michael. 'I guess he saw it another way. Fuck it. Why would I think of it after all this time?'

The camera. Calvin lifts the camera.

'Hey, man, lemme get my jeans on,' protests Michael. There is a thin grey blanket over Michael and Simone. It has slipped down over Simone's breasts but she is too embarrassed to pull it up again. Besides, she's used to Calvin coming in like this.

'Good picture,' says Calvin, squinting at the viewfinder. '*Go-ood* picture.'

Simone sneaks a glance at Michael. He's smiling, enjoying this.

'You got flash on that thing, man?' he asks.

'Sure. You want me to take some pictures?'

'What do you think?' Michael asks, turning to Simone with that look of false, teasing solicitude that only comes on his face when Calvin is here. 'You'll be going back home to England soon, won't you? How about some pictures to take back with you?'

Simone opens her mouth. Just in time, she stops herself from bleating out, 'I'm not going back' in front of Calvin. Calvin mustn't see what Simone hopes for. She pictures the winter wind flailing round the cabin in town, a fire lit and Michael striding in. He shakes the snow off his shoulders, his face softening as he sees Simone stitching his shirt-buttons on, the lamp-light a pool of melting gold on her hair. His voice is charged, husky.

'Simone –'

The two of them, the closed door. Nightmare relaxing into dream.

Calvin knows nothing. He doesn't hear Michael at night, roused from nightmare, clutching at her hair, her breasts.

Simone says nothing. She pleats the edge of the blanket and waits for Michael.

'Yeah,' he says, 'yeah.' He reaches over Simone, and takes the edge of the blanket. Slowly, looking her straight in the eye, he peels back the blanket.

'Michael!' she protests, snapping her legs together. But he pulls the blanket right away to the other side of their bed.

'Cool,' says Calvin. 'That's cool.' His spidery outline dances over them. The snout of the camera protrudes this way and that. 'You look beautiful, man.'

A little stringent part of Simone comes to life, wonders if this is singular or plural, then dies down again to the dormancy where it's spent the whole summer. The camera probes the white triangle that Michael's swimming shorts don't cover. The stir of his genitals. Their flesh touching, thigh to thigh. Simone rolls a little sideways to present the safe hairless curve of the classic nude. Calvin is much too close now, on top of them. The camera flashes, blue and white. She flinches, expecting a sound, a crackle like thunder.

'Relax, baby. Relax,' says Michael. He rolls her back. The camera shoots again and again. Suddenly Michael coils and gets up, stands beside Calvin. 'Lemme see, man.' Calvin passes him the camera, and Michael peers at the viewfinder. Simone flinches. Calvin is making Michael see what he sees.

'You need to get closer,' says Calvin.

'No closer,' says Simone.

'Please baby. Listen. It's OK if it's me taking the pictures, hunh?' wheedles Michael.

Calvin folds his arms, watching, as Michael takes the camera and kneels down in front of Simone.

'What do I do, Cal? Do I press here?'

'You gotta change the focus first.'

The two men kneel, intent on the gadget.

'I got it. Hey, relax. It's me, remember? Come on. You're so beautiful,' he croons. 'You're a beautiful chick, Simone. Give me a good shot now.'

She hates the language, the language of Michael and Calvin. But his voice melts her. She's yielding, giving way, spreading her legs for him like she always does. Calvin's nothing now but a shape in the background, out of focus. The camera flares but this time she doesn't flinch.

'That's it,' says Michael. 'That's the reel finished.'

Two

I take off my wig and settle it into the shiny box with my name on it, then clip the box shut, reach into the cupboard and put it on the top shelf. My head feels cool and light. I look into the mirror as I comb out my hair. The wig has crushed it flat, so that for a moment my mother's face peeps back at me. I reach up again, take out the wig, re-settle it on my head. It fits perfectly. It should do. All the measuring we did, following the wig-maker's diagrams.

'They haven't changed this leaflet in fifty years,' Donald said, poring over it, 'except to give the measurements in centimetres.' We stared at the illustrated head. It was lofty, trustworthy, like a phrenologist's advertisement. Not a familiar head at all.

'That's because it's completely symmetrical,' Donald said. 'No human head is like that. Come over here by the mirror and I'll measure you.'

We had a piece of squared paper and the maker's instructions. Donald measured me from nape to crown, from crown to chin, over temple and forehead. The tape tickled as it ran over my nose. Donald jotted down each measurement and then read them back to me.

'It sounds a lot,' I said.

'It's in centimetres, that's why.'

'Or maybe I have a huge head. Do it again to be sure. It's so expensive if we make a mistake.'

The measurements were not quite the same the second time.

'It's the tape,' Donald said, 'it's been in your sewing-box for ever. Look how worn it is. Why do we never have decent scissors or tape-measures in this house? And those bloody boys have taken my masking tape again. I wouldn't mind if they ever did anything sensible with it.'

'It doesn't matter,' I said, 'as long as it fits more or less. As long as it doesn't fall off.' But Donald frowned and compared the figures again. He was always more exact than I was. 'It's your hair that's the problem as well,' he said. 'I'm not sure how much I should press down your hair to get the measurements right. These measurements will be geared to men. Their hair won't be as thick as yours. That's what the wig-maker will be allowing for.'

I slicked my hair flat with both hands. 'I'll hold it down while you measure again.'

'But that won't be how you wear it in court.'

His face was very close to me. His skin was fine but I saw the wear on it, the way it crinkled dryly when he frowned. Donald would go on for an hour or more to get the measurements right, and I was tired standing. Since the boys had been born I'd been able to walk any distance but I found it hard to stand still long in one place.

'Just do it once more and split the difference,' I said.

He ran the tape round my head, pinched it still with a finger and read off the measurement. Then he looked straight at me in the mirror and smiled.

'I never thought I'd be measuring my wife for a wig,' he said. His smile was too open, too fond. It was like hearing him talk of me on the phone, with simple pleasure in his voice. 'Yes, she's pretty tired. She's still getting on top of the job. But she says it's all going well . . .' From the next room I would hear the pride and buoyancy in his voice. And then when we turned to one another there was such dark water between us. I looked away.

'Wait till you see it,' I said.

'What do they make it out of?'

14

'Horse-hair, I think. It feels like that. There's an art to it, that's why there are only these two places that make them.'

'It should be good,' said Donald. 'It costs enough.'

I shut my mouth and let him measure down to my chin again. I was not going to say, 'You don't need to worry about that. I'm the one paying for it.'

When the wig came I would have liked to go off by myself to try it on and get used to my face under it, but the boys were there, and Donald too. I unpacked it and held it up. It had tight rolls of horsehair riding on a dense scalp. It looked like an old drag queen's perm. My family crowded round and Matt snatched up the wig, saying he was going to be the first to try it. Donald took it away from him.

'Put it on, Simone. Let's see what it looks like.'

I was wearing jeans and a yellow T-shirt. I knew how the wig would look above them. 'No,' I said, 'I'll try it later.'

Donald held the thing above my head like a crown. The boys laughed, egging him on. We could have a scene, or I could put the wig on at once, as if it didn't matter.

'There,' I said, settling it on my head. My glance skinned the mirror. The tight band of the wig pressed my forehead and I wondered if Donald had done the measurements right, after all. The boys were staring at me. There was laughter in their faces still, but something else as well.

'Jesus, Mum,' said Matt, 'you look like –'

'Don't say Jesus,' said Donald automatically.

I looked straight into the mirror. My face stared back at me, knowing, severe, aloof. I was of any gender and any time. I was the judge.

'A judge,' went on Matt.

'That's what she is,' said my husband, but a faint astonishment coloured his voice. I smiled, then I let my face settle again. This face had no need to please. The wig got rid of my softness,

15

the softness that makes people smile back at me when I'm not aware I'm even smiling.

'Only a district judge,' I said.

'Take it off,' said Joe. 'Put it back in the box.'

'Why?' I asked him. His eight-year-old face creased with effort, then he said, 'Don't wear it at home, Mum. Keep it at work.'

I knew what he meant. 'It's all right,' I said. 'It's not something I'll be wearing about the house.' Matt muttered something into Joe's ear and the pair of them began to choke and spurt, farting out laughter.

'Go on out,' said Donald.

I touched the wig with my fingers, feeling the tightness and springiness of the curls. They were fixed in shape and they would never unwind.

'It suits you,' Donald said. 'You look good.'

It annoyed me that he talked of the wig as if I'd brought home a new pair of jeans. I knew why he did it. He was afraid of where I was going, away from him. He was afraid of the money I was making, and he wasn't. He was afraid of the door shutting on him and the children and me walking away with the wig in its box under my arm, to a world of judgments. The outer world where he'd lost his place. I knew how he felt though I never let him know that I knew. I wasn't sure if he'd realized yet that he might never go back. That work might not ever come back, or the lunches with clients, or the freedom to ring home and say he would be late. He was working from home, that's what we said. It was only that things were slow. The recession was going on and on. It was better to keep some illusion between us.

'Judge not,' said Donald, 'lest ye be judged.'

I looked at him. I knew he had opened his mouth and the words had come out without him thinking of them. They came from somewhere deep inside that I didn't share.

'You got the measurements right,' I said. We looked at each other: I in my wig, Donald with his brown hair that was nearly all grey now. I thought of how he'd had to fill in some form recently that asked for colour of eyes and colour of hair. And unhesitatingly he'd written 'brown'. It wasn't vanity, it was just he didn't think about himself enough to know that he'd changed. Or so I'd thought as I glanced over his shoulder.

We'd been together so long now that whatever we did out in the world it couldn't break the conspiracy between us, I thought, smiling at Donald in the mirror as I took off the wig and ran my fingers through my own hair to feel that it was still soft and alive. When I'd met Donald my hair had been down to my waist. Like all men he'd wanted me to keep it that way, even when I knew I wasn't young enough to wear my hair long any more. He always put his hands in it while he slept at my back, as if he was washing the day off them in my hair. I'd liked it for a long time and then I had stopped liking it.

Now my hair was cut to the level of my chin. I was in that stage of youngishness which seems as if it'll go on for ever, but I knew from other women how quickly and suddenly it can end. And then it seemed as if women entered a climate of invisibility. I would go out to meet that end. I'd wear the wig and no lipstick. I would be the judge. If I grew pouched and heavy, it would only add to the command in my face. I could go on for ever, almost. I was thirty-eight years old.

I hang my gown on the hook inside the door, and brush down my skirt and jacket with the flat of my hands. The cupboard smells of new, blonde wood. As its door swings the little mirror inside fills with blue sky and a brief dazzle of midday sun, then empties again to show my face. I am smiling. My face is soft. I lean in close to the glass, and pick a speck of mascara out of the corner of my eye with my forefinger. I am the face of the law here. It's nothing personal.

17

The first time I noticed the clerk of the court move back against the wall to let me pass I wondered what on earth he was doing. He had his arms spread against the wall as if to make more room. I smiled at him, then I realized that he was giving way to me because now I was the judge. It was nothing to do with me. An abstract respect for an abstract thing which was walking in and out of this courtroom in the temporary outfit of my flesh. You have to understand that right from the start or you fall in love with yourself, as I've seen some judges do. Not my sort of judge, not little district judges who handle the small cases. We are only doctors in surgery, watching the minor ills of the world pass in and out and trying to decide what to do for the best. And slowly coming to realize that we can't do all that much, no matter what judgment we give. But there are some High Court judges who can't separate themselves from the deference. They get as itchy for attention as old actors. They test their power by seeing how much people will put up with. And then add to that the odd one who dreams of a comeback in the greatest role of all, black cap on head, pronouncing life or death.

When I was first in court and frightened, I used to imagine the judge clipping his toenails. Can you imagine sitting in a shop window to have your toenails cut? It's much more personal than having your hair washed. You'd have to know someone pretty well before you'd let them see that little pile of horny yellow clippings, like rind.

You watch the judge. I used to watch that shifting and clenching of the buttocks during a long sitting, which probably meant he had piles. And now I suppose people are doing the same to me, trying to look past the wig and find a human being inside.

I'm in chambers all afternoon, starting with a bankruptcy petition. I don't like bankruptcies. This is where people end up when they've gone through the hoop, to have the stamp put on them. *Bankrupt* has a terrible sound to most people, though for some it's a matter of getting it over, waiting three years and starting again. Sometimes I see them looking at me while we pick over the wreck of borrowing and hoping and not quite getting enough time and creditors starting to press. It has a slow-motion quality, like an accident you've already had in your dreams. But no matter how slow, it can't be stopped. They look at me as if they're helpless to put that landslide of debt into words. Or they look at me if to say *What does she know?* They think I've had it easy. The sharper ones guess it's probably been made even easier for me, because there's pressure to get women into the judiciary now. But most of them don't think anything. It's as much as they can do to get through this, the petition for bankruptcy against them. They've charged themselves up to come here, and there's a strange relief in it too, that the terrible thing they've sweated over night after night is actually happening.

Two weeks ago a man looked at me at the end of the hearing. He cleared his throat, then he said, 'I'm sorry.' He wore a tidy dark suit, like the suit a haulage contractor might wear to Mass on Sunday. He was big in his suit. He would have worked for other men for years before he was able to start up on his own. For years it had gone well. The business had expanded, and he'd moved to a bigger house. Then when things started to slip, and he'd have liked to sell the house to get hold of some of the money that was tied up in it, there weren't any buyers. By the time he could sell it was all owed to the bank anyway, and more.

He wasn't one of those who can put the blame elsewhere and hold tight to the thought of starting again in a few years, when things pick up. To him, it was a disgrace. You could see it in the way he stood and listened to what was being said. He had very bright blue eyes. I knew that he was forty-seven, but apart from those eyes he looked much more. He still had years to go, with this on top of him, pressing him down. If he was lucky he could get back to working for someone else, but looking at him I doubted it. There was still assurance in his body, as if it didn't yet know what his mind knew. He was braced to cope with the bankruptcy hearing, not with what lay beyond it.

It doesn't take very long. When I'd made the order and it was over, he should have gone out of the room after the usher, but he didn't. He cleared his throat and stood there and said, 'I'm sorry.' I think his voice came out louder than he meant it to do. He wasn't speaking to the solicitor for the other side or even to me. It was something in him that could not bend to what had happened, that kept on taking responsibility even when all the responsibility had been taken away from him. He was the kind of man whose wife would never have had to sign a cheque. She'd have to, now. I was afraid of what would happen when he got home.

I calmed myself. It was nothing to do with me, and he didn't want my sympathy. I was the instrument, making the order, that was all. I nodded as if to acknowledge anything that he might want me to acknowledge. When he'd gone I closed my eyes for a few seconds and thought of a white blank wall. Then I allowed the next case to flood in on top of the blankness.

Another packed list today. Five more minutes, and the usher will start sending them in. The minutes always seem elastic when they're about to run out, as if you could do anything you want in them. And no room is ever more private than this one becomes, when I know someone's about to open the door.

It's too hot to eat. I open a can of Coke and drink it straight from the can, though it's tepid now. It was ice-cold when it clunked out of the machine in the garage on the way here, I love that sweat of cold on my hand. I never drink Coke at home. I'm always trying to get the kids to drink tap-water, or squash at least, telling them it will rot their teeth if they drink cans. But they have iron-hard fluoride teeth, not like mine. I wonder if I've got a rim around my mouth. Better check.

'You don't look like a judge.' I can't remember who said that. It could have been any one of my friends, and they are right. There is no severity in my face, but I wonder how many of the faces that look into this mirror have fought as hard to be here as I have. I have the gift of not marking easily, that's all, or not seeming to mark.

There are footsteps in the corridor, quick but never light. Someone else's disgrace, walking rapidly towards them.

Three

Most days I get up early, while the house is silent. I slide out of bed and into jeans and a heavy sweater. I work, or I go out and walk across the fields to the sea. The world feels private then. I like the chill of morning, and the quiet sea. Sometimes I see a ferry sliding past on the horizon, with its lights still on. There will be people looking out of their portholes and seeing the low line of the land. They'll yawn, say to themselves that there's nothing worth seeing yet, and lie back in their bunks.

But when you get to know them you could look at the marshes for ever. They are full of secrets. They look as if they lie open to the sky, offering everything, but they don't. You have to live with them day by day, through the changes of light and water and sky and wind. Suddenly you realize you don't know them at all. You're just at the outside edge, perhaps, of beginning to know something.

We are two miles outside the village, and the sounds come to me one by one, slow enough to count. A tractor coughs, then settles into heavy noise as it comes down the lane, stops by the gate, and passes through, dragging a trailer for the sheep which are going to market this morning. The sky is a broken ripple of cloud. It's too clear, it'll rain later. I love the sound of rain falling around this house.

Donald doesn't like it. The boys don't either. They hated me for dragging us all here, away from the city and everything they knew. They didn't know our reasons.

'I won't get this chance again,' I told them. 'If I don't go for this job, I might not get another.' The boys watched us packing up and making phone calls and being busy, and they never seemed to catch the smell of our fear. Donald was afraid, we were both afraid. As soon as I saw this house I wanted to be here, with all the light around me. I was leaving the city and the place where both the children had been born. I didn't want to have to walk past my old life every day.

This house is stone, and it's cold. We haven't put in heating yet. We got through one winter without it, and we can get through another. There is so much debt. Our last house was loaded with debt, mortgaged and then remortgaged. We'd sold everything, gone through all those bits of savings which are meant to see you through bad times. We were lucky: we were able to get a new mortgage on the strength of my new job. This house is in my name only. We had to do it, because of the debts in Donald's name. We can't take the risk. But he hates it. It makes him feel as if he's not at home here.

The boys had an electric heater in their room last winter. I told them they could switch it on for an hour before they went to bed, and half an hour in the morning. There are no carpets upstairs, but I took up the linoleum and scrubbed the boards. They are warm, wide planks of pine. We had open fires downstairs. We are paying our debts, though it's like running against the tide. The bank takes so much; the interest I can handle, but not the charges for every letter, every review, every meeting with a bank manager who isn't competent to do anything on his own authority anyway. I feel so angry. I'm not angry in my head, I'm angry in my body. It feels intimate, this pawing over of our finances, like a sexual humiliation.

Every time I walk on the beach I bring back driftwood for the fires. There's a stack of it now under a tarpaulin, at the side of the house. Some of it is white as bone, and there are planks and great knotted tree-trunks which the sea tosses up as lightly as lolly-sticks when there's a storm. We don't get much muck around here. Not too many indestructible plastic tampon applicators, or condoms. The water is grey, cold, salty.

I can't concentrate on my work this morning. I go to the window, kneel down, lean my elbows on the low sill. The flood of white light is so bright that I blink. We could be far out at sea ourselves. All summer I've heard the ewes and lambs calling to one another. The lambs are born late down here. The sheep are shorn late, too. The marsh is bleak and bare and the wind blows all winter long. It snatches your breath as you come out of the house. It makes your skin burn.

We can't see the sea from here, because the rising lip of sea-wall cuts it off. Beyond the sea-wall there's a ragged, pebbly beach. There's no road to it, so no one comes. If you look closely, you see that the grass at the edge of the beach is studded with speedwell and pimpernel, among the straw and flotsam. I walk there most days, with the sea on one side and the wall on the other. All the land here is below sea-level.

Here comes the rain. If I hurry, I've got time for a swim.

Donald sleeps. A gust of wind comes just before the rain and the house booms softly, like a touched drum. Donald is lost in the dreams he never remembers when he wakes. He tells me he doesn't dream. He frowns, his face clenched. In his sleep his easy, open smile disappears. The dream gains force, shoving him upward into day. Alarm clock. It rings on while his hand flails. He stabs down the button and subsides beneath the warm used sheets. He smells the heat of his body and my absence. Each morning it grates to find me gone and busy while he is still sleeping. He'd like for once to roll over and see me sleeping on my back, face open and abandoned, a drop of spittle at the corner of my mouth. The rain spatters on the windows. Got to get those frames repainted. One more winter like last and they'll rot through. He's never lived anywhere there's so much weather.

He hears my footsteps but doesn't turn. Let me think he's asleep. My bare feet tap on the floor. Now I'm above him, looking down. He can feel me.

'It's time to get up,' I say. He rolls over and squints up at me. I've screwed my hair up on top of my head, and I'm dressed in an old tracksuit.

'Did you go out?'

'Yes. I've been down to the sea.'

He knows I'm better when I've been out, down to the sea. I touch my palm to his forehead. My hand is so cold he flinches.

'I've been swimming,' I say.

'Jesus. What time is it?'

'I told you. Time to get up.'

'You shouldn't swim on your own down there.'

But he knows I always will. I swim naked. There's no one to see. The water is grey and clean, and I know the tides. Although it's a cool September, the sea has the warmth of the summer in it. I love it. He feels along my hand, my arm.

'You're freezing. You'll catch cold.'

'You can't catch cold in salt water.'

I take off my tracksuit top. Now I am bare to the waist, my nipples standing out stiff and dark. A trail of salt water runs down from the wet hair at my neck, hesitates, then slithers over my collar bone. I bend, and he licks the drop of salt, and tastes my body under the taste of the sea. I hook my fingers in the tracksuit pants and pull them down. He lifts the quilt like a tent-flap and I wriggle in. I am so cold that he shrinks back from me, then he seizes hold of me as if he is plunging into cold water himself, and wraps his arms around me, tight. I don't pull away, but I shudder as if his warmth is ice. He feels for the warm slippery channel between my legs, but I'm cold there too.

One of the boys shouts in the bedroom and I tense to listen. My eyes snap open. Joe.

'Ssh,' says Donald, not to me or Joe but to the listening thing in me that turns me away from him, just as we are coming close. He runs his hands up and down me, fast, trying to get the blood heat of the bed into my hips, my breasts, my cold belly with its knot of navel that is looser since the boys came. The cold has made me solid. I feel as if I'm come back wrapped in another element, one he'll never penetrate. I turn my head, open my eyes, open my mouth and kiss his wide mouth. When he smiles the rounding of his cheek looks like a distortion.

At the end of the kiss I lick my lips. 'I'm so dry. My lips are cracking.'

'You shouldn't swim so much,' he says. 'You shouldn't go so far out. How far out did you go?'

I pull against him. 'Not far,' I say, and touch the damp, sweaty hair in his groin. 'Not far.'

'You should stay with me. I'll look after you,' he says. He dives down my body, rasping his unshaven chin over my stomach. 'You don't smell of anything,' he says, raising his head. 'You're so clean you don't smell like you.'

'It's OK,' I say. I feel my voice changing, the way it does, dampening and thickening. 'You can muck me up.' I kick back the quilt and stare down our bodies. Behind his head there is the grey square of the window, the grey stone round it, the pale streaming marshes. The wind drowns the tick of the postman's bike.

I hold Donald tight. He's drifting. His body is loose and content in my arms. He gives me a drowsy smile, so open it makes my heart contract. The rain spits on the glass, the wind whines and the house seems to rock, with us inside it. I can lie here in the hollow of the bed, in the seaweed smell of sex. The bed seems to rise and fall beneath me.

I can allow myself ten minutes by the clock whose hands turn calmly on the table, at eye-level. At the outside, fifteen, if I drive fast and the gates of the level crossing aren't down. The children won't wake until we wake them. I shift my legs and Donald says, without opening his eyes, 'Don't get up yet.'

'It's all right. You stay here.'

I want this day never to begin. I want them all to stay like this, Donald, Joe, Matt, floating in and out of sleep as the house floats on its foundations above the marsh. I want them to believe they're safe. There is money coming into the house, my money, weighing down the scales against the debts. I know how Donald is. I don't need to watch him or weigh him up or check up on him, because he's always in my mind. We don't use words like breakdown, we never have. We step lightly round it. We have got past those nights when I'd find him up at two, at three, at four in the morning, sleepless and frozen. There would be little whisky glasses round him and a tide of newspaper which he'd let flow from his lap. He would order two or three newspapers a day and never read them. He'd get muddled and forget he had a whisky glass already, and fetch another. And then he left the top off the bottle so one day Matt got up before I did and kicked it over the carpet. It wasn't the drink that bothered me. It was the hot, hurt look in Donald's eyes that the drink couldn't extinguish.

One night I woke to find him sitting on the bed watching me in the light that came through from the landing. I could tell he'd been there a long time, watching me as if he was never going to see me again. I pretended I hadn't noticed. I said I felt hungry, and I got up and made us both some scrambled eggs and then we watched a film together. I remember it had Marilyn Monroe in it. I didn't follow the plot much, but the noise of the film was a way of holding things back, like the big mugs of tea I kept making.

When the children woke they were jealous of us, because we'd been up while they were sleeping. And because we were sitting close up together on the sofa. Joe crammed himself in between me and Donald, and I thought how perfect his face was, with the night warmth on it and that almost inhuman beauty children have when they're flushed and ruffled with

27

sleep. And I thought that nothing was going to destroy us. Nothing was going to make their faces clamp shut.

He was thinking of leaving us. He couldn't live with the thought that he'd failed us, lost our money, dragged us into debt. That night when I woke he was fixing our faces in mind, for when he was gone. He had been in the boys' room too, watching them while they slept. It was only a question of weeks, he said. They couldn't go on. They'd made so many mistakes. He could see that now. All that expansion, the loans, the clients who went bust and couldn't pay. Money will make money, that's what they'd thought when they went to the bank for the loans which went on bigger premises, and more staff, and a networked computer system. Money well spent will make money.

I didn't ask him then what he meant by leaving. It was too dangerous. I was afraid that any question would boot him into action. I could see the brink in front of us and how we had to move back softly, step by step, never letting on that we'd seen the fall we might have fallen.

It was going to have to go. Donald was going to come out of the partnership with nothing but debts. He had worked fifteen years to build it up. It had been the centre of his life as long as I'd known him. Donald is not the kind of man to talk of his dreams. He says he never dreams. He'd have some good years, a few that were not so bad and then three dry years when he fought to hold off the bank with everything we had. And now it was the middle of the night and I had to think quickly.

I'd been sitting as a deputy district judge for four years. I knew I was good. I did it five or six days a month, and the rest of the time I worked in my own practice. It was mainly a legal aid practice, so there wasn't much money in it, and it was tough and tiring. But I liked it and I had plenty of clients. I had my office on a street corner, with windows looking two ways down onto the pavements awash with people. There was a flower shop opposite, and a supermarket that never closed. I knew everybody and I knew exactly the hesitant sound the downstairs door made when it was a first-time client. Every lawyer is a bit of an actor. The clients would come in away from the cold street, the dust and billowing chip-papers, and I would ease it all out of them and they would believe the reassurance they saw in my face.

It was an old, crooked building, with narrow stairs where one person had to stand aside to allow the other to come up. The walls of my office were uneven. There was a little Victorian grate behind my desk, with blue tiles round it, and yellow lilies on the tiles. I bought some blacklead and blackleaded the grate so the iron glowed with a dull coaly gleam. On winter mornings I would come in early and light the fire. I liked to see the look on the clients' faces when they came in heavy with trouble or prickling with the desperate need to put their story, which no one else believed or wanted to hear. They would see the yellow flames unpeeling from the coal, and the heap of red slumped in the bottom of the grate, and they'd pause for a second, and their faces would change. What I liked best was the afternoons in midwinter, when the streets were thick with early dusk and the lights were coming on in the opposite block, and I'd have a break between clients to catch up with my paperwork. I'd put another shovel of coal on the fire and let it burn up, and I'd turn the computer keyboard and swivel my chair so I could watch the flames.

I got into computers early. It made up for the way I gave clients more time than I should have done. I was never going to make real money, but I paid my share of the bills and for the boys' nursery. I kept going, and I was always good in court. You have to focus on what's really going to win the case: it sounds simple, but it isn't. And if I thought I needed more time on a case I'd take it. There was no one standing over me with a time-recording sheet, telling me I wasn't ever going to keep my costs up if I worked like this, the way there is in most big legal practices now. If I thought I was going to get home on a case, I wasn't often wrong.

That's all gone. It went the night Donald turned to me after we'd eaten the scrambled eggs and said, 'They're going to make me bankrupt if this goes on. And I'm fucked if I'll do that to you and the kids.'

His eyes were rimmed with lack of sleep. Not red, but blackish lines that had been getting deeper for days. His voice was light, with no emphasis in it. We were going to sink. The water of debt was going to go over our heads and then Donald would leave us. He wouldn't want to do it, but the only way he'd be able to live with what was happening would be to get as far away from us as he could. Not to see our faces.

'That's not going to happen,' I said, as if he was one of the boys waking from a nightmare of losing me and running all up and down the supermarket and never being able to find me.

'Of course it'll happen,' said Donald. 'I've done the figures. And the bank's on to us now. Another couple of months like this and we're finished. More than finished. Completely fucked. And I can't do it. I won't be able to write a cheque, do you know that? I won't be able to do anything. I know we've got to close, Simone, but I'm not going to go through the hoop. I'm fucked if I'll do it.'

'It's not going to happen,' I said again. 'I'll get the money.'

Donald looked at me. 'I'm sorry,' he said. 'That's just not realistic. Even with what you get from your part-time district judging, you can't keep us going. Let alone pay off debts like this. It's a free fucking advice centre you're running down there, not a business.'

'I'll go for full-time DJ. They want more women.'

'You'll never get it. The competition's fantastic, it's bound to be.'

'If we're prepared to move, if we're prepared to go somewhere most people don't want to live . . . then I think there's a chance. Alistair Ringwood's sounded me out a couple of times.'

'Has he? Why didn't you say?'

'Because I didn't want to do it.'

'Then why are we wasting time talking about it?'

'Because I've changed my mind.'

I saw a little life creep back into his eyes, like blood into a hand as it unclenches, colouring the white knuckles. I saw how far he'd gone without me, and how easily I might have woken up one morning to find the bed blank beside me.

'I can get it. I know I can. You won't go bankrupt. I'll get the job and then we'll go and see the bank and we'll show them we can service the debt.'

'What if you don't get it?'

'I will.'

'Are you –'

'Donald, I will.'

Four

It is much too hot in the courthouse. Inland, the weather is always different, and this is a true Indian summer. By early afternoon the sun's beating through the double glazing straight onto my head. I've got a heavy list and I'm in chambers right through the day. In the middle of a pre-trial review a sharp, tight pain begins above my eyes. I blink and the couple in front of me wavers behind tears. *Disputed contact.* Our language changes all the time, and it's hard for people outside the legal profession to keep up with it. Sometimes I'm afraid that's the point of the changes. When I was still in my own practice I used to have clients say to me, '*What do you mean, contact order? I'm talking about access, aren't I?*' Or '*I don't want <u>residency</u>, I want custody!*'

They'd give me that baffled, aggressive look you get so used to in the law, as if they suspected that people on the other side of the desk were trying to put one over on them. So then I'd go through it all again gently, I hope, not too patronizingly, I hope, trying to make it clear. They had to know the language, if they were going to do more than listen dumbly while their future was decided before they knew what was happening.

Disputed contact, in this case, means that Graham Rossiter claims that his former wife and her new partner are trying to alienate the children from him, so that they will stop wanting to visit him the two weekends out of four, the week at Christmas and Easter, the three weeks in the summer to which the couple agreed at the time of the divorce.

His former wife's name is Christine, now Christine Delauney once again. She has pale hair scooped into a French pleat, and she's wearing a sober suit. I see so many sober suits. So many tiny marks at the side of a nose where someone has taken out a nose-ring on their solicitor's advice. So it goes. Sometimes it works the other way, too. There was an argument on the steps of the county court a few months ago, because when the client met his male solicitor just before they went in for trial, the solicitor was wearing an ear-ring.

'What's the judge going to think, me here with a brief with a bleeding ear-ring?' shouted the client, and wouldn't go into court until his solicitor had taken the ear-ring out. He lost the case anyway.

Graham Rossiter hasn't looked at his former wife since he came into this room. Christine says he is quite mistaken in thinking that she and Martin have any interest in reducing contact time with him. She and Martin encourage the children to maintain a strong relationship with their natural father, but, not surprisingly, the children are wary. As it happens Christine and Martin have kept a diary of the times Graham Rossiter has had to go away on business, just like that, with no notice, when he was supposed to have the children for a weekend.

Natural father. The phrase worries me. As I go through the evidence I think, 'Why doesn't she just say "father"?' The welfare report confirms that the children have a good relationship with Martin, and have accepted him as their mother's partner. The relationship between Christine and Martin appears to be quite stable.

All the tired phrases click to and fro, like counters in a board-game which each still believes can be won. The court welfare officer sits there too, her face tidy with professional neutrality. There are solicitors for both sides. All of us in the room, taking apart the lives of Christine and Graham, and of the absent Martin, and the absent children. On some points we approve, on others we disapprove. I have a sheaf of reports in front of me, from the welfare officer, from the children's schools, from the GP who has been treating the eldest child's 'persistent enuresis'. It is barbaric, this terminology, but it's what we have to use.

Sometimes you can't help seeing behind the words, seeing a boy of nine setting his alarm clock for six a.m. so he can get up and put his sheets into the washing-machine before the little ones wake up. The GP calls this 'a successful element of self-management of the condition'. And then the boy showers, for half an hour or more at a time. The child is anxious. He is developing a phobia about smelling of urine.

But for some reason the health visitor's report is not here, even though it has been requested. There's no explanation: muddle, probably. Even though we have the GP's report, the health visitor may be important. The youngest child is only three years old, and the health visitor has been involved since an episode of post-natal depression after the birth. Christine attributes her depression to the unhappiness of her marriage. Once she met Martin, once she made the decision to leave, the depression began to lift. I look at Christine's taut, fair face, carefully made up, and at the femininity of the ruffled white blouse under the suit. She will have thought carefully about what to wear. Maybe they went through her wardrobe together, or bought something specially.

There is a vicious tension in the room. Graham Rossiter doesn't trust me. After all, I am a woman, about the age of his wife. I may have children myself. His eyes flit sharply around the room and he keeps making notes in a tiny black-bound notebook, like a policeman's notebook. Each time he finishes writing he looks at me, as if to make sure I have registered what he is doing. He is keeping a check on it all. I have no desire to read his notes.

Pain squeezes in my head. My eyes hurt, too. It's the light. The light, and sleeping badly, and not having time to eat this morning. It's hot, much too hot. Sweat prickles inside my clothes. The courthouse may be new, full of pale wood and glass and rounded edges, but the design isn't good. It is meant to impress people, not to house them comfortably. I ring for the usher.

'Could we have a window open, please?'

'Certainly, Madam.' He's bulky, packed with physical power even though he's getting on. He must have been formidable, frightening even, when he was younger. A good person to have around, if he is on your side, and of course he's on my side. We all watch him. It is a relief to watch him. The double-glazed window swings back, and I wait for the air to reach my face. But before the air there comes the noise. The insistent throb and whine of an amplified guitar, a voice, off-key and howling out the blues.

Well I woke up this morning with blood on my hy-ands . . .

The usher turns, looks at me. One thick eyebrow goes up.

'Shall I close it again, Madam?'

'Is it coming from a car?'

He looks down, ponderously. 'No, Madam, it's one of those –' he pauses, fastidiously, as if the word is an obscenity '– buskers. We've been troubled a lot this year.'

As he speaks, the air reaches me. It surrounds my face, warm but fresh, easing the tightness. There's a breeze you would never suspect from the solid heat that cooks us through the windows.

'Let's leave the window open for a while, and see how we get on.'

The usher fastens the window in place.

It's not going to work. The noise has the crazy confidence of bad music. You can't think through it. After a few minutes of listening to the welfare officer through the screech of the amplifier, I say, 'This is no good. We'd better have the window closed.'

But there is sweat on Graham Rossiter's forehead. These

are his children, his and hers. Things are bad enough for them. Their lives are already under a magnifying glass. Why should they have to put up with this? The usher leans towards me.

'If I might make a suggestion, Madam. We could have him moved.'

Our eyes meet. His overbearing face is pasted across with respectful attentiveness towards my needs. Nothing, no matter how minute, is outside his attention, if it affects the process of the law.

'Get him moved?'

'I could give them a ring down at the station. One of them'll come down and move him along for you. It won't take five minutes. I know them down there.'

He is bland but conspiratorial, waiting.

'Yes, please, that's a very good idea,' I said, with the same blandness. Because I have said yes, a policeman will tap the shoulder of the blues singer. He'll make him pick up guitar and amplifier, and go elsewhere. I feel a flush rise to my skin, but the usher is pleased with me. He steps off heavily but silently, to make his phone call.

It doesn't take long. Soon we have fresh air blowing in, and quiet outside the window. The afternoon passes, the sunlight relaxes into yellow. We move forward by due process, towards a full hearing.

Five

At last my list is over. I'm tired, restlessly tired, as I go out of court to the car. There is no wind at all now, not even a breeze, and the air is warm. I take off my jacket and the sun strokes my bare arms. The car-park is almost empty and the inside of the car smells of hot plastic. Suddenly I can't face driving home straight away. I sit with the keys in my hand, thinking. I'll go for a walk, buy a newspaper, then have a cup of coffee some-where. Rare, empty time, belonging neither to work nor to home.

I feel as guilty as a thief as I lock the car again. But it's so good to walk slowly across the hot car-park, feeling myself unclench, feeling lighter than I have felt all day even though I'm still carrying the document case that I must never leave in the car. Or maybe I won't go to a café. There's a walk by the river where people go to sit at lunchtime. I've never been there, but it would be good to sit by water, not even reading.

The river is a city river, penned sullenly between two concrete banks. The banks are very steep and every few yards there are metal stanchions let into the concrete, so that if someone fell in they could cling there until their own weight dragged them back into the oily water. It makes me think of fishermen who never learn to swim. They're right, I think. Better to go down fast, between billows of storm. Better not to struggle. There's a stand for a life-belt, too, with a big notice that says, *'Please do not vandalize this safety-station. YOU may need rescue one day.'* The life-belt has been removed and the rope which held it hangs down limply. There are benches all along the water. I walk past them, wanting to get beyond the concrete, but it goes on and on, and then you can't walk any more because the path is cut off by a barbed wire entanglement. I go back.

When I was little and afraid in bed at night, my mother told me, 'Name each sound you can hear, and count them. See how many there are. When you know what's there you won't be afraid.' I counted the drip of the cistern, the rummage of feet up the carpeted stairs next door, the whistle of a man walking his dog outside, the far off sound of traffic, like rain. There was not so much traffic then.

'Only four sounds? What about the radio and Mrs Roskowski's baby?'

'And your stockings,' I said. I could hear the nylon rasp as she crossed her legs in the dark, sitting on the end of my bed.

'If you listen, you'll hear your own heart,' said my mother. I listened, putting my hand to my chest. I can remember what it was like to touch my skin, stretched flat across my ribs. I didn't believe I would ever have breasts. I was six and inviolate.

'Listen.'

I heard the bumping of my heart through my fingers. It was slower now my mother was here. It would go on and on and on. My mouth slipped open and I fought to get the words out before sleep swallowed them.

'– for ever and ever,' I said, and my heart moved under my fingers like an amen meant for me only.

'For a long long time,' said my mother's voice.

Now I shut my eyes and count the sounds, but there are too many, and besides I don't want to lie for long with my eyes closed, alone by this city river with its concrete towpath and glaring late afternoon sun. You never know who might be coming.

Then I remember the letters I shoved into the bottom of my case this morning. The postman delivers the post with a rubber band around it, and usually I flick through it as I go out through the hall. I look for bills, and letters from the bank. It's better not to leave them for Donald, who has the long day to brood over them. The letters drive him out to walk the sea-wall, head down, his fists punched into the bottom of his pockets. He can't endure it that whatever charge the bank makes, we've got to pay. He walks on and on, sunk in himself. When the boys get back from school he flares out at them, but it's himself he really wants to punish. Even in January he wouldn't light a fire when he was alone in the house. He walks too much, and he's too thin to keep warm. One week I bought him a tin of chocolate fingers.

'Don't let the boys get their hands on them. They're for you.'

'What do you think I am, Simone? A child?'

Once we ate chocolate fingers in bed. I sucked mine until they were clean of chocolate, and the pale centre dissolved into paste that spread out over my tongue. I wrote my name on his belly in chocolate. It was one of those things you do when love seems to be changing, becoming domestic. But I saw that Donald disliked it. He doesn't like Valentine cards, and pet names between couples make him gag. He wants everything in life to have a hard, adult line around it. One of those men who'd rather fuck than kiss.

I open my case and take out the letters. Strange that I didn't notice the airmail envelope. I turn it over but there's no name or address on the back. It comes from the States, where my friend Louise lives, but this letter is typed. The postmark is wrong too. She lives in Seattle. This letter comes from New York. But as I open the letter, I still believe that it will be from Louise, the more so as the envelope is big and square and reinforced with card. She uses envelopes like that when she sends me pictures of the children.

I was right. There are photographs inside, glossy as if they've been developed yesterday. All the noises I've been listening to narrow to the hiss of blood in my head as I turn the pictures up to the light and look close.

There is a girl with long hair in a cheesecloth dress, with a bead necklace dangling between her breasts. Her breasts show beneath the cotton cheesecloth. They are round and full, and unsupported. She sits on a wooden step and behind her there is the dark of a doorway. But she is out in the light of a summer sun. Her hair shines the way my children's hair shines. She smiles, not at the camera but at someone off to one side. Her feet are slipped into thong sandals and the hem of the long dress is wrapped around her ankles. I look at the sandals and immediately I remember the sensation of the thong between my big toe and the next. At first it rubbed my skin raw. When I put the sandles on and began to walk the thong of leather burned me. I stuck on BandAids, but we were in and out of the water all day and the skin beneath the plaster grew white and puffed. So I left off the BandAid and let the salt harden my skin. And after a while the thongs didn't hurt any more.

There are two more pictures underneath. In one I am kneeling by a campfire, broiling fish. I duck round at the camera, and grin. The background is hazed by a spiral of heat coming up from the midday fire. In the last picture I am swimming, on my back, only the bobble of my face visible, with my head sleeked back. There is so much light reflected off the water that I seem to bounce on it.

It's Michael's friend. Calvin. It must be. Calvin's the one who had the camera. He was always taking pictures. He must have kept them. Maybe he didn't even develop them till now. And now he's sent them to me. Why?

There's a thick panic in me. The letter has slipped onto my knee, a folded letter on thin paper, with typed words showing through. I pull it open. For a moment I can't read it. I just can't read it in a way that makes sense of the shapes I know are words. I look at my hands holding the letter. There are little white scars on the back of my hands. Battery-acid scars.

I burned my hands two years ago, trying to help a woman out of a car after an accident. She was upside-down, hanging from her seatbelt, and she wasn't injured. The smell of petrol was spreading everywhere, and I was afraid of fire. Battery acid had leaked out, but I didn't notice. It was a country road and I came on the accident like coming on a dream. Everything around me stopped moving. I didn't notice I'd put on my brakes. My door clunked. There was metal skewed across the road and then my mind separated it out into two cars. Everything about them seemed to be in the wrong place. After a second I began to understand where the doors were and that there was a caved-in roof and a body hanging upside-down in one car, suspended by its seat-belt. In the other car there didn't seem to be anyone. The air was fresh and bright then there was a smell of burned rubber and an overwhelming smell of petrol. There was perfect silence.

The letter opens with my name.

Simone. Hey, how long is it since I said that name? I said it aloud as I wrote it down. It felt almost like talking to you. You'll have seen the pictures. Aren't they pretty? Aren't you pretty, too? I can't believe we ever looked like that, can you? Can you see those beads I gave you? I remember I got them in a thrift shop and told you I bought them in a craft market.

Simone, I've been searching for you so long. Now you've got to help me. I won't tell you how I found you, because you don't need to know. It's been a long time and my life's not been so good.

Not like yours. Hey, how do I know that? You're a

41

real success story these days, and in a way I'm not surprised. If you'd been what you looked to be, you'd never have left me. That smile you had. A bright, soft, shiny smile, like a baby smile. But you were tough, weren't you. A lot tougher than me. I would never have been able to leave you the way you left me, no matter what you'd done. You didn't even look back. I can see you now.

I know you think it was all my fault, but nothing's that simple. I'll tell you my side of the story one day. Not now. I've waited so long, I can wait a little longer.

But do you really like the pictures? If you do I've got plenty more. Calvin gave me the negatives as well, so I can just keep on printing them off. Some of them I have to be a little careful where I get them printed. You probably know what I mean.

I never met a girl like you again, Simone. You've got kids, that's what they tell me. And you're married.

Home, marriage, career, kids. You've done it all, haven't you, Simone? Just like we always said we wouldn't. You remember all that talk you used to give me, about being free? I can't begin to tell you what I've done.

Simone –

The letter ends just like that, on my name, like a conversation that's been interrupted. But it's going to go on.

Two people died in the other car. It was so still, so silent. But then I realized there was a thrush singing, and I saw it in the bare hedge, where the twigs were heavy with raindrops. As the thrush bounced along its twig the rain shook off, sparkling.

The sun came out and so the bird sang. It was as simple as that. The woman I'd dragged out of her car kept on crying and shaking. I began to feel the pain from my hands where the battery acid had burned them, and then another car stopped, and it was a man with a mobile phone. After he'd looked into both cars he called the ambulance and then he climbed through the hedge and down two fields where he knew there was a stream. He took his petrol can and brought back water to wash the battery acid off my hands. When he came back he had mud all over his clothes. He must have slipped climbing down the bank. I wondered if the mud would brush off his jacket when it was dry, or whether he would have to have it dry-cleaned, and should I offer to pay. He made me sit down, took my hands and turned them over and washed them very gently.

'What about the people in the other car?'

'Don't look, there's nothing we can do for them,' he said.

'I'm sorry, I'm sorry, I'm so sorry,' the woman who'd been in the crash kept saying, and she cried with her mouth open, her smeary face held up to the white sky as if there was someone there who might take it all away. Then we heard the sirens.

'You'd better stop saying that now,' said the man. His voice was harsh, but then he'd seen what was in the other car, and he couldn't feel sorry for the one who was still alive. I suppose he may have thought she'd caused the accident. But as far as I can remember, all we knew then was that she was the only one who'd survived.

Six

I drive south and east into a rainy sky. The cloud still has windows in it which let down pale ladders of sun, but over the marsh it's already raining hard. I am shivering, and I grasp the steering-wheel tightly. I got cold from sitting still too long with the letter in my hand, then walking back stiff and slow to the car-park. All the cars were gone except mine. The streets had that desultory look of in-between times. I felt panicky suddenly, as if I might have been away by the river for a year or more, letting time flow by me instead of water. As if Matt and Joe might be gone, their places taken by two older boys with shuttered eyes.

I drive fast down the dual carriageway, past the old finger signpost and onto the sea road. Here the road is sheltered by hawthorn and willow bent sideways to the wind. Then the shelter peels away and there is the wide, drained marshland on either side, full of sheep and cloud shadows. The road is raised above the land and there are rushy ditches on both sides. The sheep are not meant to be able to climb the ditches, but sometimes they do. They pose on the side of the road with their fleece combed through by the wind and their black, foolish eyes fixed on oncoming cars. There's no guessing which way they'll bolt. They don't seem to know themselves. The whole world is a surprise to sheep, even their own nature. So I drive slowly, watching the road, while the wind tears at loose rags of cloud. At this point of the journey home the road seems to gather itself for the sky, like an airport runway. Without meaning to, I drive faster. Wind whines through the ventilation system. I love that punch of acceleration in the small of my back at take-off, when the plane rackets down the runway and there's no turning back, only flying or failing to fly.

I am so afraid. It's not only the letter, the solid thing that's in my document case, tucked well away. I have to believe it was Michael who folded those pages, stuffed them in the card-backed envelope, stuck down the flap and the stamps. The sweat of his finger and the moisture of his saliva are here, in this car, with me. He's got to me. It makes me think of criminals trapped by the DNA printed into the spit and semen they leave behind them.

I don't know Michael's tongue or hands any more. I can't imagine him as he is now. What kind of man waits twenty years and then posts a letter? The tone of it frightens me. That eerie cosiness, as if we'd been wrapped together in the same sleeping-bag just a couple of nights ago. Or as if there's been a conversation going on all those twenty years, but I put the phone down and I've only just picked it up again. He's been talking to me all the time. He's been fingering me in a life I didn't even know I had. I've been talking and smiling in his mind. It's like being followed by someone who stops dead when you do, so you have to look round to find out if it's more than an echo. But you don't dare look round.

I've waited so long. I can wait a little longer. Do you really like the pictures?

Those pictures. There were always the two of them, Michael and Calvin. Calvin would never leave us alone.

It was a hot, still day in late August. Things were slowing down and Michael had more time. He found an old enamelled bath-tub and hauled it out into the yard behind the cabin. We didn't have a hosepipe so we carried the water out by hand and slopped it into the tub. It was shady in the yard. It smelled of hemlock. When the tub was full I pulled off my dress and climbed in. The water was cold, sweet after the stickiness of the day. Michael had a dipper and he dipped it up full of water and poured it over my head so my face ran with water and strings of hair. He did it again and again until I was cold all through, shivering. I knelt up and pulled him down by me. He was wearing that blue check shirt, a plaid shirt he called it. The collar was open. I bent his head down so his hair fell forward and his neck was bare. The skin was paler because the sun never shone there. I took the dipper and poured the water over his neck onto his hair. Then he pulled off his shirt. The light was thick and green, squeezing through a canopy of leaves. The dirt smelled strong as the water splashed on it. The light wobbled on Michael's wet shoulders. His skin shone. I think he was laughing. Anyway he had his eyes shut and I think I remember the sound of laughing. He let me do what I wanted. I drenched him, he was my baby. I started to lick the water off the ball of his shoulder, where the muscle rose.

That was when we heard the yard gate squeak and there was Calvin.

'What're you guys doing?'

'Just fooling around.'

And Michael was away from me, his face shut, rubbing the water off his face. I reached for my dress.

The road turns and runs parallel to the sea, though we're still two miles inland. I'm nearly home. The road goes through the village, past the empty school, the string of houses, the flapping sail drying on someone's line. It's not a pretty village at all. You'd drive straight through it and never think of it again, unless you lived here. It's the light that makes it beautiful. There is so much more sky than land, and the sky changes so fast that sometimes the land itself seems to be moving. It's really raining now, and the houses have an inward look of tea-time and television. The boys will be at home.

My tyres hiss round the last corner of the village and I

accelerate, wanting to get home to them, to hold them tight even though they won't like it. They come home from school jumping with news, but I'm never there. By now they're glazed over with TV and all they want is more of it, sprawled out on their beanbags, with duvets wrapped round them because the house is always cold. They lie close together, but Joe has his territory and Matt has his. They scuffle if one of them crosses a border which only they could define. There's always a mess of crisp packets, banana skins, apple cores and sweet-papers round the beanbags. Childhood is a slum and they love it.

It's my home and he knows where it is. No one forwarded that letter. It came straight here, nicely typed.

It's been a long time and my life's not been so good. Not like yours. Hey, how do I know that? You're a real success story these days . . .

I should stop the car. I have got to think. I have got to read this letter again. But I'm close to the house now, slowing down, bumping over the cattle grid, turning the wipers up to full speed to shift the load of rain that is pouring down now. I hope Donald has remembered to put the bucket in the right place under the bathroom ceiling. Water leaks through where two tiles are gone. I'll go straight up and see. If there's any hot water I'll shower. That's what I want, to sluice off the dirt of the day before I go in to the children. But the heavy gate that is meant to keep the sheep out of the garden is swinging wide. Donald's rusted Escort has gone.

There's no note on the table. The house is dark and quiet. I look in the sitting-room and the boys' beanbags are plumped up, the way I left them the night before. No duvets, no food on the floor. The kitchen is clean and still. They'll be shopping, or else there's some arrangement I haven't remembered. But I find myself listening as if they're in the house somewhere. I go up the stairs, moving lightly and keeping close to the wall. The bathroom door is ajar and that's where the sound is coming from. As soon as I open the door I know what it is. The tick of water falling onto bare linoleum. Donald hasn't remembered the bucket. But there's something there. A heap of towels, pulled roughly out of the airing-cupboard and tumbled on the floor. I go back downstairs again. In the kitchen I see at once that the wall phone is off the hook. It is silent. I put it back on the rest, then I unplug the kettle, which is still faintly warm, and take it to the sink to fill. The noise of water gushing out of the tap is bruisingly loud and I turn the tap off quickly, as if it might be covering other, more important sounds.

Nobody comes. I make tea, then wash quickly, put potatoes to bake in the oven and lay a fire in the sitting-room. I think about washing the kitchen floor, which looks smeary, but I'm too restless. The wind throws rain against the windows and when I open the back door I can hear the sea too, beating up in the distance. A smoke of rain hangs over the marsh. The path is plastered with torn leaves. What are they doing out in this? They haven't even taken their jackets.

I can't work, I can't eat. I go to my document case and take out the letter. I read it through again, gathering evidence, reading it as I would if it were a document in a case. Then I fold the letter back into the envelope.

When at last the car comes, pushing through the rain with its lights on, I'm beyond anxiety. The children and Donald have died a hundred times in my mind, but I know as I go out to meet them that I look calm. The boys are in the back, huddled together. Matt has his arm around Joe's shoulder, and Joe has a thick bandage over his head. I rip the door open.

'What's happened?'

'He's OK. They were swinging on the gate and the metal bar caught the top of Joe's head. We went down to Casualty to get him stitched up.'

'There was blood pumping up out of his head. I had to press down on it with a towel all the way to the hospital, didn't I, Dad? And we had to throw the towel away.'

'Is he all right?'

'He's fine. They did an X-ray, that's what took so long.'

'They stitched inside my head first, then they sewed up the outside,' says Joe. 'I had fourteen stitches. When they take them out the nurse is going to give them to me in a little plastic bag so I can keep them.'

We get them into the house. The boys smell of hospitals and chocolate, and Donald looks exhausted.

'I'm cold,' says Joe.

'I'll light the fire. And Matt, run upstairs and get your duvets. You can have your tea in front of the TV, you'll like that.'

'I want to go back to our old house,' says Matt, and starts to cry.

'I won't be able to go to school tomorrow, will I, Dad?' says Joe proudly, and Matt cries harder. I pull them down to me, one on each side. I hold them tight, the smell of them, disinfectant and their hair which needs washing, their skin, their chocolate breath. I see the spit in the corner of Matt's mouth as he cries. They are bleached with shock and tiredness. I hold them tight, crushing the damage that's been done.

'They shaved my hair,' says Joe.

'It'll grow back,' says Donald. 'For Christ's sake, Simone, don't make a big deal. They're fine. You weren't here. You didn't have to cope with it.'

'That's why the towels were on the floor,' I say stupidly.

'Yes, and I'll tell you something. Old Matt wiped the blood off the kitchen floor while I was putting Joe in the car. *Mum'll be frightened if she sees it*, he said. Wasn't that something?'

Matt squirms against his father, scrubbing his head into Donald's sweater. I think with a pang of how often he isn't praised, Matt the older and clumsier one, the one who argues brashly for later bedtimes and a fair division of the last tinned peach, who puts up with Joe week after week then falls on him

49

savagely for no reason anyone can see and gets punished for it.

When I had children the first shock was that there would be no sacrifice in dying for them. It would be easier than living without them. I let go of the boys, kneel down and put a match to the fire.

'Can I have a dwarf rabbit?' asks Joe. 'Andy Collett's rabbit had six babies yesterday, and it only ate one of them.'

When the children are asleep Donald comes to sit by the fire. He brings a new bottle of whisky. *Don't comment*, say his eyes. *Don't say anything.* He slops whisky into two glasses and we drink.

'Have some more.'

'Not so much. I'm starting early tomorrow.'

'Aren't you always.'

'Yes.'

He drinks down the second glass and stares into the fire.

'They put this thing over his head, like a little tent with a square cut in it where the wound was. God knows why. She was good, though, the doctor. The way she worked inside the cut. It was like watching my mother picking up a stitch she'd dropped. She said a cut that deep, there was no point stitching over the top till you got the layers firmly in place. It'll heal properly now. They're good, you know, here.'

'You sound surprised.'

'Well, it's not much more than a cottage hospital really. I nearly fainted.'

He says this in the same tone, without looking at me.

'What, when?'

'In the operating theatre. It was the lights, and the smell. I can't stand that hospital smell. And she was right inside Joe's head.'

'What happened?'

'I was OK. I don't think anyone noticed.'

He smiles, fills the glass again. 'Have some more.'

'I won't, thanks.'

He drinks. 'Remember when they were born. The way that bit on top of their heads used to go up and down.'

'Yes.'

I remember. That sealed, passionate world.

He has his hand on my leg, round my ankle. 'Why do you wear jeans all the time?'

'Because they're warm.'

He kneels up, facing me. Either we'll fuck or he'll cry. At the moment I don't know which would be worse.

Late that night I wake and go in to see Joe. His door is open and Matt is there too, sprawled over Joe's bed, asleep. Joe must have cried out and Matt heard him before I did. That hospital tang is still in the air. I bend and listen to them breathe, and pull the duvet close round them. They have crept close in their sleep, and Matt is snoring softly against his brother's neck.

Once I saw them walking to me out of a sunset. The air was dusty with harvest, the light thick. They had their arms slung round one another's shoulders, and their hair was spiked with sweat from running. They were rimmed with gold. Then they came close and they were my boys again, squabbling, jostling for attention.

I sit on the end of Joe's bed for a long time. I would die rather than let anyone break into their brotherly sleep.

Seven

All night I wake and sleep and wake again, and think about the letter. I've always loved letters. It's because they've been touched by the person who sent them. Faxes and e-mails aren't the same. Letters smell of their senders. They've been handled, folded, licked. Even the shiniest envelope has the blur of fingerprints on it. Stamps get cancelled with postmarks. And the words inside grow more real by the minute. You can think of your letter tossed into a sack by a tired man working overtime, then cantering westward on the night mail. All those hands sorting and weighing and carrying as the lighted train sways on its way through sleeping cities, through the world that's forgotten about words until tomorrow. The train comes out of the night's long tunnel into dawn. The mystery of all the possible addresses narrows down to one postman with his bag and his footsteps that might pass your house, or might not.

I say that I love letters. I've always said it, but it's not true any more. When I hear the postman at our gate, I'm afraid.

There's another letter. I grab it, take it into the bathroom and lock the door. At first I think the sheets of paper are blank.

Then I see what is written on the bottom on one, in small round script:

'*You've forgotten a lot of stuff.*'

And on the second sheet: '*But I haven't.*'

There's another photograph. It shows the same girl as before, leaning cheek to cheek with a taller woman, both of them poised, pert, flirting into camera. The taller woman is wearing heavy make-up, a tight, busty sweater, a long satin skirt. Her blonde hair is teased and piled high.

I sit on the lid of the toilet. I hear a rustle and look down to see the airmail paper trembling between my hands. I remember.

I've never shaved a man before. Only my own legs, which I do religiously every morning, even if I'm planning to wear jeans. Michael lies back in the wooden chair, his eyes shut, his lips curved. His lips move.

'Go on,' he says, 'shave me close. Real close.'

I have a basin of hot water, soap, the razor. I lather him up and begin to shave him with long smooth strokes of the razor, guiding the blade around the contours I know so well. I shave and rinse and pat his skin dry. Michael feels his jaw with his thumb. 'Still feels like a man to me,' he says. 'You got to get in close.'

I stand in front of him, my legs straddling his jeans. I stand still and stare into his eyes, which are so close they have no meaning. I touch the skin of his jaw. There is bone there, under the flesh. Shaving can't take out the bone under the surface. I wonder if the feel of a man comes from the inside, or whether it can be made up.

I lather him up again, and shave as close as I can. Jaw, cheeks, chin, upper lip. Then the blade drags and there's a tiny nick and a bright bubble of blood springs up.

'You cut me,' says Michael.

'It's nothing. Just a little blood.'

I am getting into this. I wipe his face again and feel his skin. He is smooth and fresh as a baby. Michael opens his eyes.

'Great,' he says. 'Let's get going.'

First the foundation. It's not mine, because I never wear heavy make-up, but I've been into a drugstore and chosen carefully, matching to his skin tone. I rub the dark sludge over his face and massage it in. His complexion grows eerily even. He looks like a vice-presidential candidate on TV.

'Look up.' I dip the mascara wand, flick it up under his lashes. He startles, and blinks. A woman would keep still. 'Let this coat dry, and I'll do another.' Michael's eyelashes are long and thick anyway, and with the mascara on them they spray out like Bambi lashes. Someone once told me that children with cancer have the longest eyelashes. Things like that stick in my mind. I line his eyes with kohl, elongate them at the corners, then shadow them. Now he has a Pharaoh's face.

'It'd look better if I plucked your eyebrows. More elegant.'

'You kidding?'

'No. I could tidy them up a bit, anyway.'

I get out the tweezers and start work. He flinches and sits up. 'Jesus, Simone, what the fuck are you doing?'

'Making you beautiful. Lie back.'

He subsides, grumbling. I pull out a few more hairs, each with a transparent oily globe at its base. He keeps his eyes shut so as not to see me coming at him with the tweezers each time. I grasp a hair between the tweezer, test it to be sure of my grip, pull with a firm smooth movement. The skin reddens. This feels like the most intimate thing I've ever done with Michael. My hands are sticky in the heat of my shuttered room, with the glare of electric light full on Michael's face.

The blusher, then the lipstick. I leave the lipstick till last because I know it's going to be the best part. I line his lips, stroke on one coat of 'Ruby Ruby', blot with tissue, coat his lips again. It's an expensive lipstick, and it glides on smoothly, glossily, like no lipstick I've ever bought for myself. I don't wear lipstick much, anyway. I like my lips pale.

His mouth is luscious. 'Sit still. I'm going to get a mirror.'

I hold the mirror in front of him. He stares at himself, then he puts a forefinger to each corner of his mouth, and pushes his lips up into a smile. He wags his head from side to side like a clown.

'Stop it, you'll muck up the make-up. I'll go and get the wig. This is going to look good.'

It's a blonde nylon wig, coarse and cheap. Michael came with me to choose it, fooling around, cramming it on his head so the salesgirl laughed too. We told her we were going to a fancy-dress party. Now I feel like a surgeon, holding it, looking at the web inside it which holds the wig to the head. I prop the mirror so I can see what I'm doing and have both hands free. My face in the mirror is calm and ruthless as I ease the wig into place.

'You're not doing it right,' says Michael. He adjusts the band of the wig gently, tugging it into place around his hairline. He looks as if he does this kind of thing every day. And the wig is suddenly right, part of the bold make-up and the sudden pout of his lips as he narrows his eyes at himself in the mirror. He stares into himself.

'Oh my Lord!' he flutes. 'Aren't you just gorgeous?' And then in a voice as deep as a prayer, 'Oh . . . my . . . Lord.'

'You're beautiful.'

'Mm.'

Still holding his own eyes, he parts his lips, moistens the shiny red with his tongue. He starts to sing, clear and husky:

> 'And it's one, two, three,
> What are we fighting for?
> Don't ask me, I don't give a damn . . .'

'We're fighting for *you*, Ma'am,' he says to his mirror self. Only the eyes aren't right. They are restless inside their ring of mascara fibre. I am behind him, staring too. I can't tell if he is looking at me, or at himself.

'Wouldn't you fight for that, baby?' he asks me. 'Wouldn't you fight for a girl like me?'

'I wouldn't fight for anything,' I say. 'You ought to get dressed.'

'You can say that,' he says. 'That's what a girl should say.' He tries the words over twice. '*I wouldn't fight for anything. I wouldn't fight for anything.*' The first time it comes out prissy, know-nothing, don't dirty my skirts. The second it's flat and hard. Then he says to me, 'But you don't believe it.'

'What do you mean?'

'You'd fight for your kids.'

'I haven't got any.'

'You'd fight. I know you.' He looks at me. 'You're already fighting.'

'Who?'

'Calvin.'

'That's not true.'

'Yeah, it's true. And you won't win.'

He takes a cotton-wool bud, leans forward, eases a speck of mascara from the corner of his eye.

We've done things in the wrong order. Pulling the sweater over his head now will crush the wig and smear the make-up. I hook my hands through the sweater neck and hold it wide so it slips over his head. I unbutton his shirt and he shrugs it off. We haven't got the bra yet, though we will when Calvin comes to take the photos. It's hard to find a wide enough strap to go around his back, without a cup so deep no amount of cotton wool will stuff it so it juts through the sweater as it should. But I'll find one. I've finished the skirt. I made it myself, cutting it out from an old Vogue evening skirt pattern I found in a thrift shop. I bought red satin, cheap and shiny and hard to handle, and made the skirt up on a hand-operated Singer. The satin kept slipping and bunching up under the machine's foot so I had to rip out the seam and start again. I didn't mind the work, though my eyes stung from the light bouncing off the fabric. I kept on and got it done.

I stroke the red satin as I bring the skirt to Michael. It snags on the skin of my fingers, which are rough from hauling up the boat onto the shingle. Michael steps out of his jeans and I help him slither his way into the tight skirt. It is floor length, but even so I think it would be better if we'd shaved his legs. More complete.

'You can't do that, Simone. How'm I going to explain that to the guys?'

'You'll make something up.'

He stands there in the red satin, like a wolf dressed as a woman in a fairy tale. Everything is out of scale: the waist too thick, the hair is heavy, dead blonde like the thatch on photos of Myra Hindley. I see him as if he isn't Michael at all, but a stranger hiding to trap me. I am intensely aware of what is under the skirt. His penis, his balls, the thighs that lie so heavy between mine.

'How do you walk in this, for Chrissake?' he asks.

But I don't know how to tell him. I don't wear clothes like that, anyway. I wear jeans and soft, flowing skirts. I wear cotton and cheesecloth. I have never bought a tailored garment in my life, or high heels. To me they feel like uniform. I have sat on my mother's knee and felt her stiff bodice dig into me; I've tottered down the street in her stilettos. But they are not what I've chosen to inherit.

Michael steps forward and takes my hand. 'Let's dance,' he says. When he stands his red, moist lips are on a level with my hairline. The blonde wig bounces against my cheek and the thick make-up is sweating off him. He lowers his eyes and then puts his arms around me and he holds me close inside his grip. Every time Michael holds me I can't help thinking how hard it would be to break away. He smooches me up close to him and I smell the cosmetics, that sweet, cloying stink of department stores where girls in white stand behind counters looking as if they're about to be operated on. His hipbone pushes against me. We start a slow circle. I shut my eyes and there's nothing left but the movement, the heavy sweetness, and his voice by my ear crooning like it's a love song:

> *'And it's one, two three,*
> *What are we fighting for?*
> *Don't ask me, I don't give a damn,*
> *Next stop is Vietnam;*
> *And it's five, six, seven,*
> *Open up the pearly gates;*
> *There ain't no time to wonder why,*
> *Whoopie – we're all gonna die.'*

He passes me across his body as we twirl and as our lips come close I smell his lipsticky breath. Round and round and round we go. The room is warm and there is stuff on the floor, underwear, shoes, books, coffee cups. I am not tidy yet. Our feet shuffle, our breath comes fast.

Michael stops. He puts his hands on my forearms and holds them tight. The wig is slipping. It's not such a good wig. We should have spent more money. He looks hot and sweaty and tired. He lets go of me and fumbles for the waistband, where I've sewn in hooks and eyes. He tugs at the zip and tramples the skirt down. It looks like nothing on the floor. A red rag.

'Don't spoil it,' I said. 'Remember, Calvin wants to take pictures.'

Calvin is going to photograph us together. This is a rehearsal, because I want to know we can do it before we expose ourselves to Calvin. Michael slides his foot under the skirt and kicks it up into the air. I catch it, smooth out the satin, lay it down on the bed. Michael sits down heavily on the bed.

'My head's spinning around.'

'You didn't eat anything.'

'You got something?'

We are in my room, in the house where I board, with a woman of forty-two who seems to know nothing and notice nothing. She is single and she works in the town library. I have the right to cook in her kitchen between the hours of five and seven, and to make coffee when I please. Otherwise, I keep fruit in my room and buy doughnuts and peanuts. There is a bag of bananas on the pine table.

'No, I'm OK.' He's leaning back, head pillowed on hands, eyes narrow. The make-up exaggerates him. His lips purse up to whistle and I think of the film code that used to say you had to have one foot on the floor in every bedroom scene. I kneel by the bed. I put out my tongue and taste the foundation on his cheek. I want to wash it off to get at the taste of his skin, but he pulls away.

'I don't feel so good.'

We lie side by side, my body tense from fear of toppling off the narrow bed. The slight cramp in my leg seems to balance out the pain he's feeling. It is a pain I know nothing about. I'm afraid of it, too afraid even to ask about it. Anyway, Michael has already made it plain to me that his past is not my place.

We lie there for a long time. Bit by bit Michael relaxes. We smoke cigarettes and I find some cans of beer in the fridge. I wipe the make-up off Michael's face with cold cream and cotton wool, and he takes off the wig. The only sign left is a little redness around his eyebrows, where I plucked them. We put on some music, not too loud because I've already heard Miss Beecher come home. She's in the kitchen, watching TV and making her dinner. Miss Beecher makes herself a three course dinner each evening, and sits down to it with a napkin at her place, and flowers in a white porcelain vase on the table.

*

I remember the way the noise of her TV bulged into our room. Michael turned up the music. 'Let's dance again,' he said.

We hardly moved. We were tired and full of beer and we swayed on one spot, clasped close as if both of us were drowning. It was the lost wolf howl of the Doors and it made the room darken and throb. I was far away from myself, far from Michael even, though I felt the closeness of him. Then he was muttering, close and urgent as if it was the only true thing in the world: '*Don't ask me, I don't give a damn . . .*'

We fell on the bed and he struggled with my skirt for a while, but halfheartedly, as if he didn't even want to make it. The last thing I remember was that he cupped my face in his hands and stroked it smooth and then he said in a voice like stone, 'You really don't know what I'm talking about, do you? You don't know what the fuck I'm talking about.'

I certainly didn't know what the fuck he was talking about. I was eighteen years old, and this was the first time I'd been in America. The summer job at a children's camp had lasted a month, then I met Michael. He could give me work in the boatyard over in Annassett. He hired out boats to summer visitors, took them on fishing trips, and gave sailing lessons. There'd be plenty of work for me. He knew somewhere I could board, too.

'You look strong,' he said.

'I am strong,' I said. 'I'm never ill.'

'Sick,' he said. 'You mean sick.'

'I mean what I say.'

We sat late round the camp-fire, after the kids had gone to bed. Flames bubbled off the logs and the crickets' noise filled my head, echoing back into the deep woods that were full of poison ivy and snakes. They were not safe, like English woods. Michael had his hand on my breast, inside my shirt. We sat very still, for a long time, until the flames died down and we were left with stars, thicker and brighter than the stars at home. I knew I was going to go to the boatyard. Michael had a place there, and he could find me a rented room. There was the sea. How was I going to resist? I wasn't going to resist. He was everything I wanted. And what he wasn't, I made up.

You've forgotten a whole lot of stuff.

But I haven't. It's all in there somewhere. It's just a question of finding it.

Eight

Only ten minutes have passed. Donald is knocking at the bathroom door, and quick as thought I pull aside the loose panel on the side of the bath, stuff the letter in among the pipes and dustballs, replace the panel, then open the door.

'What're you doing? You'll be late.'

'I'm all right. My list doesn't start till ten-thirty today.'

'What about Joe?' asks Donald.

'What do you mean?'

'Have you looked at him? He can't go to school.'

'I thought he was still asleep.'

'Well, he isn't. He's got a headache and he's been crying. He wants you. And I've got my meeting with the bank at 11.30.'

'What meeting with the bank?'

'Jesus Christ, Simone. I told you about it. They've got a new debt policy and they want me to speed up the repayments. I can't do it. I'm going to put on my suit and take the figures in and explain why I can't do it. Does that ring any bells?'

He is pinched with rage and humiliation.

'Yes,' I say. 'Yes, I remember. Isn't there someone you could ask to keep an eye on Joe for a couple of hours?'

Donald sits on the side of the bath. I am the enemy. I see life flow into his face as the rage runs outward, hot and satisfying.

'You have no idea at all, have you? Listen. You get your job. We come here. The kids don't know anybody, I don't know anybody. You're out all the time. I've got no job. That's what people here see. Some of these women round here, if they asked me in for a coffee their husbands'd knock their blocks off. This is a *village*, Simone. Everybody knows everything about everybody, but that doesn't mean they talk to them. It's not the city. *I don't know anyone.*'

'I'm sorry. I didn't mean –'

'So one of us has got to be here with Joe.'

'I can't, Donald. You know I can't.'

'And I can, I suppose?'

And it's coming up in me too, the same anger which brings us closer than we can bear to be.

'Yes,' I say.

'Jesus, Jesus, Jesus,' says Donald in a quiet voice, and lifts his hand and smashes it against the tiles. I am watching his face, so I see how the colour goes out of it.

'You've hurt yourself. Donald, let me see –'

He nurses his hand, cradling it away from me. Tears of pain have sprung into his eyes, but he won't even blink them away. He won't acknowledge any of what's happening.

'Let me look at it.'

'It's not broken, if that's what you think.'

'It's bleeding, look, where you caught yourself on the edge of the tile.'

The blood oozes out like jam, and thick drops run down his arm as he holds up his hand to look at it.

'Perhaps we ought to go to the –'

'No. We are not going to that Casualty department again. We'll get the kids taken away at this rate.' But he's smiling, as if the pain has eased something in him. He holds the hand towards me, with the other cupped under it to catch the falling blood. 'It's all right. It's not as bad as it looks.'

It takes me a long time to find plasters, scissors, a clean old cotton pillowcase I can cut up to make a pad under the plaster. There are no bandages in the tin that's supposed to be our first aid box, but only contains an oozing tube of insect cream, a roll of plaster and some travel-sickness pills. Matt should have left for school already, but I tell him to stay with Joe. I fetch

Donald a cup of coffee, then I clean and dress his hand, taking my time, doing it carefully, the way I used to do the boys' cuts. The nice look of the plaster would take their minds off their injuries. Donald's cut looks to me as if it ought to be stitched, but I say nothing. I push the edges of the cut together and plaster down the cotton pad, as tight as I can. I can't face the hospital either. A scar on the hand won't matter.

'I'll ring the bank. I'll say there's been an accident.'

He has gone back in his mind, to a warm place where he's taken care of and the rain beating on the bathroom window has nothing to do with him. I see him shrug the warmth away, and take on what has to be done.

'No, it's all right. I'll keep Matt off school. He can cope for a couple of hours. He's got plenty of sense when he wants to use it.'

A nightmare image of the boys flashes over me, faster than thought. They are bored, arguing, tumbling over one another, Matt on top of Joe. Joe's head wound gapes wide and blood pours. Matt opens his mouth to scream for help then closes it again, knowing there is no one to help. My body aches with desire to stay with them.

'They'll be fine,' says Donald.

I leave him and go in to the boys. They both turn when I open the door, and their wide, dark gazes are identical. I sit on the bed and put my arms around them both. Matt stiffens, resisting me, resisting the boy he was only a year ago, when belief in me and in Donald was as easy for him as breathing. As if I haven't noticed their tension, I say cheerfully, 'Dad's got to go in to the bank, Matt, just for a couple of hours. I want you to stay at home this morning and take care of Joe.'

He looks at me, his face closed against me. 'I've got to go to school this morning. Mrs Rogers is giving our projects back.'

'Matt, I can't leave Joe here on his own.'

He slides me a quick, unreadable look, and mumbles something, deliberately too low for me to hear. I stand up.

'Come out here a minute, Matt. I need to talk to you.' He follows me onto the landing.

'What did you say?' I ask, bending down so his face is level with mine.

'Why can't you stay at home?'

'What do you mean, why can't I stay at home? You know why. I've got to be in court. There are people waiting.'

He shrugs minutely, looking exactly like Donald, and says, 'I don't see why it always has to be Dad who stays at home. It's not fair on Dad.'

Before I know what I'm doing, I have seized Matt by the shoulders. My fingers dig into his sweatshirt. He is mute, not looking at me, resisting. With an effort, I relax my hands. 'If I don't go to work, Matt, there will be no job, and no house, and no food in the fridge, and no car. All I'm asking you to do is to look after your brother for two hours. That's not long, is it? You often watch TV together longer than that. You can watch TV the whole time.'

'I don't want this house, anyway,' says Matt. 'I'll be glad if we have to leave it. So will Dad.'

'Will you.' I take a deep breath. I want to slap the look off his face. My lips hurt with the effort of holding in everything that Matt must never hear. 'Will you,' I repeat, and my anger hisses into Matt like a snake into its hole.

'Mum! Mum, you're hurting me.'

'What?'

'Your hands are pinching me.'

I look at him. He is my son. He is nine years old. His face is pale, his soft mouth a little open. His eyes watch me, wary and scared. I take my hands off his shoulders. I want to cry, but I smile. He doesn't smile back. He doesn't look shocked.

65

He looks as if he is mutely reckoning how long this will go on, how soon he will be able to get away from me.

'I'm sorry, Matt. I didn't mean to pinch you. Listen. How about if I give you some extra pocket money for looking after Joe? What about two pounds? I think it's worth two pounds, don't you?'

He stares at me in silence. He wants the money, of course he does. He'll do it. Then his face quivers and he says, 'I don't want two pounds. I'll *stay* with Joe. You don't have to – '

'What?'

'Be so angry. You're always so angry.'

I reach to hug him, but suddenly he's not close enough. I would have moved, I would have hugged him, he would have sat on my lap and I would have cried and he would have cried too and it would have all been different. But just then the phone rings, and Joe cries out from the bedroom. The tension breaks, and Matt turns and runs, his trainers slapping on the stairs. I know that he doesn't want me to follow him. I straighten myself and go in to Joe, and hold him tight in my arms, rocking him as the phone rings and rings. After a long time it stops. I don't know if Donald has answered it, or the caller has given up.

'Don't go to work, Mum,' says Joe, his hands twining in the hair at my neck.

'You know I've got to. I'm late already,' I say, as gently as I can. 'Listen, I'll bring you back a little surprise for being good. What about that?' Donald is yelling from downstairs, but I can't hear what he's saying. I reach behind my neck and unclasp Joe's tight, hot hands. 'I'll have to see what Dad wants. Back in a minute, all right?'

I look down from the landing and there is Donald at the bottom of the stairs, holding out the phone. 'It's for you.'

'Get the number and say I'll call back.'

'He's calling from America. Just come down, can't you?'

A charge of fear jolts through me. My legs stiffen. I put a

66

careful hand on the banister and walk down the stairs to where Donald stands, holding the phone. I take it, and clear my throat.

'Hello? Hello? Who is that?'

The silence sighs and sings. Is he holding his breath?

'Hello? Are you there?'

The phone says nothing. 'Hello?' I say for the last time. I think he has a tape machine running. I think he is collecting my voice, putting it somewhere I can never get it back. I feel the tug, the suction of myself disappearing towards the past. And then, loud in my ear, there is a click. He has hung up.

'Who was it?' asks Donald.

'I don't know. They didn't say anything.'

'Must have got cut off.'

But he is looking at me closely. He knows me too well. He'll always spot the circle of shadow under my eyes, from a headache I deny.

'Why did you say it was someone calling from America?' I ask him.

'That's what he said.'

'What, he said *I'm calling from America*?'

'No. But he was an American.'

'He might have been over here.'

'I don't think so. The call didn't sound like that.'

'What do you mean?'

'Oh, for God's sake, Simone, you know what I mean. Calls from overseas sound different. There's that tiny gap before the other person says something. What *is* this anyway? What's the matter? Who is he?'

'Nothing's the matter. I just can't think who it could be, that's all.'

'He'll call again if it's anything important,' says Donald, still watching me.

*

As I walk to the car I look back at the house. Joe is at the bedroom window, not waving or smiling, just looking out where I am. I have the feeling that Matt is watching me too, from wherever he has hidden himself. Donald is at the door. He lifts a hand, turns away, closes the door. The house folds in on itself, hunched down against the weather coming in from the sea. The front door looks as if it's been shut for ever. The windows peer, reflecting the dark sky, giving out nothing of what happens inside. A wave of senseless panic makes me fumble the car-keys as I fit them into the lock. I won't look back. I force myself into the car.

You left me. But when you say that you have to be precise. I bought the plane ticket and I walked through Customs without looking back. I carried the same bag I brought to camp at the start of the summer.

'You can keep the rest of my stuff,' I said. 'It's not worth taking.'

I went down to the boathouse and watched the grey waves tossing up weed from the bottom of the sea. I wanted to turn to you, I wanted to spit at you.

'*Old buddy Calvin is your way of leaving.*'

I would go away and I would never be that shiny girl any more. I'd known better when I was a child, before I got stupefied by love. You never believed in the shine anyway. You saw the fight in me, the scratches coming up from beneath.

Nine

'Madam.' I jump. It echoes as if this is the third or fourth time he's said it.

'Madam. If I might just –' He plants a forefinger on the list. 'The appellant in this case has been taken unwell in the waiting-area. *Stress*,' he murmurs confidentially, his eyebrows derisive.

'Oh, dear.'

'There'll be a taxi coming for him any minute now.'

Usually I am grateful for any break in the list, but today I want to work myself blind.

'It gives you about thirty-five minutes before the emergency injunction, Madam.' He lingers. Surely he can't be wanting to talk? He's always making such a point of how busy he is.

'Very different from how it used to be,' he remarks, twitching the blind cords into position.

'Yes, I'm sure.'

'Yes, in the old days, Madam, when it was the registrars we had here, before they called them district judges, it was a bit more of a gentleman's agreement, if you get my meaning. Sitting in the morning, a nice lunch, a couple more cases, then off home. They'd have been *most* surprised if they'd come in to find a list like this waiting for them. These days you'll see a district judge sitting in chambers, sandwiches on the table, crumbs all over an affidavit. Not that it isn't the way it should be,' he adds, with the air of having suddenly remembered my own quirky preference for cheese salad rolls and satsumas. 'The pressure on the judiciary these days, Madam; well, you know it as well as I do, what with litigation coming at us like a fountain. It's only a wonder they've still got people willing to take on the responsibility.'

His eyes light on mine, malicious, satirical, their quickness at odds with his menacing physical bulk. What does he get paid? I'm sure he knows my salary to the penny. But he doesn't know that seventy per cent of it goes into servicing debt. Let him think it's eccentricity that makes me carry a battered briefcase and alternate my two plain suits week after week. But I am sure he knows better. On my birthday my sister sent me a handbag. A beautifully plain envelope of soft, dull, supple leather. I left it on a table at work, and he picked it up and came hurrying after me with it.

'You never know what might happen, Madam. There are some very light fingers in the most unexpected places. Inside a bag like this, if I might say so, Madam, a thief might expect to find rich pickings.'

'It's a birthday present from my sister,' I said. 'She won the lottery.'

He laughed politely, but it was true. Jenny works in a residential home for autistic children, and she has no money. She buys her lottery ticket each week. When she won £2,458.46, she planted six beech trees in new forest in memory of our parents, and started building society accounts for the children, with a hundred pounds in each. And she bought me the bag. Jenny is the only person I've told the truth about our debts, and the collapse of Donald's partnership. I wanted her to know what was really going on. Lucky Simone, that's what the rest of the family think I am. Simone with her law degree and her handsome architect husband. Think of all the money they must be making. It's all right for some.

He is still fiddling with the chairs. Why hasn't he got the sense to go away and let me look through the rest of the list? I stare at the back of his head, his broad, spreading haunches. He turns round, catches my look, and wipes the conspiratorial smirk off his face. *How do you think I got here*, I say silently, looking him in the eye. If I was as soft as you think, I'd still be filling in green forms.

The usher goes out of the room. Slowly, deliberately, I relax the muscles of my face. I make my shoulders drop. There are a lot of ways in which an usher can make your life difficult, and no doubt he'll run through them all, after this. But he should be more careful about how he lets his thoughts show.

That silence on the phone. I know it was Michael. I have got to stop thinking about what he's doing, and think about why he is doing it. He has got photographs. He knows where I am and who I am.

Home, marriage, career, kids. You've done it all, haven't you, Simone? I can't begin to tell you what I've done.

You never could tell me much, Michael. You left me to guess. What you and Calvin talked about, those nights when I stayed with you and Calvin stayed late too, drinking and smoking grass, and I heard you murmuring while I slept, I don't know. I would listen to your voices, the breaks, the laughter. But any two people heard through a wall sound as if they are sharing the deepest secrets.

Then you would come in to me, stumbling over your shoes and clothes so I woke up. You wanted me to wake, because it was so hard for you to get to sleep. You'd unzip the double sleeping-bag and crawl in beside me and you'd be cold against me. I'd start to say something and you'd put your mouth over mine and I'd taste the beer you'd drunk and the grass you'd smoked and the apple you'd eaten just before coming to bed. You always did that instead of brushing your teeth. I'd taste you with disgust and joy and soon your cold would melt into my sleep warmth. I would swallow your smoky breath as if it was sweet as marzipan. There was so little room that the seams of the sleeping-bag creaked as we moved. You liked it that way. You didn't like sleeping out in the open. The day was for sprawling and the night was for lying wrapped tight against the dark.

You frightened me sometimes. It didn't feel like sex, it felt like burial. You buried yourself in me, deep, in the double dark of the night room and the thick quilting of the bag. I'd be hazy afterwards, sliding in and out of sleep, but you couldn't turn off your mind. You lay there on the knife-edge of sleep, and it cut you to the bone. So I understood why you kept awake. Your dreams weren't like dreams. They were another life, rippling under the surface of this one, waiting to recapture you as soon as you dipped beneath the skin of sleep. It wasn't until I had the children that I understood about night terrors. There was a year when Matt would wake crying once a week or so, unable to come up to the surface of sleep. His breath sobbed like the breath of a diver running out of air. He would stare at me, whimpering with fear, and no matter how I soothed and murmured I couldn't make him realize that it was me and he was safe. The health visitor told me not to try and wake him. *He's still asleep. He can't see you, he's still seeing the nightmare. Just wait with him until it passes.*

One night you did begin to talk, in the dark.

'I don't dream about the things you think I dream about,' you said.

'What do you mean?'

'I mean it wouldn't sound like a whole lot if I told you.'

'What did you dream about tonight?'

'Jesus, Simone, why do you ask me these things? Why do you think I don't tell you?'

'Because you don't trust me.'

'It's not that. I don't want you to be like me, Simone, do you understand that? I don't want you to have the thoughts I have. I don't want you to have the dreams I have.'

'But I want to –'

'OK. Last night I dreamed about a closet.'

'A closet?'

'A closet with a door. I had to watch it all the time. If I stopped, what was in there would come out.'

'What was it?'

'I don't know. I didn't see it. I don't know.'

'So you kept your eyes open all night.'

'Yeah. Yeah, I guess I did.' You were silent for a long while. Then you said with a bubble in your voice which might have been laughter: 'The thing you don't know about that place I was in, Simone, is it's so boring you could die. Except when you're dying.'

You were a hostage in the daylight world: you didn't belong there. That's what the hours of drinking and smoking grass with Calvin were about, but they didn't work. Sex didn't work either, not after the first few times when I felt your slack, grateful face against mine in the sun coming through the morning window. I had no idea what it meant to you that you'd slept the whole night through. Even in your dreams I think you had your eyes closed those nights. But then it stopped working. I lost the touch.

You'd lie awake, straining into the darkness, until you couldn't lie awake any more. You'd slump against me, then jolt, as if someone was passing an electric current through you. You'd scream out. You'd thrash and beat at the air and I'd wriggle out of the sleeping-bag as fast as I could because I was afraid of getting hurt. Your eyes would be open but I don't think you were awake. It was a babble of stuff I didn't understand. Names, mostly. Screaming out people's names. I never knew them, and you never spoke of them when you were awake. Once I woke to find the quilting hot and wet round us. You'd pissed yourself in your sleep. I got up and showered and wondered if I should wake you, but I didn't. I rolled myself up in a blanket and slept beside you, and pretended to stay asleep when you woke and climbed out of the sleeping-bag.

'I took the bag to the Laundromat,' you said the next day, your eyes on me, hard and challenging.

'That's great,' I said. 'I meant to do it last week, but I forgot.'

The worst thing was when you went out at night. I'd be lying there, listening to you being awake, keeping still so you'd think I was asleep. Sometimes you'd breathe fast, as if you'd been running. You would sweat, and it would smell different from the sweat of running. A sharp, acrid stink. You'd unzip the sleeping-bag almost noiselessly, and slide out. It was dark, but rarely quite dark. If the moon was on the sea I could watch you easily, as you pulled on jeans and a T-shirt and kicked around for your sneakers. You hardly made a sound. You'd go out, and I'd tell myself it was stupid to stay awake, but it was hard to sleep again, not knowing when the door would open. I was afraid you'd go down to the water and start swimming. You liked to swim at night, but you were never a good swimmer.

It was a long, long time before you told me what you'd been doing. It must have been the day I left for England. I can't remember how the subject came up. I remember the greyness of the room, and outside the first big wind of the autumn whipping the tops off the waves. There wouldn't be any boats going out. I can't believe I asked you, after all those months of not asking and pretending that the nights didn't happen and all we had to think about were the days. But I'd had enough. I was beyond all of it by then. I didn't feel eighteen, or any age. Each time I shut my eyes I saw a boy who was small for his age, going back to where the basketball game had been. I saw you climb until you could reach the little kid who was trapped in a hoop. I saw you try over and over to lift him up with your arms that were still hairless and puny, and each time his weight fell back, jamming him tighter. The hoop was iron and it dug into his belly. He couldn't see any end to what you might do to him, and he broke up then and started to cry. You were trying to make it all right, but it was too late for that.

Too late for me as well. I was going back to England to make my life.

You began to talk.

'Sometimes I just have to walk. I can't stay in the room. It's like everything's up in here, buzzing around my head like a swarm of bees. I know I'm not gonna get to sleep. So I go out and I walk miles, along the shore road or round town. The rest of the night sometimes. Mostly it feels better to be out there and moving.

'I'll tell you something. You wouldn't believe the number of times I've met another guy walking. A guy my age, dressed the way I'm dressed. We don't usually talk. He's back there and I'm back there. One time, this guy stopped me and asked me for a cigarette. I had a pack of Marlboros. He didn't look like he had much so I told him to take the pack, but he wouldn't. He said he wasn't a bum. He asked for a light and he sucked it in deep, like he wanted to suck the flame right down into his lungs. I stayed and smoked a cigarette with him. All the time we stood in the street and smoked we were back there. I heard the leaves hissing. Big, dark-green leaves like hands. They grow so fast, a village can be burned one season and the next you wouldn't find the site. You fly over it and see nothing. Maybe a wave of brighter green, if you look close, but nobody looks that close. You can hear the jungle sucking and hissing all night long. And you know it thinks it's gonna get you. Even without people, that's pretty scary.

'It was the same for him, the other guy. I knew it. The town was like a paper wrapper you could rip through any time, and you'd be back there. You can't believe in anything solid, once you've seen how quick that jungle moves.'

*

My time is up. I am behind my desk, my face poised, attentive, neither smiling nor severe. Today I'm glad of the procedure holding me in its rigid embrace. I haven't got time to think now, only time to respond, to assess, to note, to make my judgment and deliver it. Counsel is seeking an injunction on behalf of his client, Patricia Mary Coogan, wife of John Joseph Coogan of 17b Darley Mansions, Henderton. Counsel is young, thirty or so, glossed with confidence like new paint. His client has received hospital treatment overnight and has been detained in hospital today following an assault by the said John Joseph Coogan. Injuries sustained include a broken rib, contusions to the face and body, and burns to the fingers of the right hand. His client alleges that her husband threatened to kill her if she did not have a proper dinner waiting for him next time he came home.

I lean forward and ask counsel how his client sustained the injuries to the fingers. His eyes widen slightly, he bows his head equally slightly, theatrically.

'My client alleges that her fingers were forced downwards and brought into contact with the surface of an electric sandwich maker. She was in the process of preparing a cheese-and-tomato sandwich for her husband, at his request, on his return to the matrimonial home at 1.45 a.m., when the alleged assault took place.' He looks straight at me. What is he thinking? *Is this enough for you? Are you satisfied?*

'In addition,' continues counsel, 'my client alleges that her husband told her it was a pity she had not been frying chips at the time, or he would have pushed her head into the chip-pan and held it there.'

I look back at counsel, at the smooth, fleshy mouth from which these words have just issued. I imagine what it was like for Mrs Patricia Coogan, to hear them emerging from the mouth of her husband on his return from an evening with friends, at 1.45 a.m.

Counsel and I speak the same language. We know where we are. The embrace that holds me holds him too. He knows that I will grant the injunction. In this case, a power of arrest and penal notice will be granted and attached to the order. But I know that other language, too, the language Mrs Coogan has had to learn. The language of being made to do things you don't want, one by one, until you end up far down on a path that's twisted so many times you'll never find your way back again.

There's been something else on my mind all day. It's a section of the County Courts Act 1984, and it relates to the tenure of office of district judges. I read it through last night.

A person appointed to an office to which subsection (1) applies shall hold that office during good behaviour.

The power to remove such a person from his office on account of misbehaviour shall be exercisable by the Lord Chancellor.

Mrs Coogan could have been one of my clients. She would have sat opposite me, her burnt fingers twisting in her lap. I would have offered her a cup of coffee, and put an ashtray on my desk.

Sometimes I still can't believe I've left them all behind. The bull-necked removal man who couldn't turn his head, after his mate stumbled and sent the weight of a sofa downstairs on top of him. They should never have been trying to do it anyway, it was against their better judgment, but the client was being difficult. Swore the sofa'd go upstairs when any fool could've told him it wouldn't. 'All right then, we'll show him,' said Pete.

The couple who'd had their house on the Bentley estate repossessed, and were living in one room paying off the building society. And now she was pregnant at last, after years of trying. At the end of the interview her husband went down the narrow stairs first. She looked up at me out of the stairwell. Her face was mottled, her hair greasy with the changes of early pregnancy.

She said, 'We had the nursery all ready, you know, where we lived before. Five years and nothing happened. Well, in the end we shut the door on it. Funny, isn't it?' She pressed her lips together, clutched her handbag tightly under her arm, and went away down the stairs.

As I drive home I feel myself drifting. I blink and focus hard on the road, the shine of fallen rain, the low slant of evening sun making the marsh a vivid, liquid green, like the back of a snake. My hands are tight on the steering-wheel. I see her on the edge of the road. It's Mrs Coogan walking towards me, the chip-pan a halo above her head. I pass her and then she's there again, still up ahead, her arms stretched out towards me and her hair a crown of fire above the bubbling of her features and the melted pits of her eyes.

Ten

Donald is busy cooking when I get home. I go in to the boys. They are lying on the floor, heads close together, making an electric circuit on a board.

'It's going to be a burglar alarm for our room,' says Joe. I watch Matt as he fits wire into the battery terminal. He doesn't look up or greet me. Joe may have forgotten the morning, but not Matt.

'I bought you something,' I say. Matt catches his bottom lip with his teeth, as if concentrating. 'I went into a little shop,' I go on. 'They had these screwdriver sets.' I take them out from behind my back. They are well-made, with smooth, heavy handles. There are eight in each set.

'Here you are. One each.' Matt's face flushes, very slightly. He hasn't expected a present. As I give him his, I slip two pound coins inside the plastic pack. 'And thank you for looking after Joe.'

'I didn't do anything. He's all right. He could've gone to school.'

'I couldn't, could I, Mum?'

'I don't think so. The way you looked this morning, Mrs Carmody would have sent you home. Dad'll look after you tomorrow, then it's the weekend.'

Matt takes the smallest screwdriver out of the pack to examine it. He won't use it yet. He likes to pore over new things. Sliding a finger down the handle, he says, 'A man called.'

'Who?'

'I don't know. He didn't say.' His finger again strokes the metal, this time down to the sharp point of the Philips screwdriver. 'He was an American.' Joe is watching Matt closely. He knows about this. They've been talking about it. Most of the time it's Joe who needs Matt, but this phone call has left Matt needing his brother. I know how they'll have sat, heads close together, one talking, the other listening. And when the house made one of its empty sounds, they'll both have stiffened and looked up, silent, for a long moment.

'What did he say?' I ask.

'He asked if you were home. I said you were in the bath.'

'That was right.'

'Then he said he'd call back when you were out of the bathroom. He asked how long I figured you'd be.'

'So what did you say?'

'I said you'd be ages because you were washing your hair.'

I can see them. Matt in the hall, holding the phone carefully, soaking up every phrase, and saying what I've taught them to say if the phone rings while I am out. Joe at his elbow, watching his older brother's face.

'Then he said, *Who is that? Am I speaking with Joseph, or is it Matthew?*'

I hear a stranger's intonation in my son's voice, its stresses adult and foreign.

'Did you tell him?'

'Yes.' We are all silent. 'He asked me!' cries Matt.

'It doesn't matter,' I say as lightly as I can. 'It must have been someone who knows us anyway, or he wouldn't have known your names. Probably an old friend everyone's forgotten about. I'll have to ask Dad who he knows in America.'

'It was you he wanted to talk to,' says Matt.

'Never mind. Forget it. Show me how your circuit's going to work.'

But Matt sits back on his heels and looks straight at me.

'He isn't a friend,' he says. 'If he was a friend he'd know nobody ever calls us Joseph and Matthew.'

'Well, don't worry about it. You said all the right things.'

Joe squirms close to me. In a sudden rush he says, 'He said something else as well. Matt didn't want us to tell you.'

'Go on.'

Matt flushes. 'When I said you were washing your hair, he said, "That's going to take a while then, with all that long hair your mother's got."' Again the faint, disturbing echo. My face must have changed, because Matt reaches over and punches Joe's arm. 'I *told* you not to tell her.' But it's a routine punch. Matt is relieved that I know. The call has frightened him.

'But you haven't got long hair, Mum,' says Joe.

'No. He made a mistake.'

Matt stirs, as if he's going to say something more, then he turns back to wiring up the battery.

I stand up. 'I'd better help Dad with the meal. You two finish this, then you can give us a demonstration.'

There's the phone, at the bottom of the stairs. I put my hand on it. It is quite still. I can't remember if modern phones vibrate, the way the old ones used to, before they rang. If it throbbed under my hand now, and began to ring, what would I do? I want it to ring. I want to pick up the phone and ask, 'Who are you? What do you want?'

I find Donald in the kitchen.

'How did the bank go?'

'I'll tell you in a minute. I've got to measure this.' He presses mashed potato down into a cup, frowning. I always remember the smell of the chemistry lab when I watch Donald cook. The gassy smell of the Bunsen burners, the stink of scorched wood where some joker turned the flame onto a desk-top, the smell of iron oxide that reminds me of menstruation. Donald doesn't like cooking. He has to have a scaffolding of cookery books, scales and measuring cups before he begins. Donald doesn't improvise.

'What're you making?' I ask, leaning against the counter.

'Corned beef hash.'

'Oh. Nice. Let me open the tin, you'll get corned beef all over your bandage.'

The corned beef is warm from standing next to the stove. It glops out of the tin in an oblong the colour of oxblood polish, coated with melting yellow fat. Donald chops at it with a knife, then forks it into the mashed potato. Peering at his recipe, he adds salt, black pepper and grated nutmeg, then binds the hash with beaten egg. I shut my mouth as he pours sunflower oil into the frying pan, fails to let it heat up enough and then whacks in the hash. It doesn't sizzle. It flops into the cool oil and lies there.

'Maybe you could turn up the heat a bit.'

Donald turns the flame up to full. I go back upstairs to change. As I strip off my tights I smell burning and run back downstairs in case Donald is out of the kitchen. He is there, standing with a wooden spatula in his hand while the hash smokes on the table.

'Look at it, the bastard,' says Donald. 'The moment my back's turned it catches fire. Do you think it's worth scraping it out?'

'No, not really. Leave it, I'll make sandwiches. They like sandwiches.'

I open the window wide and the cool evening air floods in. The marsh is beautiful in the distance.

'Let's eat quickly and go for a walk.'

'Do you think it's all right to leave them?'

It should be me asking that question. 'Of course,' I say. 'They'll be fine. We'll walk down to the sea-wall.'

In the bread-bin there are two white sliced loaves. In the fridge there is a tub of soft margarine, a cake of soapy cheddar and two tomatoes. Donald has been to the village shop.

'I wish you wouldn't buy this stuff.'

'It's cheap.'

It has nothing to do with cheapness. I know it and Donald knows it. It is to do with punishment. I used to go to the market on my way to work, and fill two shopping bags with tight-skinned, shining purple aubergines, with russet apples, Kidd's Orange apples, peppers so fresh they spat out juice as you cut them, cauliflowers with firm white curds, turnip greens which I cooked with sesame oil and ginger, big, mild Spanish onions, fresh chillies. I would leave the bags lolling in the cool cupboard where I kept my coat, then bus home with the bags on my lap, thinking of what I'd cook. The fruit and veg from the market was half the price it is down here, in the village shop.

November was the best month for the market, when the days were dark and short and the late apples were piled up in heaps next to satsumas, clementines and navel oranges. Everything was cheap, before the frosts. I bought green tomatoes for chutney, and purple sprouting broccoli, and celery which had been earthed up and had crumbs of black soil in its grooves. The market began at seven, in the winter dark, and the lights would swing inside the canvas awnings and throw huge shadows when the wind blew. There was a smoky, bonfire smell in the air, and the stall-keepers wore fingerless gloves as they shovelled potatoes out of sacks. Later I bought bunches of Christmas greenery, and a hoop of holly to hang on the door, and mistletoe with fragile berries which dropped to the floor and had to be picked up at once in case Joe ate them. I bought nuts and sage, clementines with long sharp green leaves still on them, drums of figs and long sticky packets of dates.

Now I spread soft margarine on the bread, cut cheese and lay the tomato slices on top.

'So what did the bank say?'

'They want to up the payments on the second loan to £560 a month. They don't like the way the debt is increasing.'

83

'It wouldn't be increasing if they didn't charge so much interest.'

'I looked at the figures. We owe £3,600 more than we did this time last year. It's gone up to £132,000.'

'Jesus.'

'With the mortgage, that's £204,000. If interest rates go up again – '

'Take this in to the children, and we'll go for a walk. We can talk about it then.'

Donald turns to me, smiling. 'You'd be better off if I died. With the life insurance, and what you earn, you'd be well-off.'

'You're not going to die.'

I want him to stop talking of death and debt and go out and get a job as a petrol pump attendant. But he won't do that. The worst moment was when he sent away to one of those advertisements in the Sunday papers that promise you a new, lucrative career in your spare time. *Thanks to taking your course, one year later am earning £2,500 a month, I drive a P reg. Cavalier, and the family will be holidaying in Florida this year. Thank you, Erskine Enterprises!* I didn't see the pack arrive, but he must have read through it all day, because when I came home that night he said, 'I've got something I want to show you. Sit down and I'll make you some tea.'

I scanned his face. He looked alive, optimistic, the way he used to look when he was starting work with a new client. He put the mug of tea in front of me and planked down the sales pack on the table.

'You have to read it carefully. I've gone through it several times and I can't see any snags. It looks pretty good, Simone.'

I read the first few pages. The pack was all information bubbles, testimonials of success, charts of figures. I could not believe that Donald was taking this stuff seriously. I glanced up at him, hoping it was a joke. But his face was eager. He leaned over my shoulder and pointed out a column of figures.

'That's all right, don't you think? Of course I'd have to go into it carefully.'

I thought of the time we took Matt to the fair, when he was eight. Joe was six, and all he wanted was to be with us and go on roundabouts. But Matt was to have his own money. 'You can choose what you go on. But when the money's gone, that's it. No more.' He had five pounds. He went over to the rifle range, where a flock of enormous fluffy toys hung above the targets, ready to drop ripely into the palm of a successful shooter. I saw his eyes fixed, brilliant, dazzled. It looked so easy. I let him spend the first pound. He got nothing, but he turned to me, his face passionate. 'I *know* I'll win if I get three more goes. I watched that boy. You have to shoot to one side first, then the other.' And the second pound was spent. When I tried to stop him his eyes dilated with panic. 'It's my money, Mum! You said I could do what I wanted!'

I was stupid. I ought to have stopped it then. After the third pound, he was in too deep. He could not stop now, couldn't admit that it was all a stupid con. The stall-keeper must have seen my anger, for when Matt's fifth pound was gone he came over with a little fluffy mouse and said, 'There you are, sonny, well tried.' Matt walked away, his face a rictus of distress, grinning. Later, in the car, I heard him say to Joe, 'Here you are, Joe. I won this for you.'

The look on Matt's face was with me as I turned the pages of the pack. I drank my tea, then I said, as gently as I could, 'I'd be a bit cautious, Donald. It looks like pyramid selling to me.' I could not bear to look at his face. A year ago he'd never even have noticed the advertisement. If he had, he'd have laughed at it. That was when I first knew what the loss of the partnership had brought him to. It had destroyed his faith in his judgment so completely that he had suspended it.

I look at Donald now, as he stands holding the tray of sandwiches for his children, his head bowed.

'Let's go out,' I repeat. 'They'll be fine for an hour.'

But he won't come. I walk into the clear, cool, autumn evening. As soon as I'm outside the house I hear the sea. I untie the orange baling twine from the gatepost, lift the gate, swing it open. This is the way down to the sea. The sheep stare, then shamble away from me and take up their task of eating again. They have cropped the grass close, and it is covered with sheep droppings, black and shiny as liquorice, and with smaller, drier rabbit droppings. In the mornings, when I come down to swim, the rabbits are thick on the fields. It doesn't matter how many get shot, there are always more. A little wind makes the reeds ripple by the drainage ditches. I feel myself breathing deep for the first time that day, in the loneliness of the marsh that is like clear water.

I walk over the three fields to the sea-wall. It's been piled up and repaired as long as people have lived here. Without the wall the land would be gone in two winters. A lot of money has been spent two miles farther down the coast, where a spring tide breached the sea-wall two winters ago. But here it has grown into the landscape, with its stone face turned to the sea and its bulky green shoulder to the land. Sheep get through the wire and climb it sometimes. You see their silhouettes on top of the wall, ruffled by the wind that always blows there. I climb the stile from the last field, and go up the wooden steps which take you on top of the wall.

I turn, and look back at our house. Donald said he wanted to go through the figures again, and draft a letter to the bank. I hold my hand up in front of my face, palm outwards. Now there's no light, no house, no Donald, no boys. I move my hand sideways and the house appears, recreated. I think of all the people who have stood on this sea-wall.

Invaders landed here for centuries. It was a good spot. You could see the home fires from here, just as you can now, all the lights of the little settlements dotted along the coast.

They poured in, torching the thatch first. It would burn well at the end of summer. The flames would snap and lick and fire would jump from hut to hut. And then shouting and people plunging out of their huts with the dreams still in their heads and a waking nightmare of fire ready to swallow them. A woman dragged back by her hair because she got in their way. The bare pale throat gleaming with sweat and the knife jagging into it while the man who did it didn't even watch her die. He was shouting over his shoulder to someone else.

You don't even bother to look at death, you just make it happen. And you kick someone back to the ground after slitting her throat, even if she's not dead, because you've got more than enough deaths to get done. The way she flops about on the ground is like someone taking up time that doesn't belong to her, when you've got a busy day.

They carried what they could, and off they went, making a note of the bearings. They had an excellent sense of timing. They'd leave it for a bit, let people think they weren't coming back. If you want to make the best use of people you've got to leave them a bit of hope. Otherwise they're buggered, they'll just go off, and all you'll get next time are weeds and stray cats. You've got to judge it right. Come one year, then not the next, nor the next. Give them a couple of harvests. Let them think they're doing all right, and work their guts out getting in the corn they won't be eating.

The worst thing is when people fight back. That's when it gets ugly, and there's no need for it, if people have a bit of sense. That's why you should never disturb a burglar. He's so full of adrenaline, he might just kill you. He wouldn't mean to, he wouldn't know what he was doing. Or so they say. Those men coming inland, across the cleared ground, moving quietly in spite of their weight. Such things have always been happening. Sometimes they stop for a while, but they start up again before long. If you happen to be born in one of those happy times when nothing's happening, then the change can be a real shock.

All I've ever wanted is to live in one of those times.

'*We registered for the draft.*'

I can still see those looks that pass between them, Calvin and Michael. I could never imagine what it felt like to be them. They'd grown up thinking life was a personal thing, then history hit them. They registered for the draft. They waited to see what numbers were drawn, while I lay on the floor in the safe backwash of television. But Michael told me I was a fighter, long before I knew it myself. *You'd fight for your kids.* It sounded like a cliché to me then. Children weren't real to me before I had them. I could easily think of myself as gentle, and fighting was something other people did.

It's different since I had the children. I plot for them; I plan ahead like an army general. I would do anything to protect them.

I'm thinking of a man who built a cellar under his house, with a secret room that no one else knew about. He made a nice job of it. There was even a toilet down there, put in by a plumber friend of his. The walls were painted white, they bought a couple of folding beds and a few other fixtures and fittings. When the door was shut you just wouldn't know it was there.

Then he went out in his car and drove around the streets, just driving idly from one bus-stop to the next, past school entrances, past church halls where there are dancing classes after school. Lots of days like that, putting the finishing touches to the cellar and then driving, driving.

He saw them. Maybe there were two little girls who carried their dancing shoes and leotards in red attaché cases. It was November, a bit gloomy but not dark yet. Only half-past three. They had their hair combed back from their faces and fastened tight on top of their heads. That's the way their ballet teacher liked it. No wisps hanging down. They had long, skinny legs ending in clumpy school shoes.

Two little girls, ten years old, and this is the first time they've been allowed to walk from school to ballet class on their own. Except they're not alone, there are two of them so it's all right. 'You've got to let them have a little bit of independence,' their mothers say, reassuring one another because it's hard to let go even when you know it's the right thing. 'After all, next year they'll be off to secondary school on the bus and they'll have to be able to look after themselves then.'

Mothers are like that. Always fussing. The two little girls laugh and dawdle along, chattering. Every so often they remember what their mothers said: 'Go straight there! Don't be hanging about on the street,' and they put on a spurt, giggling more than ever.

They don't notice the car coasting along the other side of the road towards them. Why should they? The man with his elbow on the edge of the open window. They do notice a bit when the car crosses the road onto their side and pulls in, engine running. But it's got nothing to do with them. They're on their way to dancing class, and after that they're going to be met by Ann's mother who is taking them both home for tea. More chattering, hours and hours of it, and pizza and *Neighbours* and music and taking the phone up to Ann's room to phone their friends.

But look. There's another man in the back of the car. He's opening his door, very smoothly and quickly, and now he's out and on the pavement behind them. And the driver's out too, and he comes in front of them. And it's funny, he hasn't turned off the engine. And the children are lifted out of their lives.

There's my house with the yellow lights coming on in the windows, one by one. My children moving from room to room. If I had binoculars I would see their shadows. It looks so safe.

Shadows in the firelight, yellow electricity, the doors closed. The country dream that everybody wants. If I saw a car on the road now, just there between those trees, so far off that it seemed to be crawling towards the house, I would have nothing to fear.

But there is no car. It's the evening wind that stirs the hair on my neck. I want to run, and I want to stay here. It's stupid to let myself get this tired. I'm not thinking straight. I am only a judge, district judge. Maintenance is my territory, and insolvency, and disputes over contract. I don't deal with murder. I judge. I have to make shapes. I make sense of things that don't really make sense at all.

History hit you like a storm. Small for your age at twelve, and then you must have grown quickly. You'd have been able to get the little boy out of the basketball hoop.

You were lifted out of your lives, disgorged in bellyloads by planes that lumbered in looking too heavy to fly. As soon as you put your boot onto the soil it stuck. You were history now.

But you still had yourself. Your private smell buried in your armpits and your groin. The way your skin tanned, the way you always put on your left boot before the right one. Your thousand tastes and habits and instincts that you followed without even thinking about them.

I suppose that's what armies do. They bury the private flesh in uniform, they make you put on your right boot first and bit by bit they teach you to walk away from your own history and into theirs.

It was a country of small people. They had low technology and none of the wall of resources that stood at your back. But on home ground they danced while you stood still.

'It was so fucking boring most of the time you could have died. We'd even lay bets on how fast a shadow would move.

90

All the time you'd think you saw something move, but when you turned there'd be nothing.

'There was this old woman, she had her hands on me, pulling and screaming. I thought, "Why don't you take your hands off me? Why are you doing this to me?" I wasn't doing anything to her. All through these times you don't really know what's going on. Later on you get told and it makes some kind of sense. You get told why it has to happen, and now you're part of it, you're not outside any more.

'The girls would crowd around in the bars. You'd feel as if a whole sheet of butterflies was settling on you. They made us look like the pores of our skin were sandpaper. If you laid your two arms alongside, hers would look like silk.'

As you spoke I saw two arms on the bar counter. One was yours. It was dark, the windows blinded to keep out the sun. At your side her body twisted in its narrow sheath of silk. I knew what you were thinking of. Entering that girl, her smallness and her liquid softness which swallowed you. I could hear the sound of the money you gave her, passing from your hand. It would be soft and moist. A sound like suede on suede. It wouldn't crackle.

'I don't remember her name,' you said. I looked at you and I didn't believe you. I didn't say it, because it was your world, not mine. I only saw what you let me see. Then you laughed and said, 'But that's OK. I've got Calvin right here to remember it for me.'

The more you do, the more you can do. I'm trying to think about what you want to do now, and what is in your mind that you won't yet allow me to see. You haven't done much yet. A couple of letters, two phone calls that didn't really say anything. I make you bigger than you are.

Eleven

I touch the phone as I go past it, up the stairs. And again. Two for joy. I could have unplugged it. I think for a second about unplugging, then it rings.

'Hi.' It's his voice. A week ago I wouldn't have recognized it, but I've learned it again. I turn, so my body shields the rest of the house from the phone.

'Hi,' I say back.

'I've got you at last. First I get your husband, then I get your kid. He sounds like a nice kid.'

I don't say anything. I make my listening attentive. I'll pull him to me along the currents of air that carry voices. I'll undo him with my listening.

'Simone?'

'I'm here.'

'Aren't you going to say anything?'

I wait again. A roar of TV laughter comes through the door. I hear Joe laugh, loudly, consciously, proud that he has got the TV joke. Between Michael and me the air sighs.

'It's been a bitch, finding you again.'

'Has it?' I say. 'I wouldn't have thought it'd be that difficult.' I polish the base of the phone with my forefinger. I hear him breathe in. He's waiting too, for someone who doesn't exist any more. How I used to pour myself down the phone to him. All warm and spilling and eager. Hoping he would think me sexy.

'Well, I made it at last,' he says. 'I'm talking to you.'

'You know where I am.'

'I can't picture it. You could be anywhere.'

I say nothing again. I think he's telling me that he's going to come here. In this clutter of what isn't being said I can pick out a few shapes. That's my training, after all.

'Did you cut your hair?' he asks suddenly.

'No. It's still long.'

'Matthew told me you were washing it, when I called.'

'That's right.'

'I remember the way you used to wash your hair all the time. You told him anything about us? Does he know about you and me?'

He's climbing into my life, hand over hand, like a burglar. *There's no you and me*, I want to say, but this isn't the moment. All those years in my office upstairs with the fire burning, I've learned a lot about making silences for other people to talk into. It's what people don't know they're telling you that you need to hear.

'Why would I do that?' I ask. It leaps into my mind that he's not alone. He's got someone else in the room, standing close while he talks. Calvin.

'Does Calvin want to say hello?' I ask.

'Calvin?' His surprise sounds genuine.

'Calvin. Isn't he there with you?'

'Calvin's dead.'

I can check that, I think automatically.

'He died in an accident in Illinois.'

'Illinois?'

'Yeah. Way back in '86. Truck he hitched a ride in went off the highway. The trucker lived, he had a broken leg. He was fast asleep when they crashed.'

'Who, Calvin?'

'No, the trucker. He let Calvin drive. But that's not what everyone else got told.'

I see the truck barrelling along the highway like a lit-up castle, all of Illinois ahead of it, Calvin behind the wheel. The light of oncoming headlights flares in his face, but I still can't make out his features.

'When did you say he died?'

'April 26th. His birthday.'

'What was he doing in Illinois?'

'Jesus, Simone, how'm I supposed to know that? I'm not his keeper. He was restless, he was always travelling around. You know Calvin.'

The Calvin I knew stayed in one place, close to Michael. If Calvin's gone, things are going to be a lot easier. I can't think of anyone else who knew us well enough to remember much. Not after all this time. If Calvin really did drive that truck off the road more than ten years ago. Now that I have the date, I can find out. And I can't feel a shred of sadness for him, not even that fellow feeling of bones and flesh for other bones crushed, other flesh torn and letting out life.

'You think he did it on purpose?' I ask.

Michael sighs. 'I knew you'd ask me that,' he says. He says it as if neither of us has changed at all. 'I knew you'd want to know.'

'Yes, I do.'

I've changed so much you won't know me, I think, moving the phone to my left hand, hearing Joe laugh again. *You think you know me, but you know nothing.*

'I'm sorry about Calvin,' I say.

'It'd been a while since I saw him.'

'All the same.'

We are quiet for a while. The expensive silence ticks on.

'You know, Simone, the way you went, it wrecked me. I was out of my mind. Do you believe that?'

I say nothing. I hear him swallow.

'There was a storm two weeks after you left. I took off in the *Susie Ann*. By the time I got her round the point and hit the wind I knew I could be in trouble. The wind blew so hard

94

it was cutting lumps of water off the top of the waves. They were hitting the boat like rocks.' He is silent again. I see the boat buck, the water smashed into chaos by the wind fighting the tide.

'But you got back.'

'Yeah. No matter how much you think you don't care what happens, you find yourself fighting. I couldn't let her turn over and get broken up on the shore. You remember the *Susie Ann*.'

'You know I do,' I say into the mouthpiece, barely moving my lips. My heart annoys me, bumping as hard as this when I have nothing to be afraid of. And my hands are sweating. 'I'm not sure where this conversation is taking us,' I say, in a voice I know he's never heard before. He is quiet for a bit, then I hear his voice again, bubbling through laughter.

'Oh wow! Here comes the judge.'

And that tells me all I need to know. He has really done his homework, and for a reason. And I remember the two of us watching *Rowan and Martin's Laugh-in*, Calvin didn't like the show. My bare feet tucked in Michael's lap, and the taste of beer from the bottle his lips had touched before mine. Sometimes I would see the bubble of his saliva and put my lips to it slowly, for the shiver of pleasure it drove through my body.

'I've got to go now,' I say.

'But we only just got started. You don't need to worry about the cost of the call. I've got plenty of money.'

He hasn't, of course he hasn't. But it's money that's in his mind all right. The thought of money was waiting there all the time, just behind his tongue. And now it's slipped out.

'All I want is to talk to you,' says Michael, and it sounds like the truth. He comes into my mind, all of him. His shirt off and his shoulders glistening. The plume of water pouring from the dipper, spilling onto his skin. The loose drops kicking onto the dust and dirt of the yard. And his eyes closed, his face peaceful. All of him there for once and offered to me.

'I'm sorry,' I say.

'You don't know how long it took to find you.'

'I can't believe it took so long. It's easy enough to trace people if you want to.'

'Have you ever tried?'

'No. No, I've never tried.'

'You didn't need to.'

'Listen, Michael –'

'Simone, would you have recognized my voice?'

'I don't know.'

'I wanted to talk to you, Simone. Just talk. That's all I want.'

And then we're both silent. Silent for a long time, until the phone clicks. I hold it, hearing the echo of Michael's voice die to nothing. The voice is the most physical thing. It carries the grain of the man. His weight, the depth of his lungs, the tightness of his throat. His mouth wet, or dry. It wasn't true what I told Michael. I would have known it. Memory spreads over my senses like a film of oil, brilliant and treacherous.

Donald is out in the woodshed, piling wood by the light of a battery lantern. There are two big piles, and a heap of fresh white kindling. He's been splitting logs.

'Davey Berryman's going to let me have another load at the end of the week, so I thought I'd better clear this place a bit.'

'Donald.'

'Yes? Don't stand in my light, Simone, I can't see what I'm doing.'

The chopper goes up, its shadow beating on the wall, huge. It cracks down and the wood cleaves.

'Wood's still a bit green.'

There are chips of pale, sweet-smelling wood all over the floor. I pick up a handful and smell them.

'What's this?'

'Apple wood. There'll be mainly apple in the new load, too, where they're clearing the orchard.'

'Nice. Listen, Donald – '

Again the shadows leap. It's late. The children should be in bed.

'I'm going to have my hair cut short,' I say.

He straightens, looks at me. 'You're always saying that.'

'No, I've made up my mind.'

He smiles. He doesn't believe I will.

I look around the woodshed. It's not one of the stone outbuildings, it's a proper wooden shed, well-made, of smooth pine planks, with a pine floor. Joe wants to live in it. It has one square small window, so it's always dusky and sweet-smelling in here. Now it's full of warm light and shadows, the rough edges of wood, the scent of resin. Joe wants to have a rabbit and keep it in here. He says rabbits love apple wood. Splitting wood is one of the things Donald could already do, when we came here. If he finds a fallen branch when he's out walking he'll drag it home and leave it outside the shed under a tarpaulin until it's ready for chopping.

Donald balances a thick log on the chopping board. He stands back, swings up the chopper, brings it down. The wood opens, white. I go forward, and touch the cut surface. It feels moist.

'For God's sake, Simone, get out of the way. You'll get hurt.'

'Let me smell it.' I bend down, smell the tang of the wood. It does smell of apple.

'I want this shed full before the winter. It's worth putting in the time now, if it saves buying coal,' says Donald. He turns and wedges two more logs into the biggest pile along the wall. In the soft light of the lantern the shed looks like a cave. Donald is building up a safe wall of wood that won't collapse when we take out logs in the winter. He has the chopper, the logs to be tested, split and piled. I think he might be happy. The bandage on his hand is filthy, but I'm not going to say anything.

'Did that chap ever ring back?'

'Oh – yes. Just now.'

'What was it all about?'

'He was ringing up about someone else really. Someone I knew when I was a student. He's been killed in a car crash. But we hadn't been in touch for a long time.'

'Oh, I see. Nice of him to go to all that trouble.'

'Yes.'

Twelve

If it's money Michael wants, that's one thing. I can deal with that, though it'll be tough until I can convince him I haven't got any.

But I don't believe it's money. Michael never cared about money. It wasn't in his nature. He could have made plenty if he'd wanted, with the boats and the summer people. The *Susie Ann* was his own, and he could have been taking people out all season long, around the bay on fishing trips, or to the harbour bar to see the wreck which was just visible through the thick green water at low tide. That was the way other people worked, dawn to dusk for the bright, greedy weeks of the summer season. Michael worked enough to keep himself in food and drink and grass, and that was all. But he loved boats. To Michael a boat was an end in itself, not a means to make money. If he didn't like a man, he wouldn't work for him, no matter how good the pay was. That summer he spent whole days working for nothing, helping someone he'd met to build a catamaran.

'Listen, the guy's got no money. How's he ever going to get that thing into the water unless somebody helps him?'

It was a good design, he said. The guy knew what he was doing, except when it came to money. We quarrelled because Michael spent the whole of a fine Sunday working on the catamaran when I wanted to drive up to the apple festival. I picked up his clean jeans and threw them into the sea. *If you won't go with me, then don't go anywhere.* He waded after them and put them on wet, and went off anyway. I don't even remember the name of the man who was building the boat. I thought he fancied Michael. That's what I was like, on edge about everyone who came near us, and too young to hide it. And whenever I felt at ease, there was Calvin.

We did go to the apple festival, another day. I remember the smell of the apples, heaped up by the barns and on trestle tables, sharp and winy in the cold air. When you bit into them, the juice spurted and ran down your chin. They were mostly red apples, Macintoshes. Dark, shiny red, like the apple in *Snow-White*. There were pumpkins too, waiting for Hallowe'en. I had never seen pumpkins like that before, big and round and golden orange, some smooth-skinned, some rough. I'd never tasted pumpkin pie. American pie was too sweet for me: I'd tried it a couple of times then given up. I had never bought butternut squash or onion squash. I didn't even know that pumpkins grew on vines. I saw red barn, blue sky, yellow pumpkin. The largeness and brilliance of everything took my breath away. We wandered round the side of the barn and watched a pickup truck slam to a stop in a wave of late-summer dust. It was a girl driving, my age or a year more. She swung her legs down on what I was just beginning not to think of as the wrong side. Then she kicked off her shoes, lit a cigarette, and stood there with her eyes closed, resting, while her toes clenched and unclenched in the silk of the dust. I thought she was beautiful. I don't suppose she was, but she was what I wanted to be, at that moment. And I saw Michael look at her.

Some of the pumpkins were so big it took two men to carry them. I saw two men in overalls hunker down and lift an orange pumpkin and carry it to a trailer. They made a noise somewhere between a grunt and a laugh as they took the weight. I can still see the red barn walls, the clear blue sky, the round, ripe pumpkins, though when Michael told me that Calvin was dead I couldn't remember Calvin's mouth or his eyes.

We'd got up early and driven a hundred and seventy miles through a pale, cold morning. Just Michael and I. The leaves were beginning to change colour a little. A lick of colour here and there, like a mistake. Michael told me how the roads would be crawling with cars once the foliage season started. People came up from New York and all over, just to see the fall colours. I'd have liked to come up and see the trees red and orange, blazing mile after mile, but I didn't say so. I could tell it wasn't cool to crawl round Vermont gaping at maples.

Some of the apples were exhibits, some were for sale. Michael and I picked out a basketful, laying them in as gently as eggs. It was a big flat basket and we put it in the back of the car, wedged in so the fruit wouldn't spill. You could fill your basket for a dollar. Some people were piling their baskets so high the apples spilled and rolled, but we didn't do that. Michael always had a sense of grace about such things.

Michael looked them over, picked out the best one, rubbed it on his shirt-sleeve, and held it for me to bite. It's hard to bite an apple when someone else is holding it, and my teeth slipped on the tough, shiny skin. I had to grapple it in my mouth to get a grip. There's something humiliating about being fed like a baby, but it was sexy too. The guys who'd lifted the pumpkin were looking at us and smiling a bit, and I thought how their teeth were like dog's teeth, bared, and I was glad Michael was there to shield me from them. The girl from the pickup knew them. She'd gone over to talk to them. They looked at her quite differently from the way they looked at me.

I took one bite from his hand, then I held the apple myself. The woman on the stall told us she'd picked the apples the night before. She had a barn full of them, best season she'd had for years. But the price she got in the city didn't even pay for the gas.

She told us we should go walking in the woods. It was her land, no problem. There was a logging track right up the hill. I couldn't believe the way people had land up there. They'd point at a hill and say, 'That's mine.'

Most of it wasn't farming land. It was trees and scrub, the soil thin over the rock where trees clung. She had her farmstead, her orchard in the valley, a few fields. I thought how good it must feel to look out from the farmhouse window and see the hill, and know it was your own, curled around to protect you. It had light on it up there long after the sun had left the valley, she said. I'd grown up with a strip of garden twenty feet wide and thirty feet long, a sandpit where Jenny and I scuffled in the summer, and a back gate which opened onto an asphalt lane. I must have told Michael about that house, but he kept on believing that my soft English voice meant a soft upbringing. He'd never been to England. He had no idea of the kind of smallness I was used to. Or maybe I didn't really tell him. At that time my aim was to rinse the smallness off my eyes. To be like the girl in the pickup truck.

'You want to try a winter here?' the woman asked me, laughing. She could see the city in me.

Michael may have changed. People say they don't care about money when they're young. They believe that the grown-ups will keep on painting the window-frames and replacing the tiles on the roof so the rain doesn't come in. Or else they don't even notice that window-frames have paint on them, and that it doesn't last for ever. Maybe Michael wants a house now, and window-frames, and a pay-cheque for everything he's ever done. Even the debt no one's ever going to pay: the innocence he won't ever be able to get back again. The politicians and the generals who sent him to Vietnam have Alzheimer's now. Their voices slur and their feet shuffle. Without their wives they'd be left out on their lawns in their wheelchairs, with leaves falling on them. These are the same men who jumped out of helicopters on the White House lawn, ducked under the churning rotors and ran boyishly across the grass. These were the men reporters chased with microphones. Flashlights were always exploding in their faces like tiny imitations of the wars they started.

For years I watched them on black-and-white television. These were the men who backed Mayor Daly when he let his cops run wild. *The whole world's watching*, the kids outside the hall chanted, as the batons thrashed down on them and the dogs were let loose. *The whole world's watching*. I remember hearing that. I was a child and I still believed the upraised arms would fall to the cops' sides, shamed, and the hall of the Democratic convention would fall silent too, and a new world would begin. It was a long time ago, before a different generation grew up to channel-surf its way past war and famine with a bag of popcorn in its lap.

Now I remember. The guy whose boat Michael helped build used to walk the streets at night too. After Michael told me about that, something suddenly came to me and I said, 'Don't you ever meet men – guys – who think you're out there for something else?'

'What d'you mean?'

'I mean, if you were a girl out that late, men would think you were a prostitute. Do men ever think that about other men?'

The naïveté of it takes my breath now. That I thought it, and that I said it too, looking at Michael through the V of my hair, there in the room with the wind outside beating up the sea. If he doesn't want money, what does he want? And Michael looked at me and said, 'A guy did once.'

'What? You mean he thought you were – '

'Yeah.'

'What did you say?'

Michael shrugged. 'I told him it'd be twenty dollars.'

I remained silent. This was the type of situation in which I so often said the wrong thing.

'If he wanted to fuck my ass, that is,' Michael continued. 'Fifteen dollars to suck him off.'

I said nothing and Michael was quiet. I stole a glance at his face and it was calm, as if telling me these things eased him. He had his hand twined around mine. For a while I watched blobs of foam fly off the waves. It was so restful. I felt like an invalid who has been pushed out to the edge of the sea to watch the water, to recover.

'Why not,' said Michael at last, as if to himself. 'Why wouldn't I. He was just a guy.'

I wipe Joe's face with baby-wipes, so as not to get water on his bandage. He shuts his eyes, to let me. The shape of his eyelid is perfect, like something cut in wax. I can feel his breathing on me, light and quick. He says that Matt says his hair smells. I say we won't be able to wash his hair for a while, but I can't smell anything at all.

'Matt says I smell of blood.'

'No. There's no blood there. It's all healing up. Soon you'll have a little white scar and then your hair will grow over again.'

He believes me and subsides in his bed, content. It's a good, calm bedtime. Even Matt allows me to hold him close for a moment before he wriggles away to read his book. Goodnight, goodnight.

I remember what it was like to know that my parents were moving about downstairs, eating cake, talking. I'd listen to my father whistling. The pipes gagged and I turned over and smoothed the wall with my forefinger until I fell asleep. I always tried to fall asleep before my father went out, leaving my mother alone. If I was still awake I'd hear her walk from one small room into the other, drawing curtains, flicking the lights on. The TV would blare, then fade. She always turned it right down, as if there might be other sounds beneath its noise, and she didn't want to miss them.

Although the front door was shut and locked a draught seemed to blow through the house all the time he was away.

Every week he bought her a box of chocolates and she ate them alone, at night while he was away, rustling down to the bottom layer for cracknels and almond whirls. In the daytime the chocolates stayed on a high shelf. Once I balanced a chair on a box and hooked them down, but the box fell, the paper cases and chocolates spilled over the floor. I crammed everything back, and pushed the box up on the shelf again, my heart banging. I didn't eat a single one, but she knew it was me. She stood me in front of her, between her knees, and said, 'I don't ask much, Simone.'

My sister Jenny knew more than I did.

'He shouldn't go out every night. We haven't got enough money.'

I thought of my mother's fingers on the clasp of her handbag, as it shut and opened with a fat click. She had all the money, as far as I knew.

It's true that she didn't ask much, and she didn't get much, either. She didn't expect much more for her daughters. We were clever, people said. We passed exams, but that might lead to more problems than it solved. We were safe as long as we were going through the hoops of school, but the empty, rangy territory that lay beyond frightened my mother. She could not see us making our way in it.

She managed to be glad when I went to America, telling herself it was safe. A job in a summer camp, organized and timed by others, would let me combine travel with doing what I was told. And I would be getting experience of responsibility for young people, which was valuable for someone who was about to drift into teaching. I told myself this was true. But I was waiting. I must have been waiting all the time, keeping dead still so no one could tell what was me and what was the light and the leaf-shadows moving over me. At home, at school, I dissembled my own personality and hid the force that Michael was the first to see.

I met Michael. When I came back I wasn't returning to my mother's plans. I dumped the idea of a teacher training course, and set myself up to go to university to study law, which men studied. It wasn't going to be any good, ever, to wait for love to come along and solve my life. It had come and had solved nothing. Love was something in itself, I thought. It didn't come with arrows on it pointing out destinations. Michael in the gloom of the backyard, printed with shadows, the grain of his flesh nearer to me than the whorls on the ends of my fingers. I played those moments over and over and I knew they led nowhere but back to themselves.

Of course my mother was afraid for me. She believed that my A-levels had been achieved by a sleight of hand that wouldn't fool anybody for long. As soon as I got to university they'd find me out. She never said any of this to me. She'd tell me about girls I'd been at school with who'd left at sixteen and got good jobs with the Council, where they were getting on nicely. All these girls lived at home with their families and bought their mothers presents, and put money away for 'the future'. 'The future' was getting married. Janice Mackerson, Angela Crimmond, Susie Winslaw, Allie Dinford. Their names stick in my mind like the litany of a religion no one believes in any more.

Once, pushing her wedding ring back and forth over the loose skin of her knuckle, my mother told me that I ought to be aware that the other law students would all come from very different backgrounds. Not that I should ever pretend to be anything I wasn't. But I ought to take it into consideration.

She lived to see me half-way through my third year and deep in debt, though I kept that from her. Jenny, at least, had shown sense and trained as a nurse. I'd already met Donald, though my mother never did. I don't think she'd have liked Donald, but she'd have been pleased that I'd fooled the world enough to get someone like him. As term followed term and I failed

to be kicked off the law course, she must have begun to relax.
I didn't even try to tell her how easy it felt, how good I was,
what degree result was predicted for me. It would have made
her more anxious. Once I got 100 per cent in a maths test at
school, and she worried all night because she feared I had failed
a different kind of test, a crueller one, meant to teach me once
and for all that such results weren't possible.

Michael knew me before I knew myself. I can't really remember
what I was like then, and I don't want to. *You'd fight*, he said.
And on another occasion, looking at me as I totted up columns
of figures for his accounts, he told me: '*You're tough, Simone, you
know that? Look at you now.*' And I looked up surprised, really
surprised, because that wasn't how I saw myself then. '*When
you're concentrated, it comes out in your face.*'

I went back to England with it all ringing in my ears. And
the one thing I never forgot, the thing he said when we were
far out in the *Susie Ann*, and the squall blew up. When he saw
I was frightened and asked '*What's the worst thing that could happen
to us?*' '*We could drown.*' '*We could drown. That's all that could happen.*'
It wasn't fatalism, it was better than that. It was a way of
keeping your mind clear when terror came clouding over it.

He says he wants to see me. He sends me photographs that
show me naked, sprawled beside him, or clothed, embracing a
man dressed as a woman. Maybe there are other photographs.
Last night I lay still in bed, but my mind turned over and over.
It's not sin that keeps you awake, it's shame, or fear of being
shamed. My mother was right about that. She saw the law as
a temple fronted by men in formal suits, mocking her daughter
as she tried to mount the steps and go in past them. She saw
my pretensions exposed like my skin to Calvin's flash.

Calvin. The click of his camera, and his thumb winding on
the film. You had to wind on the film by hand then, and set
the exposure, in the days before cameras did everything for

themselves. Calvin had a light meter. He would hold it close to our skin and talk about light and how it changed second by second. He developed his own photographs. Once he took me into the washroom he'd fixed up as a darkroom and I watched the images of myself and Michael swim up to meet me.

And now I see Calvin's face, as he was when I was eighteen. He always knew how much I wanted to hold on to Michael. He teased me with it. *How far will you go? How far can we make you go?* But Calvin's dead now. I won't ever have to see Calvin again. When I left I told myself it was because of Calvin. If it hadn't been for Calvin, it would have worked. He took the light, all of it. He wouldn't let go of Michael. But as the plane got clearance for take-off, and speed took all our lives in its fist and peeled the land off us like a strip of tape, I thought of Michael alone, and not of Calvin. I saw him on a September morning, with the day's work ahead of him. I watched his paintbrush moving. I saw the underside of light flickering up from the water onto his face. And the look of peace which I remember because it came so seldom.

However much water I poured over Michael it wasn't going to ease him. He was hurt in some part my rooting fingers were never going to find or put back together.

I think Michael did go with the man who asked him. He took the money too, I'm sure of it. Fifteen dollars, or maybe twenty. Why he told me, I still don't know. Looking back, it would be easy to believe that he hated me, but I don't think that he did.

Thirteen

Dear Michael

 Since I spoke to you on the phone last night I have been thinking about your motives for making contact with me after such a long time. I appreciate that things have not been easy for you, but you must realize that we have gone in very different directions, and if we were to meet now we would probably have very little to say to each other. As you have already found out, I am married with children. I have to put my children first, and I also have a career which takes up a lot of my time and energy. I think the best thing would be for you to accept that I wish you well, but I do not see any point in further contact between us after a gap of twenty years. I have shown my husband this letter, and your correspondence, as I do not wish to have any secrets from him.

Dear Michael

 I am writing to inform you that any further communications from you will be returned unopened. The telephone answering system will be left on 24 hours a day, and any messages you leave will be recorded and kept on tape for future reference.

Dear Michael

 Why are you doing this? What is the point of it? You don't even know me any more. There isn't a cell in my body which hasn't changed since you knew me. I'm a woman of thirty-eight, not a girl of eighteen. The person you are writing to doesn't exist. All I am asking is that you accept that and leave me alone. I have my life to live, work, children, my husband. I can't be lying awake night after night waiting to see if there'll be another letter from you, or another call.

Michael
  It's two in the morning. I have got to work in the morning. I have a child with a head injury who needs looking after. If you don't stop calling me and writing these letters I'll

Michael, what is all this about? You were the one who fucked things up, not me. ~~You remember If it hadn't been for~~

I've often wondered if that boat ever got built. The catamaran.

Dear Michael
  You are persistent. I'm beginning to think that maybe I've been unfair to you. But if we meet, it's got to be properly arranged. It can't be here, but

I sent none of them. He is suddenly silent. No letters, no phone calls, no silences when I pick up a ringing phone. A week of Indian summer days goes by, cool and breezy, with large blue evenings when I walk miles along the sea-wall. Donald brings in his last radishes and lettuces, and turns over the compost heap. He loses his temper violently with a tractor on Saturday afternoon when we are driving to the supermarket. The tractor is stopped, chuntering in the middle of the lane while the driver leans out to converse in a yell across a hedge. Donald toots the horn once, lightly, registering our presence. The tractor-driver glances round but otherwise takes no notice. Donald holds down the horn. Slowly, measuredly, the driver gets off his seat and clambers down from the tractor, and strolls to Donald's window. He is a big man, tight-packed into his clothes.

'What's your problem then?' he inquires mildly, his fist balling on the open window. Donald leaps out of the car. His body is slight compared to the tractor-man's, but the pressure of his rage drives the other man backward. He takes his hand off our car. He looks at Donald and realizes that Donald might do anything. Physical strength has got nothing to do with this.

'This is a fucking road,' says Donald, each syllable quiet, separate. 'For fucking driving on. So you don't park in the middle of it for a chat with your mate.'

The tractor-driver shrugs largely, appealing to his audience. It's a token. His friend is silent behind the hedge, listening. He gets back into his cab, and drives forward, out of Donald's way.

'You can't carry on like that here. He's bound to be related to half the village,' I say.

But Donald is happy. Rage has made him happy. Joe and Matt bounce in the back seat, jabbing one another with gleeful elbows.

My work goes well. Each morning I am in early, with plenty of time to do box-work and go through the files. A judgment of mine that has been appealed is upheld. I stop having nightmares where I am naked in front of a table of judges, and a long document that lists my errors is being read off, page by page. The machinery of the court moves smoothly round me. Little by little, I begin to let out my breath.

I keep a stone on my desk, which I picked up on the beach early one morning. It was wet from the outgoing tide, a flat white stone with chips of black in it. I'd been skipping stones far out on the flat morning water. Everything around me was grey and white and dun, layer on layer of colourless colours. The seagulls shone as they flew, though there was no sun on their wings. The sea looked so beautiful that I wanted to put out on it at once, to hear the sound of the oars dipping then rising to break a skein of water into falling drops. All the time the boat would glide on.

There's a rowing boat that's lain above the tide-line all winter, under a tarpaulin. No one seems to use it. The oars are there too. One day I'll row out in that boat. I'll go as far as I can, keeping clear of the shipping channels. Those oil tankers are unstoppable. They slide on the water as if it were grease. I think of what it would be like to ride their wash in the grey sea. The waves would be huge and my boat would bounce and toss. Would I be afraid? I don't believe I would. Not with the fear I feel now, as if someone has his hand inside my ribs and is squeezing my heart, slowly, intimately, not too hard in case it kills me, not too soft or I won't feel it.

On Sunday we planted two apple trees. We brought them home from the nursery with their roots covered in sacking. I know that the autumn's not the best time to plant them. The gales will catch them before they have spread their roots. New trees need a lot of care, and they cost more than we could afford. But Donald wanted them, and to plant a tree means something. It might not mean you're going to stay, but it means that you intend to. We bought a Bramley, and a James Grieve. There's a corner of the garden which gets sun and is sheltered from the worst of the sea-gales by the house. There's room for five or six apple trees there. Land is cheap down here. It's salty, wind-blown, poorly drained. And it's too far from London for commuters to drive the prices up. There's no motorway, and the railway's not electrified. There is just sea, and sky, and flat grey-green land which crouches under the whip of the wind. I don't know which is more beautiful, the huge pale sky of summer with tiny clouds that take half a day to cross it, or the hoary sky of winter, when the sun hugs the horizon and goes down brighter than it has been all day long. People come and they say there's nothing here, and they go away without seeing it. Sometimes on a cold night the stars look as big as eggs, hanging over the marsh.

I'm not sure the trees will live. Donald dug the holes for them. I blended the soil with compost, and dug in fertilizer. The boys came out to watch us, but they didn't ask to join in. They stood and stared as Donald unwrapped the root-ball, lowered the tree and held it straight. His back was bent, his knuckles tight on the smooth grey bark. The little leaves whipped around in the breeze. They'd want to set fruit next year, but we wouldn't let them. Otherwise the trees don't grow. All their strength goes into swelling the apples. I mixed the soil on a piece of polythene sheeting, turning it over with the spade. The damp earth had the same rich colour as the stones on the shore where the sea has touched them. I shovelled it in around the roots to feed the tree. You have to press the soil down, so there are no air pockets. If the new roots grow into air pockets, they'll die. Donald had his heavy boots on and he tramped around the stem of the tree once it was planted, firming it in. I watched the marks his boots made, deep patterns on the fresh soil at first, then the patterns were trodden out, and all that was left was the bare, flat soil. We planted the second tree, and staked them both.

'That's where we'll plant the other trees, when we get them,' Donald said to the boys, pointing out the spaces where four or even five more trees could grow.

'How big will they grow?' asked Joe.

'Way over your head. You'll be able to walk under them.'

'We'll sit out here in the summer, and have picnics,' I said.

I watched Joe. In his eyes it was happening already. He was still young enough to be able to see two things at once. He saw the near-naked saplings staked in bare soil, and he saw a green canopy, rustling with birds and ripe with apples. He saw himself lying on his back, his mouth full of apple. Matt came forward and touched the stem of the Bramley.

'It doesn't look as if it's going to grow big,' he said. 'I could easily pull it up.'

He didn't want to. It was only that the idea came to him and he had to say it.

'Get indoors, if that's your attitude,' Donald said. Matt flushed and turned away, kicking at the soil as he went. Joe looked from face to face, wanting to be good enough for two.

Later the wind was blowing again and I kept thinking of the apple trees. Had we planted them firmly enough, and would their stakes hold? Salt was the worst thing. A bad salt-storm could scorch leaves miles inland.

The phone rang. Donald was upstairs, so I took it.

'This is the blackmailer,' said the voice. It was a voice I didn't know, an English voice. My mind jumped everywhere. Michael had enlisted someone, feeling that he was getting nowhere himself. It was an English voice, a local voice. He was coming so close he was almost touching me.

'The blackmailer,' said the voice again, puzzled and on the edge of irritation. I heard him right this time. The bricklayer.

'The bricklayer,' I repeated.

'That's right. Your husband asked me to call. It's about the base of your wall, where it's rocking.'

'Oh, I'll get him for you.'

I sat down at the kitchen table. Words hissed in my ears, but I didn't want to hear them. When Donald was finished, he'd come in and find me here. He'd know something was wrong.

'He sounds all right,' said Donald.

'What?'

'He's going to sort out the base of the wall. He might have to take it down. It's unsafe as it is.'

'What's it going to cost?'

'He's going to give me a quote.'

'But how much?'

'Oh I don't know, Simone. Maybe a hundred. It depends how long it takes him.'

'A hundred!'

And then anger burnt through me, a hot wind from which I had no shelter.

'You've got to stop doing it,' I said.

'What do you mean?'

'Acting as if we can do things we can't. *Leave the wall*. What's it matter if it falls down? There's no one to see it except us.'

'It's dangerous.'

'Then tell the boys to keep away from it.'

'Jesus, Simone.'

'Can't you do it yourself?'

'I'm an architect, not a fucking bricklayer.'

I smiled. 'Which would you rather have,' I asked, in a soft, new voice. 'A wall, or dinner for the children?'

'That's not the choice.'

'I think it is. I think it is. And they're not getting any free school dinners, remember, because we're so fucking fortunate, one of us a judge, the other an architect – God knows what we do with all the money. I think that is the choice, Donald, and I know what choice I'm making, if I have to knock that wall down myself.'

He looked at me. I saw the hot, hurt darkness in his eyes, and I knew how unbearable I was, and how unbearable it was for him to listen to me. I would have liked to take back those words, and I would have liked to scorch him with them until there were no flowers or foliage any more.

'You've changed,' he said, 'I can't believe –' and he broke off.

'What? What can't you believe?'

'How hard you've got,' he said finally. 'When you used to be so . . . I don't know. Never thinking the worst of anybody.'

'If I've got hard, it's because I've had to. If I'd been soft we'd be in bed-and-breakfast by now.'

'Don't exaggerate.'

'Do the sums, Donald. Do you think I like it? You don't know how frightened I've been, sitting there, making judgments that could be wrong, having all those eyes on me waiting for me to be wrong. Making people bankrupt, telling them how often they can see their children. Changing their whole lives, I wasn't experienced enough. I got the job because I'm good and they wanted more women. But you don't know how it's been. They all know, you see, they know if you make a mistake. It's all written down. You can't hide anything. And all the time *you* resent it. You know we've got to have the money, but you resent it. Me with my big job while everything's fallen apart for you. Do you think that's what I wanted?'

Donald looked back at me. The heat and pain had died from his face.

'No,' he said. 'No. I don't think that's what you wanted.'

'But it's what I got. And I tell you, Donald, if I have to get harder, I'll get harder. I won't let anything kick us out of here. We'll go when *we* want to. We're going to pay back those loans. We're going to tell that bank manager to fuck himself for breakfast before he forecloses on us. No one is going to tell me what happens to my children.'

There was a long silence. Slowly, Donald sat down in the chair opposite me.

'I'm sorry,' he said. And I knew what he was sorry for. He was sorry that I had changed and I could not change back. I couldn't even take the hand he had laid on the table between us, half-way, half-open.

Fourteen

In the dark before dawn time belongs to no one. I lie on my back and listen to Donald's breathing. I can hardly hear it. He must be deep in his dreams. But day is coming, and even as I watch it becomes not quite dark. Our wardrobe bulks against the wall. My suit and clean white shirt hang in there, ready. It's not even a uniform; it's just a disguise, a cheap copy of what men wear. Clothes for a day where all the hours have been sold and belong to someone else.

But I steal back an hour, even if it means I don't get enough sleep. I'm out of the house in jeans and one of Donald's sweaters, snicking the door shut with the key so it won't bang and wake them. It's dawn now. The grass is wet with dew and starlings fly up as I come out, then settle again, cautiously, watching me as I go down to the gate. They cock their heads and fix me with their lizard eyes. I don't like starlings, I never have.

The hollows of the fields are full of mist, which wraps round me as I walk so that soon the house is hidden. A circle of visibility moves forward with me, like a hoop around my hips. Sheep thump away across the field. They cry their blundering cries, then they forget about danger and through the mist I hear their teeth tearing at the close-bitten grass.

The mist smells of marsh. Sometimes, walking on the drained fields, you forget that marsh was everywhere once, and it's waiting to come back. The sea's penned back, but it wants to rise. They say the climate's changing. That'll be its chance. Two miles down the coast there's a boggy place where the ribs of a wooden ship stick up through reeds and cotton-grass. I don't know how it came there, or how big it is. It might be a fishing-boat. Maybe there was a flood once and the ship sailed in on it and was wrecked here. There are buried ships on what was the sea-floor, and they rise up through the bog as if through water. The bog preserves everything: butter, bodies, boats.

I tried to get close enough to the ship to touch it. I thought I was going to make it but then my foot went through a tuft of grass into a cold soup that rose to the top of my thigh. And then the bog tightened on my leg like an iron band. I was lucky. I didn't fall forward. I threw my weight backward and left my boot in the bog and crawled out soaking wet. Water doesn't frighten me, but the bog does. I saw how I could have drowned in it, still not believing it.

Our house lay empty for two years before we moved in. That's why it was in such a bad state, and why we got it cheap. We couldn't believe no one had wanted it.

'Some people find it quiet down here,' was all the estate agent said. He was getting out of the car, and he had his back to us as he said it. In the village shop they said it was nice we'd come. It had looked as if the house was going to be left to the wind and weather. But there was a girl in the shop stacking the shelves, a Saturday girl, and as she packed my box she looked straight at me and said, 'I wouldn't want to live down your end.' Her made-up face was impassive. Her hands moved fast, fitting in cornflakes, baked beans and tomato paste.

'Wouldn't you?' Why did I need her to like the house? She wasn't going to live in it. It was ours. But she didn't answer. She smiled slightly, as if we both knew something but weren't telling, and went on tucking matches and clothes-pegs into the corners of the box. That's village life: it doesn't make room for you. Everyone's packed in already, and there aren't any gaps. But the tang of salt swept over the marshes and through the open shop doorway. It was the wind that rotted cloth and rusted cars and burned the leaves off trees, and would pick an empty house to the bone in a couple of winters. It worked through every season, scouring the marsh flat so as to show the beautiful curves of the earth. I smiled at the girl and met her eyes. She had to pause and look back at me.

'I was here a long time ago,' I said. 'Before you were born,' and I wrote out a cheque, picked up the box and carried it out to the car. It felt like going on holiday, with an armful of small, necessary things. Matches and salt and candles. We would have everything we needed, whatever happened.

I walk on. The mist seems to be thickening, not thinning, until I reach the sea-wall and climb the steps to the top. Up here the air is clear. Down below me, on the seaward side, the little waves mamble at pebbles. It's lonely here, that's why the girl didn't like it. I don't know if I like it or not, but I am at home. I stand for a long time, watching the waves flex, turn, collapse. The water runs in among the stones, drains, floods back. There is a bone-white stick at the edge of the water. It stirs with every incoming wave, but never floats free. I watch for a while but it is lodged by something I can't see. A big stone under the water, perhaps.

I don't know what it is that makes me turn. You do get walkers down here sometimes, following the coastal path, missing the sign that should take them inland instead of along the sea-wall. I turn. There is a man coming towards me, along the sea-wall. He walks steadily, head-down, as if he knows the way. I'm not worried. One of the things I decided when we left London was that I would not allow myself to be frightened here. You can use up a lifetime on being afraid. I was going to walk alone wherever I wanted.

I move slightly, towards the steps, so as to be out of his way. We won't even need to say *good-morning* if we don't want to. He's fifty yards off now, hands in pockets, shoulders hunched and head down. A big man in a dark tracksuit with its hood pulled up. Although there is no mist up here there is a graininess in the air which makes it hard to see his face. Anyway he's looking down. But walking very fast. And moving loose-limbed, like –

My body knows before I do. My foot is down, on the step. I should run but the air is sticky round me, the mist congealed to greasy wool. I turn and he is with me.

'Hi,' he says. 'Hi, Simone.' My name swells between us into an object so solid I could put out my hand and touch it. As if he is naming me for the first time. *Simone.* It leaves his mouth as breath, and enters me. It is no longer solid, but a net, spreading as it falls. And I am caught.

He doesn't touch me. He stops six feet away. If we stretched out our hands our fingers would brush. He is a big man, bulky in the shapeless tracksuit, breathing hard. He pushes back the hood. And then he vanishes, the man I've carried in my head for years though I never looked at him. He is swallowed up like a caterpillar in the chrysalis of now, as it splits before my eyes. Eyes, nose, lips. The look which used to swing to greet me, watchful, guarded. But not always like that. Not always watchful, not always guarded. He could be as sweet as my own children. I still feel his skin, his flesh, so young, the sweat lathered on it, swimming in my arms to lose itself deep in my body. His head back, his throat exposed, his eyes shut.

He has consumed himself. He has made himself not exist any more in this middle-aged man with bulky flesh and face. He has lost his fine sharpness. He is loose and blurred, like a photograph out of focus, stickered with a note from the laboratory that tells you where you've gone wrong. I look for what I knew before. I see his eyes, the mist of sweat on his forehead as he pushes back the hood. The hair is crisp, greying. I never knew Michael's hair would curl like that when it was cut short.

'How did you know I was here?'

'I saw you leave the house.'

'You were watching me.'

'Sure I was watching you. How else would I have known where to find you?'

His face creases into a smile, inviting me to share it.

'But you didn't come across the field,' I say, working it out aloud.

'There's another path, from the village.'

'I know there is.' But he shouldn't know that. He must have been watching a while, getting to know the place. Staying nearby? Who's he met? Who's he talked to?

'You don't look a day different,' he says. He is watching me intently behind the genial half-smile that stays on his face as if he's forgotten to switch it off.

'I think I do. Twenty years different.'

'No. No—oo. I would have known you anywhere.'

I am terribly afraid. My body pounds out fear. He mustn't guess it. That's why he's come like this, so he'll catch me off-guard. What does he want to make me do?

Then I do it. I look at the bulk, the tracksuit, the flesh that carries on it the fat of poverty, and I say: 'You've been in prison.'

He sighs deeply, as if in relief, looking me straight in the eyes.

'It's like I said, Simone, I could never hide anything from you.'

'What was it?'

He shrugs vaguely. I smell his sharp smell, the sweat I used to lick off him. My memory short-circuits and I taste him, the way he was. I taste his semen, chalky, marine. I stare at him and he fills my mouth. Look. He's afraid too. He's jumping with adrenalin.

'Not the way you mean it,' he says. 'I never committed any crime. I just had to go away from people for a while.'

'You had to go away from people for a while,' I repeat, trying to match the cadence of his voice. I don't know what he means, and he looks at me as if I should know everything.

'I was sick,' he says. 'Depressed.'

'You were in a hospital?'

'Yeah.' He wipes his forehead. 'For a while.' He looks up and adds quickly, 'I was a voluntary patient.' A long pause. *Voluntary.* He volunteered. It makes no sense to me. *We registered for the draft.* He smiles suddenly. 'But it was hard to get out of there because they made it all so easy. They did your thinking for you. You keep on telling everyone you don't belong there, but they won't listen. They don't know how to any more. All they know about is being doctors and nurses.'

'That doesn't sound like a good hospital.'

He moves his shoulders slightly, as if shrugging something off them. 'Maybe it was what I wanted,' he says.

'How long were you in there?'

'A while, the first time.' He stops, looks at me. 'It wasn't voluntary the first time. I told you a lie, Simone. I was going through a lot of stuff. Nothing you'd want to know about.'

I don't contradict him. The chill of the mist rises round and I suppress a shiver. He won't feel it, he's a big man. But all the same I have the terrible feeling that he isn't solid at all. I could look through him, through the heavy flesh, the yellow marbled layers of fat, and pluck out the man he was. If I held his hand, would I feel the original grip? The touch of his fingers, with little nicks and hard places on them from his work. But I'm not going to.

'How did you know, Simone?'

'What?'

'That I'd been hospitalized. That I'd been in an institution.'

'I didn't know. It was just a guess.'

'You must've seen a lot of people who've been in jail.'

'That's different.'

'But isn't it what you thought? It was the first thing you said. If I'd told you yes you'd have believed me.'

'It was a guess,' I say.

'You're a good guesser.'

'Not so good. I can't guess why you're here.'

I look at him straight and hard, as if he's someone else. Minutely, his face flinches and hardens. He really must have believed I would feel differently when I saw him. I've got to be careful now.

'It's been so long,' I say, and I let myself smile very slightly, for the first time.

'I know it.' He turns and looks north. 'That's your house there.'

'You know it is.'

'And your boys. Good-looking boys.'

I cannot speak. I can't say anything about Joe and Matt to Michael. I don't want to believe that he has seen them, that his eyes have touched them. They are another life and the two lives can't meet without one flying apart. I would gag on saying their names to him. He steps forward, puts his hand on my arm.

'You have to help me, Simone.'

His hand lies on my arm. It is heavy and it could tighten. He looks sloppy but he could tear me to pieces.

'How do you mean, help you?'

He takes his hand off me, laughs. 'Don't be like that. I didn't mean anything. It's OK. Don't be paranoid.'

I haven't heard that word for a while. *Paranoid*. And Michael would not have used it before. I see him face to face with a doctor, across a desk. The doctor writing something, then waiting, her face professionally smooth. The apparent relaxation of Michael's body masking his coiled wariness. He must have been a difficult patient, hard to judge, sitting there with his blue-collar body and his intelligence sunk down deep behind his eyes. 'So that's why you came?' I ask. To tell me everything's OK?'

'No, I didn't come here for that. Why would I lie to you? You can see how it is.' And he offers his hands to me, palms upwards, in the old gesture of nothing, of emptiness. *I have no weapon. I can do you no harm. Trust me.*

'So tell me why you did come.'

'Give me a minute, Simone. I don't feel so good.' And he doesn't. There's a glaze of sweat on his forehead and upper cheeks. He is pallid, sick from a cause I don't want to know. Put him on the street squatted on an old blanket with a mongrel at his side and I'd throw twenty pence into his cup. *But he was mine.* Michael breathes heavily, his shoulders rounding, hunched, protecting himself. Automatically and without wanting to, I find myself checking him as if he's one of the children. The way he's breathing, the rasp and wheeze of it –

'Have you got an inhaler?'

'Mm. Back at the motel.'

'Just relax.' I put my hand on his arm. 'Don't struggle to breathe.' He bends over, sucking at the air. Something's triggered this. He never used to be ill. Sick.

'It's all right,' I say. I could run now. I could be down those steps and across the fields and he'd never catch me. He couldn't run twenty yards in this state. But I don't move. His breathing quietens slowly, and he lowers himself and sits on the ground. I kneel down opposite him. Sharp pebbles dig through my jeans.

'You OK now?'

'Better.' After a while he smiles and says, 'I'm just an old man, Simone. I can't even take my boat out any more. Once I'm out on the ocean I get afraid. It feels like the water's closing in around me.' For a second there's a fellow-feeling between us which has nothing to do with the past or the present. It's just the feeling of flesh for flesh, as meaningless or not as the smile you give a stranger on a sunny morning.

'It'll pass,' he says. 'That's what they say. I have to keep on doing these relaxation exercises.' He offers me a small, cynical, complicit smile. His eyes lock on mine as they used to do when he knew everything and I knew nothing. I look through them into the dark fields of the night where he used to take me.

'Why'd you come?' I say.

'I had to come.'

Fifteen

'You had to come.' We walk slowly, side by side, along the sea-wall, above the wrinkled sea. I look at my watch and see that it is still early. Scarcely any time has passed.

'I had to see you.'

'You had something to tell me? Was that it?'

He stops and I stop too. We face one another.

'You can't *tell* these things, Simone,' he says in a low voice. 'I say to you I was in hospital. What does that mean?' He clears his throat. 'It's taken me all this while to tell myself what happened. Stuff I'd never looked at. Never dared look. It was like opening the furnace door then jumping back because the flames lick out and burn you. And so you slam it shut and tell yourself it's not there. But it keeps on burning until you're burnt away inside.'

'You're talking about yourself,' I say.

'Yeah, that's what I'm doing.' He looks at me out of the heavy grey face that isn't beautiful any more. 'I tell you, Simone, there were things in that furnace there I would die before I touched. Things I did and I never looked at them again. I had ways of getting around my mind without looking at half what was inside it. Did you ever play that game when you were a kid, where you have to get around a room without touching the floor?'

'No. There wasn't enough furniture.'

He gives me a sharp, gleaming glance. 'No kidding?'

'No kidding. We weren't all born in the richest country on earth.'

'You haven't changed, Simone.'

'Of course I've changed.'

An oil tanker crawls east over the quiet sea. I think of the quiet ignitions it's destined for. No sheet of flame swallowing the surface of the water. Michael sighs. I hear him draw in a deep, shaky breath. He goes on in a low, close voice with the laughter burnt out of it. 'I used to wake at five every morning and watch that square of window coming blue. If I kept watching I'd see a bird flick across, too fast to know what kind it was. For a while if I really tried I could still imagine what the air was like out there. Blue so wet it looks as if it'll come off on your hands like paint. But then I got too tired and there was just the room and the window and a mess of noise as everybody else in the building woke up. Get up, make the bed, go to the bathroom. Take a shower in a stall that's open at the front so the attendant can walk up and down and watch us. Did you know you can commit suicide with a shower-head, Simone?' He kicks small pebbles and they rattle away down the sea-wall.

'But you got out.'

He pinches a fold of flesh above his waist. 'I ate my way out.'

'What?'

'I was the Donut King of Thoreau Ward. Once I got over two hundred pounds and stopped watching the window they let me out. But they told me I could go back any time I wanted. You think that's stupid, don't you, Simone? You think the last thing anybody would want is to go back? You don't understand. Once you've been in those places there's a part of you that always belongs there.'

'Michael. What happened to that little boy who got strung up in the basketball hoop, when you were a kid?'

He is silent for a while, and I think he's going to say he doesn't remember. Then he says, 'He was OK. Some guy came along and got him out.'

'I bet he never tried to join in your game again.'

Michael laughs. 'That's the weirdest thing. That's where you're wrong, Simone. He did. The next time we played, there he was. Just as if nothing had happened. Waiting. Almost as if he was waiting for us to do it again.'

'That can't be true.'

'Yeah, he was. He was there. It was as if he didn't have any choice. And it's taken me all this time to know why he did that.'

'But it wasn't a good idea,' I say.

'You have to go back. You can't leave things. You can't pretend the past didn't happen.'

'No one is pretending the past didn't happen.'

'The more you hide the more you dig yourself down. You know what I'm talking about, Simone.'

'You tell me.' I'm angry now. Let him say it right out.

'I'll tell you. I'm not going to be kept out of your life any more.'

'All right. You tell me something else then. Tell me why you sent me those letters.'

'You know why.'

'You shouldn't have done it. You haven't got the right to break into my life like this.'

'And you're the judge, is that right?'

We haven't gone any distance. When Michael turns and looks back across the fields we can still see my house. 'So that's it,' says Michael. 'That's where you live. You bought a little bit of land with the house, Simone? Is this your kingdom? What you worked so hard to get after you left me.'

'I didn't leave you.'

He smiles, a pitying smile as if I am a stupid child. 'I guess it must have been me that got on the aeroplane then.' He pauses, then goes on, 'I brought the pictures.'

'What pictures?'

'You know what pictures.'

'Let me see.'

'I don't have them here. They're back in my room.'

'Where're you staying?'

'Oh. Someplace.'

I smile broadly. 'This is *ridiculous*, Michael. You mean you've come all the way over here to see me and you're not even going to tell me where I can visit you?'

He smiles too. 'Well, if you're planning to *visit* . . .'

'Never mind. It doesn't matter. Don't tell me.'

The idea of breaking into his room and stealing the pictures vanishes as soon as it rises. It is ridiculous. *Judge caught burgling motel.* 'So you brought some pictures to show me.'

'That's right.'

'Why do you think I would want to see them?'

'I don't think that you want to see them. I think you believe you're happy the way you are. I don't think you believe you need me *at all*. But you do.'

'Why?'

'Why? Because I'm your past. I'm what you were. I'm what you think you left behind, but you can't do that. If you do you're lying to yourself, your husband and your kids and all those people who have to stand there waiting for you to judge them. You make me into nothing. You make everything we did into nothing. You make your past into nothing.'

'That's not true. I don't talk about it, that's all.'

'We're not discussing something we watched on TV here, Simone.'

'What are we talking about? You tell me.'

'We did everything, Simone. We did *everything*. You know it. That's how close we were.' He holds finger and thumb together, narrowing the space until the flesh touches. 'That was *you*, Simone.'

'Was it?' I ask, and it's a real, pure question, the only one I've asked so far.

He doesn't answer. The mist is clearing fast and there's going to be sun. Down on the beach two black-backed gulls are stabbing between the stones for something buried there. We look at the water.

'Is it always as flat as this?' he asks.

'Not always.'

'It doesn't look like the ocean to me.'

'You should go to the west coast. Cornwall or Scotland. It's the Atlantic there.'

'I don't know those places.'

'Haven't you travelled around at all?'

'No. I came to see you.'

'Do you have friends in England?'

'Why would I have friends in England? I came to see you. You remember the ocean at Annassett?'

'Of course I do.'

'Remember how you used to swim? You were always swimming.'

'I still do.'

'Is the water clean?'

'Clean enough.'

'It looks pretty grey to me.'

We look at the grey, smooth water.

'D'you ever get storms?'

'Oh yes.' I glance at him. 'A long time ago, this is where Viking raiders used to come in.'

He laughs the laugh of a man from a big country.

'A long time ago, huh?'

'I suppose so. The first time they came, no one was expecting them. They stripped the church, killed the priest, killed the fighting men, filled their ships with cloth and gold and grain. The second time there wasn't so much to take. There'd been a warning. A beacon was lit on that hill: there. They ran to the woods with everything they could carry. The Vikings were angry this time, so they fired the thatch. Then they found a woman who hadn't been able to run away far enough because she'd just given birth. So they all raped her and when they'd finished they threw her on the fire to roast with her baby.'

'How d'you know all this?'

'Wait. I'm going to tell you about the third time. As you can imagine, it was a while before they came again. They raided farther up the coast, where they hadn't been before. But one night, I don't know how long afterwards it was, the fire burnt on the beacon again. Everyone ran, as they'd run before, except for one woman. She waited until everyone had gone then she ran the other way, down towards the shore and the marshes. She ran bent double with the weight of her bundle on her back. The marshes hadn't been drained then. There were bogs here that would swallow a herd of horses. She reached the place she was looking for, a piece of high ground which looked over the bog and the sea. There was no sea-wall then. She knew that the light of her fire would shine out to sea where the Viking raiders were coming in on the tide. It would look like the light of food and hearth and home. She took out her fire-pot from under her cloak. It was a wild night, with the moon racing between scraps of cloud, and the wind blew her charcoal red. She knelt and built her bundle of sticks into a pyramid and she set a fire under it. As the flames began to catch she fed them until the fire leapt high with the wind. She stared through the darkness and she thought she heard the chink of oars over the noise of the water, and then the scrape of the longboats being dragged up onto the shingle. She crawled forward, wrapped in her cloak, to the edge of the bog that lay between her and the sea. She came so close to the bog that she heard it muttering to itself. She lay down and whispered to the bog and she looked back over her shoulder and saw her fire burning brightly. The bog was moving deep inside itself with hunger that never goes away.

'"Lie still," she said. "Lie still and you'll get what you want."

'And the bog lay still, making itself look as quiet as a field full of fat sheep. She saw them coming. They were less than a hundred yards from her. It looked as if they would be on her in a few seconds. They came in a pack, like wolves. Then the men in front wavered like the air over a fire and they went down. She lay low, watching. She drank up the sound of their cries as the bog swallowed their bodies. Sometimes the bog swallows a man quickly, and sometimes it plays when it has him in its mouth. It lets him think he's going to get out if he struggles hard enough. But he's never going to get out. The more he struggles the deeper he goes. She lay there and listened to the play of the bog as if it was the sweetest music she had ever heard. At the edge men were stumbling, pulling on one another, dragging one another down. Those at the rear were already in flight, back to the ships.'

'How the hell do you know all this? Those people couldn't read and write.'

'They found the men when they were draining the marsh here.'

'Jesus. Why would she do that? The woman?'

'Maybe it was her mother who couldn't run away fast enough. Maybe she was a little girl in that wood, knowing her mother had been left behind. Maybe she went back and found her mother and her baby sister. I'm only guessing. Or maybe I'm just making her up.' I smile. 'It's full of history, this area. When did you arrive?'

'Five days ago.'

'Is that all?'

'Long enough.'

'You knew where I was. How did you know?'

'It wasn't hard.'

He's right, it wouldn't have been hard. Now if I'd been called Jones or Carter he would have had his work cut out. What a gift it must have been that I'd kept my name. But it's not so hard to trace people. And then he would have had to make arrangements, once he was sure where I was. The flight, the accommodation. Spending the money must have felt much more real than posting a letter. He doesn't look like a man with money.

'So what are you doing now?' I ask him.

'I've got a little boat-building business. You know I could always do that stuff. It's nothing fancy. Mostly repairs, but I get by.'

'It must have been hard to get started again, after being in hospital.'

I know about that. Employment chances down to zero. No chance of a bank loan to start anything.

'I know what you're saying,' Michael agrees. 'It's like you kill something and you have to carry the carcass on your back the rest of your life.'

'But you didn't kill anyone.'

His eyes narrow a little. 'No.' But there's a hesitation, a thickening in his voice.

'That's history,' I say. 'Anyone can have a breakdown.'

'But not you, Simone,' says Michael. 'You're tough.'

I want to spit at him. Spit it all back at him, everything I've done and been since I last saw him. I breathe deeply, move back a little. I am not going to let myself give way.

'I've changed too,' I say. 'I'm not the person you knew.'

'But what way have you changed, Simone? Good or bad?'

The way he repeats my name is getting on my nerves. The more he does it, the less it feels as if he's really talking to me. And it's like a stranger taking hold of your arm in the glaring white-tiled corridors of the Underground, and walking you away. Everyone's glance slides over you as if you're just another couple, arm in arm. Already it's too late to cry out.

'So how did you get started again with the boat-building business? It must have been hard.'

'I went back home. They know me there.' He looks up with a half-smile. 'They'd had plenty of time to clear up.'

'What do you mean?'

'I was out of my head. That's why they put me in the hospital.'

'What did you do?'

'Oh, I don't know. I believe I smashed up the front of the store.'

'Was anyone hurt?'

'Nobody got hurt. I don't really remember.'

I visualize the front of the store in Annassett. The porch, the flight of wooden steps, the narrow door then the smell of oil, wood, apples. Mac lounging behind the counter working out the next move of a correspondence chess game. There was nobody in Annassett good enough to play him.

'Lucky the windows were small,' I say.

'It's not like you remember. They've expanded. There's a parking lot for forty cars now. They're making money.'

'Is it still Mac and Lucy?'

'No. New people.'

'Did they cause trouble?'

'They were OK.'

'What about work?'

'I get plenty of work. I'd rather work than do anything else. I don't care about the money. People know me, they know I won't screw up. I treat every boat as if it's my own.'

He says it all like the plain man I know he isn't. *They trust me. Why don't you?*

'I must go,' I say, 'I've got to be at work.'

He reaches forward. He takes my hands. I don't resist as he folds my hands together and places his around them.

'I tell you this, Simone, you need to look at yourself before you have the right to judge your fellow human beings.'

134

'You don't understand. I'm not a judge in a criminal court – '

'I know what you are,' says Michael sombrely. His hands rock mine as if they are babies. 'Nobody here knows what you are, Simone, but I know.'

Suddenly I am angry. *You're letting him win*, I think. *You can do better than this.*

'Nobody here knows what? What exactly is it that people don't know and you're going to tell them?'

'I'm not going to tell anybody anything, Simone. But I think you are. I think you won't find happiness until you do.'

'*Happiness*. How old are you, Michael? OK. Let's get down to details. Let's talk about what we're really talking about. Sex with you. Letting Calvin photograph us. Letting Calvin use a time-delay switch on the camera so he could show the three of us in bed together. Smoking grass with you and Calvin. A bit of cross-dressing. A few more pictures. And you've kept the lot. Headlines, is that what you want? *Saucy secrets of sexy Judge Simone*. Go on. Is that it? Is there any other stuff I haven't remembered? Is that the whole big deal? It was fine with you then, as far as I remember. I don't recall any objections.'

'It was never fine,' says Michael, with a spurt of anger that seems real now. 'It was shit.'

'You're getting two things confused here. Either this is a moral issue or it isn't. It doesn't matter how you feel about it. It's not about feelings. If it wasn't wrong then, it's not wrong now.'

With a visible effort he recovers himself and relaxes his grip on my hands. I slide them free.

'The thing that's wrong, Simone, is that what you are doesn't match what you do. You sit in judgment on your fellow human beings, but you turn your back on me.'

'I don't see what that has to do with anything. I haven't seen you since I was eighteen. I hadn't even started to study law then.'

He steps back a pace. Behind him the sea is light-filled, crossed by the silent, sailing gulls. How far they fly without a wing-beat. But Michael blots it out.

'That's why I'm here,' he says, 'that's why I've come, Simone. To help you find a way back.'

I look at him. He's a man who's been cracked open and scrubbed hollow. He wants me to be like that too. He won't hurt me. When I saw him first I thought he'd come to kill me, out here where the nearest house is almost out of sight and the sea carries away as many sounds as it makes. But he doesn't want to do that. Through me he's going to prove himself. He's going to earn himself back.

'We need to talk some more,' I say, slowly, watching him still. This is where I must tread forward lightly, not making a single mark that'll give me away.

'I'm glad you feel that way,' he says.

'But I must go now.'

'OK.'

Again that waiting, confident pause, fuelled by emotions I can't begin to gauge. The strangeness of him sweeps over me. This man is absolutely unrecognizable at every point, and yet I know him. I have sucked him, bitten him, swallowed him, sunk into exhausted, sweating sleep at his side. I've known the taste and smell of every inch of his body. I told myself every cell was changed but that doesn't work now, not when we're face to face. His closeness is like a vertigo, throwing me down towards him.

But the body I knew has gone all the same. It's all gone. It's been washed away in those hospital showers for him, with the attendant patrolling the pale, pulpy bodies of his charges. It's been washed away in long baths for me, with baby Joe or Matt sitting between my legs and playing with their toy boats. They have washed me clean of Michael. They have laughed and put their pudgy hands on my thighs, and wallowed in the water knowing that if they slip for a second my hands will be there quicker than thought. Everything I knew of my body was turned inside out in childbirth. And what happened to him? I can imagine it as if it comes to me through his touch. The lack of solitude. For his own sake there would always be someone watching. Ties and belts would be taken away. He would have no landscape but the square of morning sky. The lights would burn late, for the convenience of the staff getting through their shifts with a crossword. Every night would be full of cries and murmurs. And by day the slop of feet, the blank, astonished faces on their way back from electric shock, the smells of drugs and urine and the sharp sweat of night terrors. Visiting times when nobody comes. The weight going on, the jaw thickening, the walk round the hospital yard a slow shuffle.

'Well,' he says.

'I'll meet you here,' I say. 'We can go walking. I talk better when I walk.'

'You don't want me to come to your house.'

But he knows the answer. It's not a question.

'Not yet,' I say. 'Can you come here early, like this, the day after tomorrow?'

'Sure. I've got nothing else to do.'

'Nobody else to see?'

'I don't know a soul in this country.'

'Are you comfortable where you're staying?'

He laughs, a little, surprised laugh, a bit shy. 'I'm OK. It's fine. It's just one of those places. You know.'

'A bit anonymous.'

'Yeah, that's it. They don't even look you in the eye when they take your money.'

We both smile. I'm facing the steps down.

'Goodbye.'

He doesn't answer. It's hard to turn my back and climb down the steps with him watching, but I do it, and my feet touch the clean, springy turf. The sheep are settled now, grazing easily in the full morning light. They don't even startle as I walk across the field. At the first stile I look back, and he's still there, standing with one hand shielding his eyes and the other lifted in an awkward salute, held too long, its meaning evaporated. He could be anyone.

Sixteen

There's a red post van at our gate, its engine running. The postman's sorting through a handful of letters. He sees me, picks out three envelopes, gives me a long stare. He's new. I hold the letters in my hand, not looking at them.

'Where's Pete?'

'Taken a sickie.'

'What?'

'That's why I'm here.'

'Oh, I'm sorry – '

'That's how it goes,' says the boy who can't be more than twenty-five, with his yellow hair pulled back in a ponytail and his look of doing the job as long as it suits him and not a second longer. He wouldn't dream of bumping a bike down here, over the ruts, the way Pete Titheradge's had to do. Fifteen years, he's been the postman down here. But the yellow-haired boy has got his smart scarlet van and his bad news and he's happy. He gets back in the van, reverses sharply so his rear wheels spin into the turf, then shoots forward.

The top letter is airmail. The stamps are US stamps. I don't have to open it to know that it's a letter from Michael. I don't have to open it, either, to tell by its weight that there is more than a letter inside the envelope. I stuff the other two letters into my jeans pocket, and rip Michael's open. For a moment it frightened me, his trick of being in two places at once. Michael is here, a few fields away, down by the sea. Michael is between my hands, in this letter. But I know he meant me to feel this way, and the thought makes me recover. He might have posted this letter himself, just before leaving. Letters from America can take five days to arrive. Or he might have left it behind for someone else.

'*Mail this for me Saturday, would you? I don't want it to get there too quick.*'

I can almost see the hand taking the letter. I could put my own hand out and push it down, gently. *No, don't do that. You don't know what he's asking you to do.*

He's got me jumping at shadows. I open the letter, see the slick backs of photos. I don't turn them over. I unfold the letter first.

Dear Simone

Do you like getting mail? I like it because it's been touched. Faxes and e-mails don't give you the same buzz, do they? Mail smells of people. Don't you believe that? Did you just lift up this letter and smell it? I knew it. I know you so well.

I'm here now, here with you. You know that already. Do you remember that time we barbecued chicken and shrimp, down by the water? Then we went back up to the cabin and Calvin came with us and took some pictures. We had to hold you up. You were out of it, Simone. You won't remember a thing. But it was a beautiful night.

Remember I love you. You can't get away from that.

He hasn't signed the letter. I turn the photographs over. They are close-ups of me and Michael. I'm lying on my back, wrapped in a long blue cheesecloth dress, my hair long too, spread out so that Michael is lying on it. He holds my left hand in both his hands, and he presses it against his cheek. There seems to be nothing there but tenderness. We smile slackly, at space, not at the camera. In the second picture the cheesecloth dress is rucked around my waist. It is Calvin on the cushions at my side now. He is naked. I might be asleep. My eyes are closed, though the smile is still on my lips. Calvin's hand rests between my thighs. He is not asleep, but resting, deep in some peaceful place I would have said he never visited. In the third photo I am back with Michael, both of us sleeping or pretending to sleep. Michael wears the blue dress, and I am naked.

The pictures are sad, but only because everything in them has long since disappeared. They describe that time twenty years ago in a way that bears no resemblance to the descriptions in my head. We look at ease. We look as if we all belong to one another.

Now I remember the barbecue. Michael built a circular stone fireplace on the beach, choosing heavy, smooth grey stones. He made a fire of driftwood and let it burn for a long while, feeding it fresh wood until the stones were hot and there were layers of red ash under the flames. As it grew dark the ash glowed. I sat opposite him and watched him. I remember his face in the firelight, and his hands which knew just where to place each lump of wood so it would burn right. I had my knees drawn up to my chin and my blue cheesecloth skirt stretched tight over them. When Michael moved out of the firelight he seemed to disappear. One gulp of the shadows and our fire would be swallowed.

Calvin was going to come later with a jug of white wine and some grass. We hadn't drunk anything yet. I'd been swimming just before dark and my hair was still damp; now I had my back to the sea and I listened to it retreating. There was a breeze which flagged the flames then blew them straight again, but it was warm. Every so often flakes of fire would break off the wood and smoulder on the pebbles, then die into darkness. We didn't talk much. Michael was putting the shrimp he'd marinated in garlic sauce onto the barbecue rack. He had chunks of white fish on skewers, too, brushed with oil, wrapped in long coils of lemon peel, with lemon mayonnaise to dunk them in when they were browned. I didn't know much about food then, and I didn't know what kind of fish it was. But the texture was firm and the flesh meaty, with sweet white juice. The lemon peel got singed but its oil had already flavoured the fish.

Michael knew how to cook crab and lobster. He'd gut and fillet the fish he caught, or a friend gave him. I would watch him hold the fish still in one hand, a last shudder kicking through it, then knock it against a stone. When he gutted the fish his knife seemed to find its way into an invisible seam and open it, a bright red spilling line. I never realized that fish had so much blood in them. And a heap of glistening innards that he threw on the fire. We gorged because fish was no good if it wasn't fresh. It seemed wonderful to me, what he did, though when I got used to it I realized that everybody who lived year-round in Annassett had the skills Michael had. They all fished and hunted and knew how to use a knife and a gun. They all knew what the tides were doing and which channels to follow when they took a boat out of harbour, and where to place lobster-pots. They didn't need to think about it. But I was a city girl, and from England too, and it was like a door opening wide onto a world I'd never thought I could live in. The way Michael would take a boat out, so easily, as if it was the same as walking down the street.

He took me out from the beginning, in the *Susie Ann*. I thought he didn't notice that the sea frightened me. One day we were out beyond the harbour, fishing. The sky piled up with cloud and the wind chopped the tops off the waves and threw them away in spume. I held onto the side of the boat as it rocked, and willed Michael to notice, to look up at the darkening sky and pull the lines in and turn the boat home. But he kept on baiting up hooks. Suddenly he looked up at me and I realized he'd been aware of me and of the weather too, all along.

'What's the worst thing that could happen now, Simone?'

'What do you mean?'

'You don't like the weather. What's the worst that could happen?'

'The boat could capsize, I suppose.'

'Yeah? And?'

'We'd drown. I couldn't swim to shore from here.'

'Me neither,' said Michael, and it was true, he was a poor swimmer. 'So we drown. That's the very worst thing that could happen, right?'

'Well – yes, I suppose so.'

'OK. So help me with these hooks.'

The boat pitched, and we stayed out a long while, not catching anything because the weather wasn't right for it. But after that I felt easy in the boat. Michael taught me to take out a little dinghy, and then I capsized, lots of times, and learned what to do when I did. It was hard at first and I felt as dumb on the water as someone learning a new language. But I began to see what it would be like when I wasn't clumsy any more but was going the way the sea wanted me to go, with bubbles racing along the side of the boat, and the kick of the tide.

Michael's fire burned down to a mound of ash. The stones around it were too hot to touch. I thought we could have broiled the fish on them, but Michael balanced the barbecue grill over the fire. Oil dripped and hissed on the stones. He kept turning the skewers so the fish would brown evenly. The lemon peel crisped and frizzled. Michael threw a coil of it into the fire. Flame burst out of the ash and swallowed it. The flame ran for a while over the surface of the ash, like blue brandy fire on a Christmas pudding.

We sat back on our heels and ate. Michael handed me a skewer of fish, and put the barbecued shrimp down on the hot stone in front of me. They kept on cooking, seething in the frill of oily bubbles around their bodies. I pulled off the heads and tails, stripped away the body shell and shucked out the naked sweet flesh. Calvin was late, so we had nothing to drink with the food, but I didn't mind that. I dug out fish fibres from between my teeth, and threw my wooden skewers onto the fire. Then we went down to the water and dipped our hands to wash off the fish and oil. The sea was black, with no reflections. It was a warm night, but clouded. I pulled up my dress and waded in up to my knees, then to my thighs. The water swayed and wobbled around me. It was warm too, and quiet, with the waves collapsing softly on the shore. Michael waded the other way, looking into the water as if he could see things there, though I knew he couldn't. It was habit. Behind us the fire glowed. There was no one else on the beach that night. I stood still and felt the tug which meant the tide was still going out. I looked towards England and I was happy I wasn't there. It seemed far away and unimportant. I was deep in something, and all the unhappiness I'd felt with Michael was caught up with an excitement that made me cling onto where I was like someone on the dazzling top of a wheel.

So now when I stand in front of my house and look at the photographs Michael has put in his letter, I see the way these pictures would look on the desk of the Lord Chancellor, or on the desk of a newspaper editor who cares about the morality of Britain's judges. But I see other things. *It was a beautiful night.* And is that blackmail, or is it something more? The third thing I see is the youth of our flesh. If you put out a finger and dented those buttocks, the flesh would spring back. I am so used to the tired softness of my own body that it's almost shocking to see what it was like once, before the children were born. There are no thread veins on the thighs. The stomach lies snug between the smooth hipbones. The face, drugged, drunk, out of it, is smooth as a plum. Even Michael is more like my sons than my husband. I used to think he looked so much older, his face grooved by experience. Now I see how young he was. His black hair shines like my children's hair.

I've missed a photo. It was stuck to the third one. I peel the two apart, and there they are, Michael and Calvin, face to face, breast to breast, naked, entwined. Michael's face is covered by his hair. Calvin's is closed, all the features drawn tight. A rumpled scrap of blue cheesecloth pokes out from under Calvin's thighs.

I've lost a lot of memory. Sometimes you have to, when there's no way of organizing the past into a pretty shape, or even a shape you can live with. And when there's no need to, either, because you've closed the door on it and you're never going to see any of those people again. Those must have been my hands that squeezed the shutter, my eye that looked in the viewfinder and checked that everything I wanted was in the frame. But I don't remember any of it. It's all been wiped away with a clean click; and not just that night, but night after night after night.

'Simone!'

It's Donald. It's Donald at the window, leaning out. How long's he been there?

'It's eight o'clock!' he shouts. 'You're going to be late. Where have you been?'

Seventeen

'Any letters?' asks Donald.

'Just a couple. Here.' I take them out of my right-hand jeans pocket, keeping the one from Michael in the left pocket.

'What were you looking at, out there?'

'What? Oh, nothing. Just some notes for today. I must go and get changed quick, I'm late. What's that you've got?'

There's a whisk of lettered paper, but Donald folds up the letter without showing it to me.

'Oh, nothing,' he says, baring his teeth in a smile. He's very thin. He's lost so much weight since we came here. And he's stooping. If it was me I'd go out and get a job in a shop. How many times have I thought that to myself, vindictively, on the way home. Or on a petrol forecourt. Anything. But it's clear that he can't. The fight's over. He looks ill and old this morning, and evasive too. No use thinking of that now. I run upstairs, unzip my jeans and trample them down while I pull on bra and blouse. I'm dressed and washed, hair combed, shoes found, in less than ten minutes. I look awful. Matt grabs me on the landing and begins a frantic story about handwriting homework. I cut him off.

'Tell Dad to write a note and say your pen broke.'

'I can't do that! If he puts that you'll have to get me another pen, because she knows what my pen looks like.'

'Don't be stupid, Matt, how can she know what thirty-two children's pens look like?'

'She does! She does! She's going to kill me and then she'll give me so much homework I won't be able to go out all weekend.'

'OK.' I run to the bathroom, bang open the cabinet, seize the bandage. 'Give me your right hand.'

I run the bandage round and round his first two fingers and his thumb. 'Hold it there while I get a plaster.'

Matt holds it, staring at me dumbly. I fix the plaster on, as tight as I can.

'There. Now that's why you didn't do your homework.'

'But she won't let me play football at dinnertime if I've hurt my hand.'

'That's your problem. Take it off if you want.'

We lock eyes. Slowly his head droops. 'Take it off, Mum.'

'Good. Come in here where I've got my scissors.'

I scissor it off. Matt rubs his hand. 'She'd think our family was always having accidents, anyway.'

'That's right. She'll be ringing up the NSPCC any day now, so watch it. You might get taken away.'

'I could ring Childline!'

'Yeah, that's right, go on. Give me a break.'

His face curls into a smile. I hug him, trying to lift him and pull him tight as I used to do, but he's too heavy.

'Listen, say goodbye to Joe for me. I don't know what he's playing at but we're all going to be late. And I've got a horrible day.'

'Have you?' His eyes fix me again, and widen, wondering. I don't usually talk about work like this to the children. 'I thought you liked being a judge.'

'No one likes what they do all the time.'

'Oh Mum.' He wriggles his shoulders, scenting a moral. I turn and go down the stairs two at a time, clattering on the bare boards. The back door is open – Donald getting wood. There's a piece of paper on the floor. I pick it up, unfold it. It's the headed letter he hid earlier. Jesus. Jesus. He's been writing to a loan company. I note the name quickly, scan it. They haven't lent any money yet, but they'll be glad to. I'll bet they will. I drop the letter back and run out of the door. Jesus, Jesus.

There's Donald coming out of the woodshed, laden with logs. He smiles at me vaguely.

'Get Joe up, he's late.'

Donald's smile fades. 'He's all right. We'll manage, Simone, we always do.'

He's going to let me go without saying goodbye. I yank the car door open, ram in the key so hard it won't turn until I joggle it loose again. My files and case slither on the back seat. Shouldn't have left them there, what if someone steals the car? All that confidential stuff. I've been forgetting too much, getting sloppy. My mind's not on it. *But I've got to be good.*

The car jerks forward and stalls. I try again, and this time it starts and I reverse out. Donald is just going in through the back door. He must have lingered to watch me go, but now he won't look at me.

'I am pleased to inform you that I have been authorized to offer you a loan of up to five thousand pounds . . .'

That letter didn't come from a bank. Donald has gone to a loan company. I don't need to think about how much it will cost to repay those five thousand pounds. I see the procession of clients in my mind's eye, smoking and sometimes weeping, telling me of the one-off loan, the innocence of it, the ready money that was supposed to pay off all their debts and maybe buy the children's Christmas as well. That was when I was there to advise them, not to judge them. They told me about the men who came round to the house to collect when they couldn't keep up with the payments. One man the first time, then three big men. The threats to torch the flat, mark their kids, pour petrol over them and then throw a match on it. Not idle threats, but alive and active. Sometimes I went to see them in hospital. And they still couldn't pay it back. The loan grew faster than cancer. It seemed to double itself every night they

148

slept. They hadn't read the small print. I knew clients who disappeared, and one client who killed himself. He did it badly. He jumped out of a window that wasn't high enough to kill him, then he took an overdose after coming back from hospital with a broken thigh. A few weeks later his wife came to see me, because the men had been round to see her. Now she'd had time to get over her nasty shock, they wanted their money back.

Donald knows all this. I must have told him some of these stories. Sometimes I came home and I couldn't sleep for thinking of nicotine-soaked fingers that shook when they picked up a cup of coffee, or a woman living in an eighth-floor flat with her three-year-old son, her baby, and two Dobermanns she didn't want and didn't like, but knew she had to have. She was afraid to leave the flat without them, or sleep without knowing that they slept by the front door. She knew what might be waiting out there for her. She asked me to visit her at home. I didn't see anything as I came in. Only the empty forlornness of the grass outside the flats and the sag of rubbish in black plastic sacks. The Dobermanns circled us the whole time we talked, while the little boy played with a heap of toy cars, and the baby cried. She hadn't been able to take the dogs out that day, because the baby had a chest infection. She had stopped the boy going to nursery school, just in case. I was afraid of the dogs, and afraid in case they scented my fear. If they went for me, what could she do? Round and round they went, their jaws level with the three-year-old's face.

Donald knows this. He must do, I've always talked to him about my cases. And he's trying to borrow money. Maybe he thinks we're immune.

I've got a hearing today; Rossiter v. Delauney. About the children. He's still fighting to see them, and she's still frustrating him week after week. It's been one of those cases that you know right from the beginning isn't going to settle easily. They've gone through all the stages: Conciliation Appointment, Directions Appointment, they've filed all their statements, we had the pre-trial review that hot day when the usher sent the busker away. There's a new statement from the health visitor. She thinks there's something wrong. It's hard to put a finger on it, but I can tell that guardedly, professionally, she is not at all happy about these children. The three-year-old has eating problems. He has learned how to make himself sick after eating, and he is now doing this two or three times a day, to his mother's distress. The mother says that this began after a weekend with his father. The older children told her that Jamie cried all through suppertime, and went to bed still crying.

However, in response to this report Mr Rossiter says that no such incident took place. His wife, Christine Delauney, formerly Christine Rossiter, is herself bulimic, and so it is possible that the child has observed her eating and then making herself sick. But there is no evidence of bulimia from Ms Delauney's medical records. She has suffered from post-natal depression and anxiety, but she has never mentioned an eating disorder to her GP. Mr Rossiter submits that his former wife suffered from bulimia throughout their marriage, and that her eating disorder was one of the reasons for the collapse of the marriage. He further submits that it is a well-known feature of bulimia that sufferers go to great lengths to conceal their condition from doctors, dentists, etc.

The case is listed for half a day, and just as well. I had an ambivalent recommendation from the welfare officer back at the pre-trial review. Let's see if we can get things clear today. But I look at Christine Delauney and Graham Rossiter, and I don't think it's going to be easy. I've had cases like this before. There are two people here who are both fired by the strongest, most primitive emotions most of us ever feel. Passionate love for their children, and hatred and contempt for their former spouse. They cannot swerve. It's the hardest thing in the world to believe that life won't be easier if you can get the ugly, inconvenient past right out of your life, as Christine Delauney hopes to get her former husband out of hers. Why should she see him walking up her path, hear him ringing her bell, see her own children run past her with cries of 'Daddy!' Why should all that rage and pain get stripped bare two weekends out of four, a week at Christmas and Easter, and three weeks in the summer? When all she wants is to start a new life and put it all behind her . . .

I'm putting words into her mouth. Maybe she doesn't feel like that at all. But she feels something, so strongly that the room is thick with it, and so does he.

By half-past ten I know what I'm up against. We've been through the health issues. There's no clear evidence that the visits cause distress to the children. Yes, the little boy's got a worrying eating problem, and the older boy wets his bed. But the older boy has stated clearly that he wants to see his father, and he's old enough for that to be taken into account. To quote from the report: *'I don't wet my bed because of seeing Dad, if that's what you think. And if anyone says I do she's a liar.'*

If anyone says I do, she's a liar. Hmm. Now that is worrying. These children know exactly what's going on. The big one knows it in words, the little one vomits it up. The middle one, the girl, seven, is very close to her mother and to her mother's new partner. According to Christine Delauney, this child asked if she could call Martin 'Daddy'. Ms Delauney clearly thinks that's a strong argument in her favour.

'Can we come to the question of reliability, now, please. Ms Delauney, you're saying that your husband fails to keep arrangements over collecting the children and bringing them back. You have given me some examples, and Mr Rossiter has responded to these in his statement. For example, on April 2nd 1997 it was your daughter Zoe's seventh birthday. Mr

Rossiter had arranged to collect her at 5 p.m., to take her to his flat for presents and birthday cake. This had been agreed between you. When he arrived at 5.23 you were not at home. You had taken all the children to McDonald's, "because you didn't want Zoe to be disappointed". Mr Rossiter says he was delayed in traffic by an accident, and he tried to call you on his mobile phone, but could only get your answering machine.'

'Yes. That's what happened.'

'Do you think it might be helpful to the success of the contact arrangements if you could both be a little more flexible over times?'

'I'm sorry. I don't understand what you mean.'

'Well, it's not so very unusual to be twenty minutes late for an appointment, is it? People do get delayed.'

'It seems to me that if people make arrangements then they ought to keep them. I can't hang around all afternoon, every weekend.'

'I see. And you also said in your statement that the visits to their father were preventing the children from seeing other members of your family.'

'Yes, that's right. I mean, their grandparents want to see them, and my mother's working all week. The children are always asking me when we're going to see Nana and Grandad. They love them to bits.'

'Yes. I see.' Loved to bits is what these children are, all right.

Graham Rossiter is staring straight at his former wife. The air between them is loaded with his anger. But she ignores it. She won't look at him. She looks straight at me, and her fair, rather lovely features show simple concern and a desire to get things clear.

The only good to look for here is the least bad. Graham Rossiter's solicitor isn't too happy with the welfare officer's report, but he isn't going to call her. And I don't think it would do any good. She's picked up the same as I'm picking up, and though her phrases are careful and professional, they breathe a lack of hope which I'm beginning to share. In the end, if Christine Delauney consistently and determinedly does her best to make it difficult for her former husband to see the children – and for the children to see their father – then there is not much the court can do. I can make orders. Contact can be supervised. But there's no underestimating the power that their mother has. After all, she's a perfectly adequate mother. A 'good mother'. She cares passionately about her children, and they are the centre of her life. She provides them with a warm, comfortable home, food, toys, outings, clothes; she is better paid than their father, and then she has the family home, as well as the income of her partner. Graham Rossiter lives in a two-bedroom flat, with a mortgage he can just about manage, if interest rates don't go up. When the children stay he sleeps on a pull-out sofa in the sitting-room, so that the little girl will not have to share a room with her brothers. He's not going to risk that. Christine Delauney has parents living nearby, and a sister with three children, two of whom go to the same school as their cousins. They are a close, loving, supportive family, says the welfare officer.

One weekend the children will have a bug. Fair enough, only the little one is actually ill, but she'll be convinced that the older two are coming down with it, and anyway the little one will be miserable if his brother and sister go away without him. Another weekend there'll be a big family gathering, at her parents. And then in two weeks' time she wants to take the children to Legoland, and that means an overnight stay, and the special offer at the hotel ends before she's due to have 'her' weekend with the children.

The easiest one, and the hardest to fight, is when the children 'don't want to come'. They're upset. They have all their own things at home, and their toys, and their friends calling round.

Well of course they don't want to pack up their little suitcases and trail off to a flat without a garden, with none of their own bits and bobs round them. They want to sleep in their own beds. It's not that she's against the children seeing their father, but little ones need to know where they are. This 'two homes' business is a pantomime. It doesn't do anybody any good. It makes them feel as if they're different.

And Graham Rossiter had better be completely reliable. If a work trip takes him away, and he isn't back until Saturday morning; well, that's his weekend gone as far as she's concerned. She builds her whole life around those kids, week in, week out. Too bad if he can't tell his employer he's got to be back on Friday night.

The children have not seen their father regularly for over six months now. That is a sixth of the little boy's life, so any order I make has got to take that into account. I make a defined contact order, beginning with 2–5 p.m. every Sunday. Get that going, and later on it can be stepped up. I explain to both parties that the aim is to build up the contact, to repair the children's relationship with their father, and to work towards an arrangement where both parties can be flexible. I talk about advance notice. I suggest that Ms Delauney should discuss family gatherings in advance with Mr Rossiter and make sure that the children do not lose time with their father in order to attend them. I say that the situation will be reviewed in six months' time.

Nobody looks happy. Mr Rossiter's solicitor glances at him, a quick assessing glance. He knows there'll be trouble later. I'm tired, and frustrated too. There's no better solution, but even as I make the order I am almost certain it is not going to work. And there's the rest of the list to get through.

By the time I leave it's late into a warm, yellow afternoon. I'm the last to go out, apart from the usher.

'Good night.'

'Good night, Madam. I'll come out and open the gate for you.'

Of course, the new car-park gate. Even small courts like this have had to put in more security. A man in blue overalls goes by, carrying a tool-case. The usher frowns at his retreating back.

'Suppose to come at 3.30, and didn't get here till a quarter past four.'

'Is that going to keep you late?'

'Well, it will do, Madam. But the work's got to be done.'

He looks round proprietorially. The place will soon be his once more, empty of judges, parties, solicitors, clerical staff, catering staff. I bet he prefers it like that. I can see him walking down the corridors, peering into chambers, his solid, meaty face turning from side to side. He picks up everything, knows who's had a bad day, who's had a good day. The ushers always do.

'I hope it doesn't take too long,' I say. Why am I always trying to placate this man? He moves forward and opens the door for me. I step out and warm air moves over me. A smell of roses drifts by, aching, captivating. I look to the left. On the fence there is a trellis with swags of small cream roses dripping down it. And they are still flowering, breathing out scent into the autumn afternoon. I have never noticed them before. I take half a step towards them, but the usher is standing there behind me, still holding the door, his face blank and observant. I turn to my right, shifting the weight of my briefcase, and walk towards the car.

As I drive out the security gate swings up. I nose the car over the ramp and through the gate I see a man get out of a blue Sierra opposite. I don't recognize him for a second, then I see his face. It's Graham Rossiter. He hurries across the road and bends down to my window.

'Could I have a word with you? Please. It's very important.'

I glance sideways and see the usher frowning, shifting his weight to come forward. I am still in his charge.

'It's all right,' I say to the usher. 'I'll park over the road and have a quick word with Mr Rossiter. You carry on, I'm fine.'

The usher retreats slowly, his heavy black shoes crunching the car-park gravel. I park the car on the other side of the road and get out. Mr Rossiter clears his throat with a dry sharp sound. 'I hope you don't mind,' he says. He is paler than he was this morning. His rough brown hair isn't lying down flat any more. He has loosened his tie, and undone the top button of his shirt. There is something pitiful about his pale, sweaty face, his dry lips. He's only thirty-two, years younger than me.

'The thing is,' he says, 'I know I probably shouldn't be here, but I went back to the flat and it all just kept going through my mind and I knew I had to try and catch you. I mean, I don't know if it's illegal.'

'No,' I say. 'It's not illegal. It doesn't often happen, though. I can't discuss your case with you, I have to tell you that.'

'I know,' he says quickly. 'I know. I didn't expect you'd be able to. It's just that –' He raises his hand again, and flattens his springing hair. There's a wide patch of sweat under his arm. But he smells clean. 'I was back at the flat and I had this delivery. A new bed for Zoe. She said she couldn't sleep properly at the flat because her bed smelled. Well, it was secondhand. I got it from this woman I know at work. It was her daughter's. It didn't smell, but there was no use telling Zoe that once she'd made up her mind.

'After the delivery blokes had gone I took all the plastic wrapping off the new bed. And I was just looking at it, then I suddenly thought, "What's the point? Zoe won't be sleeping in it." It wasn't really like it was me thinking it. It was like I was being told, clear as daylight. *Zoe won't be sleeping in that bed.* It's not going to happen. And that order you made, well I just had to tell you it's not going to make any difference. There's nothing she won't do, to make sure of that. And there's nothing I can do. You know that, don't you?'

He has put one hand on the side of my car. His wrist is shaking as if small shocks are going through it. His voice is dead level.

'I'm sorry,' I say.

'But you do know it, don't you? You do know that it doesn't matter what you do or what you say, or what anybody else does or says. She's just going to keep on and on till they don't even want to see me any more. I know her. Only she won't ever say it. She's too clever for that.'

I reach out. I put my hand on his white shirt, just above his elbow, and squeeze his arm, quickly, then take my hand away. His flesh under the thin material is hot and dry. If he were one of my children I'd say he had a fever. 'I'm sorry,' I say again.

'So that's why I came back. I didn't know what to do. I can't get violent or anything, I'm not that sort of bloke.'

I can still smell the roses. He leans forward, places the palms of both hands against my car, and bows his head. He remains there, quite still. I think of the plastic sheeting from the new bed, slowly expanding in his rubbish bin, like something breathing.

Eighteen

Dear Michael

Maybe you're right. I'm not much of a judge. Just a couple of years ago I saw the old black-and-white footage taken when they bombed the American Embassy in Saigon. Some TV retrospective: yet another look at the roots of the war. And then on through until it hit scenes I was sure I remembered. Not that I'd experienced them, but they'd been part of the blue and white light I'd lived in, newslight, playing over me while I did my homework or drew with my Lakeland pencils. The TV was always on. I was in history, without knowing it. Every night they came on our screen, men jumping out of helicopters, heads down and doubled over as they cleared the whirlwind of rotor-blades. Then the map swallowed them up. All those young American faces under helmets that made them look the same. Even before they'd been in action and got that dazed, bleached look on them, as if the colour had been scooped out. It all happened in black-and-white for me. And something else was always going on at the same time.

But they weren't all the same. They were you and Calvin and all those other boys who are men now, heavy in middle age. Or they lie changed in death and whatever they may have wanted their future stays the same. You can't get away from the dead, and I know you didn't. They're young all the time now, the men

you called 'Sir' because they knew more than you
did. You hoped they knew enough to keep you alive.
They grow younger and younger, as you sag and seam
and grow old.

I wonder if I ever saw you? Maybe I was lying on the
floor doing my homework while the news was on and I
looked up because I was trying to do subtraction in
my head, and I stared straight into your eyes on the
TV screen. But if I'd been asked five minutes later I
wouldn't have been able to tell you what I'd seen.
The television talked to itself, full of troubles.
My mother used to say that if you let yourself worry
about what was going on in the rest of the world,
you'd go mad. You had enough to do worrying about
your own life. She spoke with feeling. The news was a
throwaway kind of truth. Nothing like the truths you
learn for yourself.

I wouldn't have been listening to my mother then.
I wasn't interested in her judgments. I flicked the
button and the channel jumped. One, two, three. The
war in Vietnam, the first moon launch, an
anti-apartheid march. Sometimes the camera went up
so close you could see the spit in their mouths. They
were close but distant, beautifully distant. They
could all be switched off. When it came to something
about war my mother would perch on the side of the
armchair, a lighted cigarette in her mouth, and drag
in smoke with a look on her face that I didn't
understand then, and only partly understand now.
Watchful, wary, faintly mocking. *'There they are,
at it again, just as I thought,'* her look might have
said. *'As if they haven't learned anything.'*

You and my mother would have had plenty to say to
one another, if you'd ever met, Michael. I think you

would have got on. She would have understood you. She would have known what not to say. She was good at being quiet. Good at smoking, too. That was the one thing she wouldn't give up for us.

The usher was there all the time I was talking to Graham Rossiter. I'm sure of it. Watching through one of the windows that give onto the car park. He'll have seen me talking. He'll have noted the way I put my arm around Graham Rossiter's shoulder and walked him back to his car. So much for judicial impartiality, eh, Michael? But I said nothing I shouldn't have said.

You told me things you shouldn't have told me, Michael, and I've never been able to forget them. They went into my mind like dirty water and turned everything dark. You remember that village you went into, on your first tour of duty? Your platoon had information that Vietcong were in there. Trouble was, you couldn't tell them apart, not once they were deep into a village and dressing the same and going out to the fields the same. They all looked about fourteen at first, until you got used to the way they were. The girls were slender and quick moving. In the city they had narrow feet but in the villages their feet were horny and splayed from walking barefoot. But all of them had small feet, compared to western women. You told me that when you first came home the American girls looked gross, with their big tanned thighs and their shorts and their way of laughing with their mouths open that showed all of their white teeth. And their tits bouncing, not like the shallow breasts of Eastern women, that rise and fall under silk.

The village was quiet. You all moved forward like

you'd been trained, but there was nobody there. You looked in one empty hut and then another. They'd all run off where you'd never find them. The frustration of it came up into your throat like a physical thing. It was like trying to grab hold of water. Calvin was there. You told me how he crouched and went forward into the last hut. Then there was a shout from the back of Calvin's throat. Afterwards a cry. He came out pulling a girl, who looked about fourteen as usual. She had a baby in her arms and she was shaking it and its head was flopping about. Even from the distance it looked bad. It had nothing to do with Calvin. It was dead before he went into the hut. Still warm and soft, as soft as it was when you picked it up out of the girl's arms, because Calvin wouldn't touch it. And she let you. She was so far gone that she looked at you as if you might have come with medicine to put it back together again.

She'd suffocated it. Not meaning to, but being left behind somehow and panicking because of the noise of the soldiers, and knowing what that meant. Not knowing you didn't mean her any harm. Not being able to run fast enough, probably. The baby was quite new. It had started crying and she'd been so afraid she hadn't known what to do. That thin cry newborns make, which gets everywhere. She pressed it against her closer and closer. Probably it was her first baby and she didn't know how to stop the crying. Or she tried to put her nipple in its mouth and it was too distressed to suck. It arched back from her and screamed again. And there was the baby in your arms and she was crying and wriggling on the ground as if she would force herself down through the dust into the earth. Her face was streaky with spit and tears. Calvin said, 'And when they come back she'll say we killed the fucking baby.'

And you'd never touched it. In fact you'd never held a newborn baby before that you could remember. But you reached out. The baby was light and limp. However much you cradled it, it hung from your hands. You didn't know what to do with it. Your platoon commander came over and gave orders and the girl was led away. The priority was to get the men out of there. There were Vietcong in the area for sure, or why would the whole village have cleared out like that? It might have been a grenade she was cradling in there. You were just lucky all it was was a dead baby.

You told me, *It was as soft as a little kitten. And you know, Simone, I don't believe I've ever held another baby since then.* You poured out more white wine and drank, staring into darkness where the stars weren't sparkling but just hung there so close they lit the sweat on your skin. I knew you were still feeling the lightness of the baby. Its non-weight. *I don't know why I keep thinking of it*, you said. *The thing about war that you don't expect before you get there is that things keep happening without anyone wanting them or intending them or planning them. There's no shape to it. Afterwards you make a shape and you call it history. You can argue about the shape, but what you can't say is that there never was a shape at all.* Then you said, *I kept thinking of the Bible, Simone. That part that says 'Dust thou art, to dust thou shalt return'. Because that's what the baby was like. It was like the dust over there, warm and silky. And then it spills out*

through your fingers. Not because anybody means it.
Because of carelessness and because it's so easy to
do. The worst things just got done, like that girl
with the baby, not even knowing he was dying.
Because fear makes you stupid, you'll do anything if
you think you're going to die. He had a line of dark
blood coming out of his nostrils. I can still see it
now.

Then we drank the rest of the wine, the whole jug
of it. It was tasting warm and metallic by then, but
it lifted us away from what you were saying. I
stumbled getting up and there was a clink of stone,
but you didn't notice. You didn't want me to say
anything or be anything, only listen while you
poured out all that stuff as if once it was in me it
wouldn't be in you any longer. Or at least, not so
much.

But you were wrong, Michael. Talking made it grow.
It grew in me and it grew in you. My listening to you
didn't help anything.

Maybe you're right, and I'm not a good judge. I
have to do a lot of listening still, but in the end I
have to act. I have to move forward. I have to make
orders even if they aren't going to make any
difference. Some things can't be changed, but I
think what I'm saying to you now is that you have to
go along with the idea you can change them. And maybe
that's all the law is: an idea of how things could
be, and a belief in change.

I get home, park the car and walk round the side of the house.
They're shooting in the garden. An arrow flies past me, then
another.

'Look, Mum!' yells Joe. 'Look what we've made.' He runs

up and shows me the bow. The wood is fresh cut, already darkening at the notches.

'It's holly. Dad showed us how to make them.'

The bows are thick and tough, the strings taut. I forget how Donald can always do things like this, giving them time and getting them right. Matt glances across at me with Joe, then he poises himself, fits an arrow to the string and draws back his bow. There's a target of crayoned red and white circles pasted onto a piece of board. In his haste to show me how well he can shoot, Matt mistimes and yanks too hard on the string. His arrow drops to the ground. He flushes and darkens. A year ago he'd have trampled the bow into the grass; now he picks up the arrow, fits it against the string again, squints alongside, draws and lets go. The arrow rises high, missing the target but cutting the air with a sharp, satisfying hiss.

'Good try,' says Donald. 'Hold the bow level next time, and look straight through at the target. You're coming on.' Matt nods, accepting it.

'Watch me!' shouts Joe. Scarcely looking at it, he lays the arrow to the bow and lets it fly. His coordination is so sweet that I can scarcely bear it for Matt. But for once Matt is relaxed. He shows me the shaping of the bow, the notches cut for the string. I smooth the wood with my finger.

'Dad did it. He said yew would be even better, but holly's OK. It bends right back but it doesn't break.' He looks at Donald then ducks his head down shyly, hiding his pleasure. Donald smiles at me.

'You know those nests in the eaves?' he asks. 'I've found out what they are. I looked them up in the bird book. They're house-martins. They'll come back year after year.'

'Will they?'

'The book says they will. They're colonial.'

'They've colonized us, you mean?'

'That's right. They're supposed to be lucky.'

'Does it say that in the book?'

'I'll show you later. There's a bit from Shakespeare.'

'We're lucky, then.'

I look at the cluster of mud cup nests under the eaves. Back and back, year after year. I wonder how long they've been coming? I love this long, sloping light. The children look as if they have grown out of the ground and don't belong to us at all.

'Come on Matt, have another try.'

I step back. The three of them are caught by the sun. The grass shines as if lit from another world, and their pointed shadows cross it like ladders, meeting and parting. They confer, heads together, as Donald makes a minute adjustment to the depth of a notch with his pocket-knife. Joe bobs, liquid around the solid shapes of his brother and father. Then they all turn to the target, and one by one they shoot.

The boys would go on shooting for ever. But the light's thickening, and I'm hungry.

'I was going to cook us something,' says Donald.

'It doesn't matter. I'll take the boys and get fish-and-chips, when they're ready.'

Donald frowns. 'Isn't that a bit – '

'It's Friday.'

Straightaway I'm thinking of the loan. The thought of money drags too many other ideas after it, and too much anger. I want to yell at him, 'I work like a fool all week and you're telling me I can't even get fish-and-chips for the kids on a Friday night?' But I know that Donald feels just the same.

We walk slowly round to the back door. The light is beautiful, and the air blows over the marshes, warm and sweet.

'Just sometimes, I think I could get used to living here,' says Donald.

'You'll get to know people.'

'I don't want to.'

'I'm going walking in the morning,' I say. 'Early on. I need to walk the week out of me.'

'I'll come with you, if you like.' He doesn't look at me as he says this. The air brushes us softly, and I look up at the house-martins' nests.

'Well, if you wake up,' I say. He knows what that means. His face stiffens, he pushes the door open and the smell of the house surrounds us, still damp even now, before winter comes. My clothes have a tang of damp on them when I shake them out of the wardrobe.

'Could you light a fire?'

'I'm trying to stock up with wood for the winter, Simone. It's not cold yet.'

'No, but it feels cold. Just for tonight.'

I see Donald's hand on the doorframe, as sharply as if I'd just given birth to it. He has beautiful, long, articulated hands. He is never clumsy. I look at his hand and shiver at the thought of it touching me. Everything is too cold in this house. Damp, cold crevices. I try to drive out the smell of mice with disinfectant. The sea rots everything.

'Light the fire.'

'All right.'

'I'll take the boys in a minute. I don't know how they can still shoot in this light. I can't see the target.'

Because from one moment to the next, as I look, the dark comes closer. The dark comes like this, like grandmother's footsteps. It's the end of September, after all. The end of every warm day is threaded with cold. Soon the sea will be warmer than the land, and it will send mist inland which won't clear until midday and will start to creep back at two o'clock. I remember last autumn, the mists and the white pastille of sun that kept appearing and disappearing. I would drive across the marsh with my fog-lamps on, and the windows wound down so I could stick my head out and peer to see the edge of the

166

road. I don't like the fog. Once or twice I'd feel panic bursting in me, putting a distant, ringing sound in my ears and making my heart beat thickly and swallow up my breath. I would make myself breathe slowly. I would make my shoulders drop, and relax the muscles of my face. I would drive on, taking the car forward steadily over the wet rope of road slung over the marsh. Sometimes I was afraid to look in the driving mirror for fear of the square of fog looking back at me. And I know all I'm afraid of is fear. If I took the car out of gear and let it glide to a stop, the fog would be all around me. It would come into my body at every breath. And then I'd open the car door and step out onto the road which would be slicked over with fog, and I'd climb down the bank, jump the ditch and walk off across the spongy ground that sucked at every step. I don't think I'd be afraid then. Maybe I would, when I looked back and realized I couldn't see the ditch, or the road, or my car, but I think I'd just walk on with my hands in my pockets, smelling the salt through the fog and feeling the faint beginning of the breeze off the sea that was going to clear it.

The boys are outside in the dusk. They can still see, though we can't. The electric light has made us blind. They are calling to one another, whooping as they run to pick up their arrows. They are like wild things in their own wild world. I'll call them in a minute. I'll have to call and call before they come in. They'll bump in the doorway, blinking at the light. Their cheeks will be cold and fresh. They'll look at me but they won't see me, only the arrows that dazzle them. All evening the memory of shooting will flood back on them: racing to the target, crouching over it to see just how close they've shot, jumping aside when the other one yells *Out of the way! I'm going to shoot!* Then back with the arrow, running, feet thudding, ready to spin round. Turn, aim, shoot. The arrow vanishes into the dark air, then strikes the board with a dull *puck!* Nearly in the centre. If they could do it one more time, just one more time, one more last time.

I drive back with the boys the six miles from the village to the crossroads where a fish-and-chip van parks for three hours on Friday night. The warm, greasy smell fills the car and the packets rustle in their plastic carrier every time we corner. I drive fast, to get back before the fish-and-chips go cold. It's never the same warmed up in the oven. The car swings and jolts through the dark. The boys sing to the Oasis track that blares from the deck, and we plunge between the hedges which will thin and die away any minute now as we come back onto the marsh.

We draw up outside the house and see that Donald's lit the fire. The lights are switched off and there's a shadow of flames in the windows. The boys shove their way out of the car.

'Matt, you take the fish-and-chips. Don't both grab unless you want it all over the floor.'

The fire burns bright. The boys sit almost in the hearth to unwrap their parcels of fish-and-chips. It's still hot. Joe pulls the batter off his cod and eats it separately.

'Here you are, Mum,' says Matt, handing me his longest chip, and I dip it in a pool of salt. Joe lunges for the salt packet and spills it.

'Quick.' I reach over, take a pinch and throw it over my shoulder, into the fire. The flames burn blue, then yellow again. The soft chips spread a film of grease over my tongue. The van doesn't do good chips, but the cod is perfect: crisp batter, not too thick, and flesh which falls apart in milky, juicy flakes.

'Want some more vinegar, Mum?' Matt souses his own chips again, and holds the vinegar bottle over mine.

'I've had enough. You can have the rest of my chips. Share them out between you, mind.'

Donald eats silently, staring into the flames. Sparks spatter onto the stone hearth and he kicks a log deeper into the nest of fire. The heat is wonderful. My stomach is warm and heavy with food, my skin flushed from the fire. We'll finish this, then we'll go to bed. I don't want the lights back on. The house laps round us, dark and safe as a cave.

Then I feel the window behind me. The glass is bare, naked to the night. My back prickles with cold. I want to turn, but I don't turn.

'Joe, close the curtains.'

He stands up, stumbles, crashes over Matt's feet.

'You stupid bastard, watch where you're going. You've spilled my chips.' Matt grovels in the hearth, picking chips out of the ash.

'Don't talk to your brother like that,' says Donald sharply. 'And don't eat food that's been on the floor. Throw it in the fire.'

Joe hunches over the chips, eating fast and watching his brother.

'OK then,' says Matt, and hurls chips, paper, batter scraps and all into the fire. He stares at his father, daring a response out of him as the greasy paper catches light.

'Don't, Donald. Matt, come and sit by me. Come on.'

I always keep the plumpest, most succulent end of my fish till last. I pull Matt down beside me, keeping my arm tight around him.

'You can share mine. Come on.'

He might twist free of my arm, run upstairs and rage in his room all evening. But for once he doesn't. He doesn't know how to nestle into me any more, the way Joe does with his easy way of getting the love he needs. But he stays, stiff inside the circle of my arm. The best he can do is to stop himself from turning away from what he wants.

'Do you want some fish?'

He shakes his head, lips pressed together. But I think he wants to be here. His want pulls on me.

Here they are, and here I am. *Is this your kingdom, Simone? What you worked so hard to get after you left me?*

And now it's late. They're all asleep; the boys curled in their beds and calm, sleeping their sleep which is just beginning to lose the sweet, grassy smell of early childhood. Even Matt is quiet, and when I looked in on him his face was still, flung open on the pillow, both younger and older than he really is. Donald is sleeping, humped up in the bed as if fending off something he can't forget even through layers of unconsciousness. He cries out, but the words are never distinct enough for me to hear what he's saying. I sit up in bed, holding my knees, and watch him. You can't watch a person sleep without some stir of tenderness; or pity, though there's nothing to pity. Only the state of sleeping. I remember my father when he died, how carved and hard he was. I pushed my finger into him and there was nothing there but resistance. Even when he was angry, I had never before touched him without him yielding. I had touched a pig hung up in the butcher's and felt its solidity. That white, stiff stuff was fat. If you leaned close you could smell its intimate, charnel smell. In me, fat was warm and yellow. I didn't understand that my living flesh could change to that hard white. And then change again, and soften as it began to decay. My father's eyes were shut. I touched his eyeball and it felt hard, too. I was eight years old.

Donald sighs and sleeps. Our house creaks, settling around us for the night. If I knew the house better I would understand every sound. I'd know that each crack meant the heat dropping by a degree as the fire downstairs sank into ash. I'd know how the wind behaved as it hit the mass of the walls, and where it found its way through the window-frames. I'd know where the condensation would collect on a cool autumn morning, and where there'd be ice inside the windows in February. But I don't know any of this. I don't really belong here.

That's not unusual. It's normal these days to live in a house you don't really understand. I knew our London house. That was where I brought the boys back, after each of them was born. I was awake every night, the way you are when you've given birth, bleeding into a wad of sanitary towel between the thighs, leaking milk and skimming the surface of sleep like a flat stone spun out on water. I had the babies in my arms in the green and red shawl I used for them both. I heard them mewing, and then the central heating would light in a whump of flame and I would hear the house shift and sigh as the heat began to move all through it. I knew the blackness of the windows at 2 a.m., and the hiss of tyres on the road outside, and the reassurance of the traffic that was always moving somewhere, off there. Sometimes Donald would climb out of sleep to make me tea and toast. I was hungry all the time. He would carve butter off the pat in the fridge and layer it onto my toast, then spread apricot jam, digging the whole transparent fruit out of the jam-pot for me because he knew I liked it best. He would cut the slices of toast and heap them on a plate. He would watch while I ate and the baby fed.

'Don't get up in the morning. Sleep as long as you can.'

We'd talk for a while then he'd fall silent, and after a while I'd realize that he was asleep. And the baby was sinking into sleep too, his tongue shivering on my nipple one last time. And I'd fall asleep suddenly, like someone walking over a cliff without even seeing the edge.

I remember the grit of dirt on the bathroom floor that I was too tired to sweep; the flakes of paint from the kitchen ceiling that fell into the saucepans when I cooked. I knew what it was like to paint that house, and sand its boards, and bump the boys' pram backwards up the worn stone steps, one by one, the jerk of it pulling the same muscle in the middle of my back each time.

Now this house is floating on sleep. I go to the window,

and stand to one side of it, and draw the curtain very slowly, an inch, then another inch, so that anyone watching from outside won't notice that I am watching back. It's light outside. The moon is riding high where it has sailed out of a curd of cloud. The space around it is bright and will be bright for hours now, because the wind is pushing away the last of the cloud. I look into the shadows which crowd around the walls. More shadows are heaped at the gate, by the low, bent trees and bushes. And then there are the drained fields that lead to the marsh. They are spread out under the moon, but not for clarity. The light makes them into a puzzle of themselves. I keep very still. I can see so far, as far as the rise of the sea-wall. Beyond it there's the sea; maybe I'd guess that, even if I didn't know. The whole landscape wears an air of possessing something beyond itself. Wind moves, and the shadows of branches poke and rummage on the ground, as if they are coming towards the house. The distant barking of a farm dog hammers at the silence.

I think I can see him. Just there by the gatepost, where the darkness is thickest. I think he is standing very still, so that the moon won't catch him and light him as he moves. He's standing still, and looking towards me. He doesn't see me. He sees the house, its windows white with reflected moon. He counts them. He knows how many of us there are.

I have shut all the windows on the ground floor of the house. But maybe, without knowing it, I have left one open.

Blackmail doesn't smash through the clean pane of a life like a stone through a window. It's always an inside job. Somebody in the house has left that little window open, just a snick. But it's enough. The hand reaches up, and the window creaks as cold air streams through the gap. I can see that hand when I shut my eyes before I go sleep. Sometimes it is heavy and alien, the hand of a stranger. But on other nights I feel the fingers move and I know they are my own.

Nineteen

When you are a child there are whole days in which you believe your body could do anything. I suppose that's one reason why people like to dwell on their childhoods. You remember what it was like to wobble your bike over the Tarmac, with your Dad's hand under the saddle, your Dad walking and then running and then suddenly gone. Only later did you guess the moment when he let go and you shot forward out of his touch, and he slowed to watch you, head thrown back, eyes narrowed against your possible fall.

I can just about remember running down the street with my legs pumping and shoes slapping and nothing in the whole world between me and running. No scribble of thought over everything.

The sky is like pearl. This is my time, before the day begins. I don't mind losing sleep to wake early and watch the light grow strong round the edges of the curtains.

Matt used to be ill so much when he was a baby. It always seemed to start after a day when he'd been perfect. His skin like a peeled almond, his eyes flickering with light. He would laugh. He didn't laugh very often, and it was a reluctant, grainy sound, deep in his belly. It made my eyes sting with love. After a while I got to dread that moment when Donald and I would look at each other, wanting to say how beautiful and lovable he was, but not daring. In the middle of the night I'd jerk awake, hearing the rusty scrape in his cry, knowing already before I picked him up that he'd be burning up. Once I'd got him cooler he'd sleep close to me, and I would put my hand behind him to support him in his sleep, and feel the sharp little knuckles of his spine. The first winter was bad. He was ill all the time, and by March he looked like a baby three months younger than he really was. His pelvis showed when we washed him quickly in warm water. We didn't bathe him, in case he lost too much strength and heat. His head looked too big, the way it had been when he was newborn. And although he'd learned to sit up, now he slumped sideways, his eyes filmed over, sunk deep in their sockets. At night he'd fold up his feet and cross them over, as if he was still in the womb, and I'd rock him while we got through the dark together, skipping the surface of sleep. I've never concentrated so hard on anything. My head was empty of everything but the times of his next medicine, the box of wipes, the bile he vomited, the tepid flannel to wipe him down, the water I dipped my finger into, and let him suck.

One night he began to shake. I put the light on and saw that his hands were blue. Even the nails were blue, but the rest of his skin was like wax and he was cold. I screamed out to Donald, but by the time he was properly awake Matt's temperature had roared up again and the blue had gone. When he was getting better we'd lie together in bed in the morning, long after Donald had gone to work. The baby would be asleep, and I'd watch the ceiling and the shadows on it, as if the whole world was floating past me. I was immune. I remember a sky like pearl, and Donald bringing up some letters, and then the drift back into sleep, the baby's temperature lower each time he woke. I didn't get dressed. I brought toast and apples upstairs, and read case law, watching him over the heavy book as he slept and grew stronger. By four o'clock he'd woken properly, looked at me, and smiled. Immune. If someone had lifted off the front of the house it wouldn't have touched that peace.

Donald isn't asleep.

'Simone,' he says, when I begin to slither out of the bed without waking him, as I've done so many times.

'Yes.'

I lean over him. I smell the morning sourness of him that I know as well as the smell of my own body. His flesh is rumpled, his eyes puffed. He blinks into a smile.

'I'll bring you a cup of tea,' I say.

'You're going out on your own, then.'

'You're tired. Why not have a lie-in? The boys will watch TV.'

'Come here.'

He puts up an arm and pulls me down beside him. 'Do you love me?'

My mouth moves stiffly. 'Of course.'

'What does that mean? Why don't you say it? Why don't you say the words?'

'I love you.' I say the words. They are not true as they come out of my mouth, but somewhere they are still true. Whether he knows that or not, his arm draws me closer.

'I'm sorry,' he says.

'There's nothing to be sorry for. We're all right.'

'I don't like to see you – ' Suddenly he rears up on one elbow, bringing a swoosh of tired air from under the bedclothes, and takes my face between his hands. He pushes back my hair. I was naked before, but I don't feel it until now, with my face bare to him. He scans me. 'I can see what it's done to you.'

'What?'

'You work too hard.' He wipes his hand over my face, as if he would wipe away the morning greyness and the lines I know are there.

'I don't work too hard.'

He touches the corner of my mouth. 'I wish you didn't have to.'

'It doesn't matter.'

My mother rises in my mind. I used to be afraid she was going to die too, from exhaustion, those years after Dad died. She was due to have a hysterectomy because of fibroids, but we didn't know that. I remember the way she'd come back from work and peel the potatoes before she took off her coat. The buttons undone, the coat swinging as she bent to reach the potatoes out of the rack. She'd put her fists in the small of her back and lean against them, shutting her eyes. She had a beautiful, slanting, slightly Slavic face: I see that now, though I couldn't then. I hated it when she shut her eyes. I can see her now, dragging sheets out of the twin-tub. We didn't know why it hurt her. We ought to have helped more. She ought to have asked us to help more.

And then one day she slipped down. I thought she'd fallen over, but she hadn't. I came in and she was jammed up between the wall and the twin-tub, her legs sticking straight out in front of her. She had her eyes shut. I was frightened because her closed eyes looked like Dad's eyes when he died. She didn't open them, but she stretched her mouth into a smile and said, *'I'm all right, Simone, just a bit dizzy. Get me a cup of tea and put sugar in it. I missed lunch, that's what's the matter with me.'* She never took sugar.

That's working too hard.

Donald strokes my hair back from my face with strong, steady sweeps of his hand. 'What are you thinking about?'

'My mother.'

'You still miss her, don't you?'

'Mmm.' I haven't cried about Mum for a long time. Once I was asleep and she came to me. Suddenly I opened my eyes and she was there, her outline clear in the darkness. She was standing, watching me. I wanted to say something but I was afraid that if I spoke she would disappear. I pushed myself up very slowly on the pillows, so I could see all of her. She was wearing a blue woollen dress, which curved softly around her hips and thighs. Even in the dark I could tell she was smiling at me. I knew how that dress would feel if I rubbed my face

176

against it, and wrapped my arms around her body. She had that dress when I was four or five. Why could I see the colour of it so clearly, when the room was dark? Not a bright blue, but a soft colour, like sky appearing behind mist.

She stood quite still, not touching the bed, looking at me. It went on for a long time. I felt warm, although the room was cold and I had pushed myself up in bed so the covers fell back from me. I could have watched her for ever, wanting nothing more. At last she said, 'I'm all right, Simone. You don't need to worry about me.'

Then after a while longer I must have looked away. Or maybe I fell asleep. But when I looked back again, at the foot of the bed, she was gone. Donald was lying in the bed beside me. It was strange to see him there, as if I'd found a husband while I was still a child. Then I did fall asleep again, and when I woke I was myself, and I had two children who were already beginning to forget their grandma.

'You're crying.'

I'd never told Donald about it. I didn't think he'd believe me. He'd have believed I thought I'd seen something, but that was different. If I'd had a daughter, maybe I'd have told her, later on when she was grown up. I couldn't tell Jenny. She'd been closer to Mum than me, that was the funny thing. It would have seemed as if I was saying, 'I was the one she loved most. It was me she came to after she died.'

'Don't go yet. Lie back,' says Donald.

He's drawn the curtain a little so the wet grey light falls on us both. I can see pale streaks of rain running past his shoulder. I think of the house-martins' nests, under the eaves, and water dripping onto them, softening them until they peel away and fall on the ground in clots of mud. But I know the birds build more carefully than that. They know which way the wind blows, and how the rain comes in, and they leave their dry nests to wait for them from season to season. It's our house of stone and wood that will crumble, while they come back to their nests year after year.

I think of my mother with her hand in the small of her back, planning for the days when she would have to be in hospital because of her operation. Planning every meal we were going to eat. She left nothing to chance. I can see her so closely, her fine dark hair slipping forward over her ears, her pale skin with the groove between nose and mouth. She had a face that could look dull and worn, then suddenly so alive that she could have been any age, as young as me and Jenny. She loved it when we talked to her about things at school: the day Bridget Connolly came in wearing false eyelashes, Lucy Rydal who fainted when she got her mock O-level results, a girl called Aileen who couldn't act but was playing Richard III through brute force of personality. But often we wouldn't tell her things. We wanted to keep them to ourselves.

Donald knows how to touch me. Already last night and the day to come are sliding out of my mind. His breathing changes, he moves forward, shifting his weight and putting his knee between mine so my legs part. There's a moment when I nearly turn and roll away from him. But he won't be left. He breathes in my face, sour but familiar. I'd forgotten how soft the skin is on his shoulders, and how it makes me want to dig my hands into his flesh and see how much he can take without flinching. He didn't flinch when the boys were born. The blood and mucus and the strange white grease on their new bodies didn't seem to shake him at all. Later he said that it had shaken him. I'd gone so far away from him. He'd thought it would make us closer, being together while our baby was born.

'I could have been anyone.'

Now he lifts me up and cradles me. I say nothing, and shut my eyes. In that moment I believe that he can still take it all away, and make it not happen. I want it to go on for ever, the rain and myself expanding like a dry thing thrown in water. A bit of old dry seaweed. I laugh against Donald's shoulder.

'Why are you laughing?'

'I'm thinking how old I'm getting.'

He squeezes me tight. 'You're not old. Listen, I'm going to buy you something beautiful.'

'Don't say that.' The thought of the loan crawls across my skin and I want to push him away. Make him learn what the truth is. But that smile, that innocent, lighted little smile I haven't seen for so long.

'I want to.'

He's inside me now, his eyes shut again, his face blank and blind with concentration. I think of where I'm going, down by the sea, where the grey water's always turning things over and over. I think of the way the sea falls down sheer from the edge of the Continental Shelf, miles deep. A stone would drop through it, shining at first in the light from the surface, then falling slowly through the thick darkness, past fish and whales and the shaggy monsters of the deep. I want to think of that, not of Donald.

'You're still crying,' said Donald. 'You didn't enjoy it.'

'I'm all right.'

'You should relax more, Simone.'

I sit up in the bed, pushing away the tears that were leaking down the side of my face.

'Why didn't I think of that,' I say.

'I wish you'd tell me – '

'What?'

'Nothing. It doesn't matter.'

'No,' I say, kneeling up, my face six inches from his. I know that he's afraid to ask the questions he should ask, and a scorch of anger calms me. 'It doesn't matter.'

He doesn't want to know anything. He is safe in his own world, and he's taking care not to know anything that would take him out of it. Let me do whatever has to be done. And yet he expects me to lose myself in fucking. How can I let myself go when he could take his hands away from under me at the last minute? But he can't help it. It's his nature. He does know: somewhere in himself he knows everything. Every phone call, every letter. He's holding his breath, too, waiting to know what's going to happen.

'You know who I hated, for years and years?' I asked him. 'My father. Because he just fucked off and left us.'

'He died, Simone.'

'He shouldn't have died. He needn't have died. I can remember it now. Jenny and I were drawing. We had these Lakeland pencils; they were mine really, and we were quarrelling over them. They were spread out all over the floor. I was lying on my stomach, and I looked up where he was standing, with one hand on the mantelpiece and his body bent sideways where it was hurting him. My mother was begging him to ring for the doctor, but he wouldn't. He made himself straighten up, then he took three aspirin and went to bed. My mother sat by the fire with us and looked at Jenny's homework, but she kept going in to see how he was. Every time she went out of the room the draught ran over my back. And by the morning it wasn't hurting so much. He just couldn't wake up properly.'

'It wasn't his fault. He didn't know how serious it was.'

'He could have bloody well guessed. He was so fucking obstinate.'

'Your mother could have phoned the doctor anyway.'

'She couldn't. That wasn't the way things happened. He made the decisions. He earned the money. He was the one who was going to look after us all. The trouble is he didn't realize that when it stops hurting is when things are really bad.'

'I don't suppose he was thinking straight by then.'

'No. Kids at school used to ask about how he died. They'd been told not to, but of course they did anyway. In the corner, at the back of the kitchens, where the steam came out of the ventilators so it was warm, and the dinner ladies couldn't see us. The steam always smelled of stew and boiled cloth. And there'd be a whole crowd of the big girls round me, being nice, asking more and more questions. But I didn't know the answers. I never saw him in hospital. All I remember is the doctor coming to the house, then I suppose an ambulance must have taken him to hospital. We were playing in our bedroom and we didn't come out. Maybe Mum had told us not to come out. There was a lot of bumping. I thought it was Mum moving the furniture round to clean, but it must have been the stretcher going downstairs. I didn't see him after that. But I saw him when he was dead.'

'I know.'

'How do you know? I never told you.'

'Jenny told me. She said your mother asked you both if you'd like to see your father, and she said no, but you said you would. When you came back she asked you what it was like but you wouldn't tell her. You said she should have gone herself if she wanted to know.'

'Did I really say that? What a little cow.'

'That's what she thought. Listen, you're not still going out, are you? It's Saturday morning, you can relax. Don't get up. I'll make you breakfast in bed.'

He pulls on a sweater and goes out to make toast. I lie flat and stare at the window, which only shows the sky from here. Michael's waiting, out there. He needs me. He won't go away. He's out there in the rain, not far away.

Donald brings mugs of tea and a plate of toast. The toast is thin and dark brown, the way I like it. I bite, expecting the greasy slur of margarine against my teeth, and taste butter. The toast is still hot, the butter solid but beginning to melt. It's white, salty butter, the kind I like. He must have gone out and bought it yesterday, thinking that he was thinking of me. But he was thinking of the five thousand pounds he's about to borrow. It will wreck us.

'We'll be all right,' says Donald presently, out of some train of private thought. I look at us both, and the crumpled bed, and then Donald smiles at me. That's when I realize that I don't hope for anything from him any more. I bite into the toast. I look up at him and say, 'We're not going to fail, not any more.'

I know too much about failure. I've had it in my office, the pain and shame of it, and in front of me in chambers. There are people who fight it to the last drop of blood. There are others, and you get to know them, who have made friends with it secretly, behind their own backs. They'll follow failure, and they'll be able to smell it in the air like a disgusting and familiar perfume, even when no one else can smell anything. They will follow it because somewhere in themselves they recognize it, and they want it. Only when the worst has happened and everything has been pulled down around them can they begin to feel safe.

I say they, because I can't bear to say 'we'. I've been stupid. All these weeks of reacting and not thinking. I've let myself be panicked in the direction Michael wanted me to go. He wants to pull me down, and I've let myself run, swerving this way and that until I'm easy meat. But he's not going to do it. Blackmail is a crime, not the basis for a relationship.

You think you know me, Michael. But you don't know me any more. You don't know who I am, what moves me, what I am capable of now that I have two children sleeping in the next room.

'We're fine,' I say to Donald, touching his hand which is exactly the same temperature as my own. He turns his hand over, clasps mine. Our hands hold tight, melting together. I dip my head and kiss his knuckles.

'You don't need to worry,' I tell him.

Twenty

I've got Michael's last letter in the pocket of my waterproof. *I'm here now, here with you . . . Remember I love you. You can't get away from that.* It's the word love that frightens me. It's a stocking full of presents, dumped on the end of your bed while you're asleep. You can pinch it and feel the crackle but you never know what's inside. The letter slides down inside my pocket, against my thigh. *You can't get away from that.*

The fields and marsh are misted with rain. It's fine rain, but it soaks its way into everything. I've put on Donald's waterproof trousers, rolled over at the waist, and my own waterproof jacket. The fields are soggy, as if the marsh is already taking them back, after one night of rain. Autumn's here. I shut my eyes and I can smell it, hurrying in from the west where the weather comes from.

The next stile is a shallow step on this side, but four steps deep on the other, where the level of the field drops. As I put one foot on top and swing the other over, he rises from the shelter where he's been waiting.

'Here I am.'

He holds out a hand, but I don't take it. I grip the wood of the stile, polished by all the hands that have ever gone over it. Then I let go, and jump. I land beside him, jarring myself.

'Here I am,' I say back, as if I've expected him. 'Have you been waiting long?'

'I've been waiting a while.'

He is not dressed for the weather. His jacket is already sodden with rain, and water must be coming through the seams. The weight of it seems to bow him forward, or else it's the cold that has made him hunch over. His hands, that used to be so tanned and supple, are waxen now, and puffy.

'Are you cold?'

'No. Is the weather always this bad here?'

We've fallen into step, going down the field to the sea-wall. Already a fog of rain has swallowed the house.

'It was so hot two years ago that the fields burnt brown and cracked open. Or so they say. It was before we came. I don't think the marsh ever dries up. There's water seeping into it all the time. Where it turns into bog it's not really land at all.'

'That must be farther down the coast. This land's been drained, right?'

'These fields have been drained. But all that – look – that's marsh land.'

'So where's the bog land?'

'I told you, it's just a couple of miles down the coast.'

'Maybe we could walk there.'

'If you like.'

'That ship you were talking about – were you serious, Simone?'

'Of course.'

'I can't believe that no one's dug it out for a museum.'

'This is England, Michael. There are more things under the earth than there are on top of it. And more people too. If we find a few bones we just throw them back in again.'

He laughs. He doesn't seem to feel the rain. His shoes are light trainers, cheap ones with spongy soles. They must be letting in water.

'I didn't think it would rain like this,' he says. I look again at the jacket and trainers. They look as if he doesn't care what he puts on. He's not even thought of protecting himself from the weather. To him this is just a holiday place, so small and cosy that nothing real can happen here. English rain won't soak

184

you to the bone, English seas won't drown you. I remember the way he looked out at the water: *Doesn't seem like the real ocean to me.* He is off his guard. I wonder if he has really been thinking of me all these years, as he says he has. He's lain in my mind, a place like a bruise which I don't visit. I would never have thought of seeking him out.

'It won't take us long to get there, if we walk along the top of the sea-wall,' I say.

We are up on the sea-wall. The rain blows in our faces, lightly, soaking in everywhere.

'We're not going to see a lot if it goes on this way,' says Michael.

'It'll clear.' I take his letter out of my pocket as we walk. I unfold it and hold out the sheet of paper for the rain. At once the letters start to blur and bleed into one another. 'Why did you write this, Michael?'

'It was just a letter.'

'Was it true what you told me, about Calvin dying?'

He looks at me, indignant, affronted. Play-acting, I think. Play-acting. Nothing is as true as Michael tries to make it seem.

'Why would I lie about a thing like that?'

'You might have a reason. Tell me. Were you outside my house last night?'

For a dozen or so paces he keeps on, head down, then he glances sideways at me. 'You know I was.'

'Were you here all night?'

'I slept in your woodshed.'

'You slept in the woodshed?' Next to Donald's wall of wood, the defences he is building against the cold of the coming winter. In Donald's place, the only place where he feels at home here. That was a good choice.

'You shouldn't have done that,' I say.

'Hey, I'm sorry if it upsets you.'

'Don't be sorry, Michael. You haven't come all this way to be sorry.'

This letter is dissolving. It is written on open-pored recycled paper, and now the paper is saturated. It can't take any more. I flag it down hard, and the paper gives along the seams where he has folded it. I do it again and again until his letter is torn into wet ribbons. *Mail smells of people.* But your letter smells of rain now, Michael. *It was a beautiful night.* The words ache in my head.

'Why'd you do that?'

'I didn't want to carry it with me any more.'

The cloud coming in from the sea is the colour of mussel-shells, bringing heavier rain.

'If we hurry we can reach the pill-box before the rain gets too heavy.'

'Pill-box?'

'It doesn't look like anything from here. It's mostly under-ground. They were supposed to knock them down after the war, but no one ever bothered. It'll be dry in there.'

We step out. I lengthen my stride to his in a way I remember from a long time ago, and heat flows through me. I am stronger than I used to be, and I can walk a long way now. This is my country, this rainy country which stretches all around us. More sheets of rain come in from the sea, one after the next like closing curtains. The curtains shiver. Each time you look they are hiding more. He's soaked. Why doesn't he feel it? Why doesn't he wipe away the rain that is trickling down his face as if down a pane of glass?

The pill-box is covered with marram grass and sea holly, sunk into the land. It's a smooth hump, and you can't see the entrance until you go around the back. We get to the steps and peer down, smelling the public toilet smell of raw concrete and urine. I stand aside to let him go down first, and the cloud reaches us, rattling down rain on the surface of my waterproof.

I watch the top of his head, moving, going down. The space is enclosed and the windows are tiny, much too small for anyone to climb through. There's only one way back out once you're down there, and I don't want to be down there with him.

'You coming, Simone?'

'I'm all right up here. My clothes are waterproof.'

I hear him moving around. 'It stinks of piss down here,' he calls up. I know it doesn't. There's a faint tang of urine, almost homely. A few kids from the village might make it out here on a summer night, to drink cider and piss it up against the wall. But in the winter the storms scour the pill-box and fill it up with pebbles, razor shells, seaweed and bits of cork.

The rain pours steadily, parting on the peak of my hood and running down the front of the jacket. To come out he's got to go past me. To find me again he'll have to come up these steps. There is something frightening about the thought of it, a stranger rising from those dark places. I look around quickly, my eyes tracking the driftwood. A defence, a barrier. But there's none, only a worn, white piece like an owl's breastbone. And a heap of wrack speckled with polystyrene. The entrance to the pill-box is scrawled with red paint graffiti. Angry symbols and numbers that mean nothing to me.

'Simone?'

I let him wait a little while. Then I call back, 'I'm still here.'

'Why don't you come in out of the rain? We need to talk.'

'In a little while.'

But I know I won't go in there. I won't talk now. From now on, I'm choosing the territory. I watch the way rain and wind are combing down the marram grass. Out on the sea a ferry hangs, seeming not to move. Below us the shore is cut by a concrete breakwater. They have worked hard to break the power of the waves here, building up the sea-wall, replacing the old wooden breakwater. The sea idles at the foot of the wall, beyond the pale strip of pebbles, biding its time.

I want to swim. The sea will feel warm, coming out of the cold rain. Turn my back on all this, climb down the sea-wall, take off my clothes and wrap them inside the waterproof jacket, then weigh them down with stones.

I step back slowly, so there'll be no sudden change in the light coming through the entrance. I don't want him to have any warning. Just to come up and find me gone. Sometimes the most powerful thing you can do is not be there. It's like silence in court, an unwillingness to be led where your questioner wants to lead you.

There is a paler strip of sky behind the rain. I run along the sea-wall until I get to the rusty metal hoop that marks the steps down, cut into the concrete. I climb down onto the beach, and crunch across the pebbles. I look up at the sky then strip off my clothes quickly, wrap them inside the waterproof jacket and pile stones on top into a cairn. The air is not as cold as I thought it would be, but the stones are sharp under my feet. I start to walk carefully down the steep beach, placing my feet on the roundest stones, wanting to run. The stones slither and a small avalanche of them breaks away. There's just enough wind to turn the waves.

The water is cold, but not too cold. I put one foot forward and the stones kick away and dissolve into nothing. The water is dark. There must be a steep shelf here. I don't even have to wade in. All I have to do is lean forward.

I lean forward. I close my eyes and let go.

Twenty-one

It isn't cold once you start to swim. Once I'm in deep water I breathe out until my lungs are empty of air, then I let myself sink, closing my eyes against the thick salt. I curl tight, wrap my arms around my knees and let myself hang in the water. It's noisy inside the sea, not peaceful at all. When holding my breath begins to hurt, I kick upwards and let myself rise to the surface. As my head bursts through the skin of the sea, I open my eyes. The rainy sky is dazzling, brilliant. I float on my back, sculling with my hands, and the little waves rock me. A drop of rain falls in my eye. I lie low in the water with only my lips and eyes above the surface, breathing quietly.

I should keep swimming, but I don't want to. I don't want to make any effort at all. I'm far enough now, a hundred yards out, beyond a stone's throw, moving quietly with whatever currents there are here. Beyond everything but water. I don't know if I'm cold any longer or warm. It must still be raining, though the sky is white when you look straight up at it like this. White sky and grey water. You should never be afraid. I've been afraid for a long time. The breast of the sea moves easily, as if it's breathing, and I move with it.

After a long time I open my eyes. I've let myself drift quite a way, but the current runs parallel to the shore and I'm not much farther out than I was. Perhaps two hundred yards. Certainly not more than a quarter of a mile. It's hard to tell, across the water. A quarter of a mile isn't far. I can swim a mile; I used to be able to swim a mile. Michael always said if you fell overboard, swim like hell. The boat moves much faster than you think. You've got about five minutes. One minute

189

the boat would be there then a wave would hide it and you'd be left swimming, your hair plastered to you, your clothes pulling you down.

I stop floating and tread water. I can't see far, because of the rise and fall of the swell. The land looks small from this angle, so much less real than the cluck of water in my ears. There's an enormous pale sky behind the sea-wall. When you're walking on land you don't realize that it's just a little strip between sky and sea. Land is like being alive. It slips away when you're not looking. That must be the pill-box, there. And there's someone walking along the sea-wall: Michael, or someone else? Not many people walk here. The figure is moving, I'm sure of it. It must be Michael. He'll be looking for me. He'll think I've walked on while he was sheltering from the rain.

I've been in the water quite a while now. Why do I feel so warm? Warm and sleepy, as if I'm slipping deep into a bed where someone else is already asleep. The heat of another body close to mine. Who'd have thought this grey water had such comfort in it?

Michael's letter opens in my mind.

Do you like getting mail? I like it because it's been touched. Did you just lift up this letter and smell it? I knew it. I know you so well. No, Michael, I didn't lift it up. I didn't want to touch you. I don't want you any more. I want this. The sea; every inch of me entered by it. There's nowhere to hide from it, but I don't want to hide. I can put my head down now, and soon I'll sleep.

But not yet. The word 'sleep' sharpens as I think of the boys. They appear before my eyes, their mouths parted, their eyelids down. Joe sleeps at ease, but Matt twitches and throws out an arm, and cries out. He's fearful, like me. Every day he has to brace himself. He shoves me away as Joe never would, because he's afraid of how much he needs me. It used to squeeze my heart when I waited for Matt to come out of school, and saw him come out alone, head up, and knew he'd had a bad day. Then Joe would burst out of the door in a puppy scuffle of little boys.

'Had a good day?' I'd asked Matt, casually, while Joe yelled his goodbyes.

'Yeah, it was fine.' And then a sudden, bitter punch at Joe behind my back.

When they were babies Matt was the beautiful one. I used to stare at him in the crook of my arm and look at the pearly bubble of spit on his sleeping mouth and wonder what he'd say when he began to speak. I couldn't imagine being separated from him for an hour.

I roll over in the deep water, take a deep breath that lifts me, put down my head and kick out for the rim of land.

'You know what it was I couldn't take in the hospital?' asks Michael.

'No, I don't know.'

'It was the smell. All those guys packed in together like a zoo.'

'You'd think you wouldn't notice it after a while.'

'No. It was always there. You'd shower and an hour later you'd smell it on yourself again. And there's the smell of the drugs. It comes out in your sweat. I used to think if I walked out and went into a bar everyone would know where I'd been. They wouldn't know how they knew it, but they'd move away all the same.'

When Michael catches sight of me in the water he begins to run back along the sea-wall, even though he must have seen I was swimming strongly. He crashes down the bank of pebbles. I am in my depth already, and I stand with the water at my shoulders.

'Jesus. I thought there was a problem there, Simone. What the hell were you doing out there?'

'I'm fine. I'm used to the water.'

But I am tired to death. My knees hurt, and I have to climb

191

the steep bank where it falls away into the water. I turn on my back and scull in until I'm right by the pebbles. They slide away underfoot as I try to stand. The pebble bank is too steep. On a rough day you'd be thrown up against the stones. My legs shake as I come out of the sea. The air touches me and the wet on my skin turns to cold. My feet are numb and slow, blundering for footholds.

'Let me help you.' He holds out a hand but I don't take it. I look up the beach for the cairn of stones where I left my clothes, but I can't see it. My skin runs into gooseflesh, and the wet tangle of hair at my neck sends shivers trickling down my back.

'Where're your clothes?'

'I put them up there somewhere.'

'You want my jacket round you till you find them?'

'It's too wet.'

I clamber slowly up the beach, lugging my legs as if they are separate weights.

'Someone might come,' says Michael. I turn and stare at him.

'*Someone might come?* So what? Someone might see those photographs too, Michael. Isn't that what you want? I thought that was what this was all about.'

I shake my hair back and squeeze the water out of it. The drops run down my shoulders in a domestic way, just as they do after I've washed my hair. It isn't raining any more, and there is the cairn of stones, where I left my clothes. A grey heap that might have been there for a hundred years.

'Aren't you cold?'

'I'll get dressed in a minute. I need to dry off first.'

'You've really changed,' says Michael.

I laugh. 'Michael, this is what having a couple of kids looks like. And being twenty years older.' I know what he's seeing.

'You look OK,' says Michael. 'You look fine.'

I kneel and begin to unpack the cairn of stones. I have my

back to him for the first time. It's not because I trust him. But it's strange to realize that after all this time I can still be naked with him easier than with anyone else I've ever met. It's strange that everything else can change, and that doesn't change. He makes me feel easy. Easier now than then, too, because I'm not trying to please him any more. He is still the man I knew.

A pebble slithers out from under his foot. He is right behind me, but I don't look up. I keep on moving the stones. I know he won't touch me yet. I think how strange it is that another man can have all the qualities Michael's never had, and yet it's Michael I'm easy with, not him. I rummage my clothes out from under the stones. The stones fall on one another with a sharp, quick sound.

'It's pretty quiet around here,' says Michael.

'Yes, it always is. That's why I like it.'

I pick out my jeans, T-shirt, sweater, bra and pants. They've all kept dry inside the waterproofs. My boots are full of little stones. I shake them out and the stones spatter on my thighs, sharper than I expected. I flinch. Michael comes forward. He is kneeling beside me, not close enough to touch. The ground rises a little in front of us, towards the cairn. Michael puts his hands on the stones, flat, palms down. He leans forward, rocking his weight forward. His head sinks down. There is the back of his neck, worn like the rest of his skin with years of tan. I shift a little. Some drops of water run off the ends of my wet hair and onto his skin. They trickle around the side of his neck and disappear.

After a while Michael pushes himself upright. He turns and I see the pupils of his eyes shrink as they meet the light. He must have had his eyes shut. He is too close now for me to see any expression on his face. Only the spread of the lighter iris as the black pupil retreats. He puts out a finger and tracks the silvery stretch marks on my left breast. He runs it around the stiff coldness of my nipple.

'Two kids,' he says.

'You didn't have any children?'

He shakes his head. 'I took care of that,' he says. 'You've got those marks on your belly too.'

'I got really big, with Joe. He weighed nearly ten pounds.'

He is following the marks, where my skin goes into folds. His knuckle grazes my navel and I jump.

'You OK?'

I nod.

'I think skin's the thing that changes most. I can't tan any more, my skin won't take it. It's the drugs. Can you move your knee?'

I move my knee, opening my thighs.

'You want to go in there?' he asks, inclining his head towards the pillbox.

'No. I don't like it. It feels shut in.'

'Me neither.' He didn't say any more about it then, but later on I understood what he was remembering. 'So this is OK?'

'I don't want any more little babies, Michael.'

'That's no problem. I've got something in my pocket.' He feels me stiffen. 'I always carry them, Simone.'

'Well, that's nice.'

'And you've got these little marks on your thighs too. Where'd they come from?'

'I don't know. They just came each time I lost weight after the babies were born.'

'You know, Simone, if I take off this wet stuff I'm afraid you won't like what you see. I'm not like I was. I'm forty-eight years old and I've got a big beer belly.'

'Do you like what *you* see?'

'You know I do.'

He stands up. A shudder of cold passes through him as he kicks off his trainers. He's been in his wet clothes too long.

He is right: he is not the same. He is a heavy man now, the

kind of man you'd find in a diner, eating fast before driving on. He has a blue-collar body that would fool anyone who didn't know him. He has thick shoulders and a belly that spreads over the belt of his jeans. Under the jacket his clothes are drier than I thought they would be. There are stains of wet on the shoulders where the water's come in through the cloth of the jacket, and his jeans are sodden from the thigh down.

He undoes his belt and flies, and pulls off his jeans, then his underpants. He unbuttons his shirt slowly, as if we've got all the time in the world, then tugs his T-shirt up over his head. There is a moment when his head is caught in the cloth and he can't see me. I stare at the place where his heart is, covered with flesh. His body is exposed, his penis thick and erect. Then the T-shirt drops on the pile of clothes and he hunkers down on the uncomfortable stones beside me.

'I'll spread out the clothes so we can lie on them,' I say. 'These stones are too sharp.'

I have never fucked a fat man before. But this fat man was waiting for me, inside the bones of the Michael I used to know. His flesh draws me into it, as if I am entering him too, coming into him at the same time as he comes into me. He is much warmer than I'd thought he'd be. It's the weight: a fat man doesn't get so cold. He smells of last night's beer and smoke, and this morning's sea air.

It's awkward, arranging ourselves between his weight and the pebbles. He folds up his jeans and puts them under my hips, and we have his shirt and mine to pad my shoulder-blades. 'You're pretty thin, Simone. I don't want you to get hurt. That's where you get the pressure.' He is very practical. And then he is right there, his eyes open, pinning me to the moment and what we are doing. His pupils are wide now, as if we're in a dark room. He moves a little sideways to adjust his weight and then he plunges deep into me as if he doesn't know where he is or where I am, as if he might be going anywhere. I remember that he has always done that. I remember how he swam towards me in the dark, in the tight embrace of the sleeping-bag. He breathes the same, his breath rising, catching. That's how it always was. His flesh laps over mine, thick and warm, smelling of motel shower gel. And under the bland lemony scent there's his body smell, that hasn't changed at all.

Afterwards we don't move away from one another for a while. One of his arms lies across me, and the bulk of his left side weighs me down. He turns his head and says, 'You feel a lot different now you've had kids.'

'You're joking. You don't really remember.'

'Sure I do. That's the kind of thing I do remember. You really let me into you this time.'

'There've been two babies going the other way, that's what makes a difference.'

'It's not just that. Hey, you're shivering.'

'I stayed too long in the sea. I'm going to have to get dressed.'

I dress quickly, though I don't want to. I am cold and clumsy and aching, as I struggle into the clothes. I've been much too long in the sea. With a nicety I didn't expect, Michael is burying the condom we've used, under the stones. He doesn't seem bothered by the cold. He lies back, folds his arms behind his head and says, 'You know what it was I couldn't take in the hospital, Simone?'

That's when he talks about the smell of men packed in together, making their lost circuits of the garden among the flowers that someone has planted to cheer them. I can guess what kind of flowers they would be. Too stiff, too bright, without a scent to trouble the senses back to life. The patients would troop back indoors and the smell of the wards would cover them.

'My father wouldn't go into hospital,' I say abruptly. 'That's why he died.' For the first time it occurs to me that my father didn't have a choice either. He didn't choose to leave us. I've been told it so many times, but always I've received it with a sour reticence in my spirit. This time it goes home.

'There's a smell men have,' Michael goes on. 'You don't notice it outside, not even when you're jammed up together in the subway. Because when you're inside all you've got is your smell and your shit. You're a piece of meat. Sometimes you believe you can smell yourself rotting.'

And there's his body, stretched out on the stones. The same body that went through those years, and somewhere in there the body I knew twenty years ago, and recognized as soon as it touched mine. He is right: those are things you don't forget. Michael could make me feel like velvet. He could draw the juice out of me like syrup running down a tree.

He has a ridge of scar on the fleshy ball of his right shoulder. I touch it. 'Was that from smashing up the store?'

He moves his head slightly, sideways. 'That was before. Some kid out of his head on crack. I didn't see he had a knife. He said he thought I was someone else.' He smiles without opening his eyes.

'Are you serious?'

'Sure I'm serious. You know me.'

'That's why I don't know what to believe.'

'I just tell you what I think you want to believe.' He stretches up his arms as if to embrace the sky. 'I like it here. I could really get to like this place.'

'It's not your place, Michael. You've got to go.'

'You don't have a knife there, do you, Simone?'

'A knife?'

'Somewhere down in the pocket of your jeans maybe. Or in your jacket?'

'If I had, you'd have seen it before now.'

'Maybe.'

'Why would I want to hurt you?'

'Don't be a hypocrite, Simone.'

197

'I don't think I'm a hypocrite.'

'You're not a hypocrite when you're fucking, for sure.'

I kneel beside him. 'Listen, Michael. I'm not a game for you to play with. What I am is a woman who's got two children to bring up, a husband without a job, bills to pay and work to do. You don't like it, but it's my life and it's none of your business. I'm not going to let you screw it. I can't see any reason why you'd want to screw it.'

'We want to screw each other, and that's the truth,' says Michael. 'Isn't that the truth? Isn't that the best truth you've heard in a long while?' He looks at me straight, and I think he's entirely serious, then he smiles his teasing, lazy smile. I sit back on my heels. 'Not for me,' I say after a time.

'I really, really liked it with you, Simone. If there's a knife in your pocket, now's the time. I'll die happy.' He shuts his eyes.

'I've told you. I've got nothing.' I hold my empty hands wide. 'Nothing.'

'Then why don't you look in my pocket and see what I've got?'

'What?'

'You heard me.'

'Your jacket pocket?'

'That's the one.'

I turn over his jacket.

'Right pocket.'

My hand digs down, and brings out a packet wrapped in plastic.

'What is it?'

'Those photographs you were talking about. Why don't you take them out and have a look at them?'

'No.'

'Go ahead.'

'No, Michael. There's no sense in it. It's the past, it doesn't mean anything now.'

'Then tear them up.'

'You mean that?'

He watches me through eyes narrowed against the increasing light as I unwrap the plastic and take out the sheaf of photographs. I turn them over so I can only see their white backs, on which Michael has written dates. I never want to see those faces and bodies again. There are too many photographs to tear at once. I take a few and rip them across and across until they are a shiny confetti of bright colours, with the images unrecognizable. I take more, and go on tearing until all the photographs are destroyed, then I clear a patch of beach until I'm down to coarse wet gravel, and dig a hole where the water seeps. I bury the remains of the photographs and pat the sand down over them. Michael watches me all the time.

'You've got copies back at the motel, I suppose,' I say, as I wipe my hands dry against my jeans.

'I checked out of the motel. My bag is at the station.'

'With the rest of the photos in it.'

'No. These were all of them.'

'But you've kept the negatives.'

He rubs his forehead hard with a fist. 'Sure I have the negatives, back in a drawer. Don't you keep your negatives?'

'So I'll never be safe.'

'Simone. Why is it that you believe all the bad things and never believe anything good? What do you want me to do? Hand my whole life over to you to tear up so it'll never get in your way again? I can't do that. That's one thing I finally learned.'

'That's what you want to do to me.'

'You've got it wrong.'

I sit down beside him. The increasing whiteness of the sky suggests that some time the sun may come out. A pair of terns dances over the water. The tide's turned, laying bare a strip of fine shingle where there's a sandpiper looking for food. It's quite warm now.

'You don't bite your nails any more,' says Michael. I glance down, already knowing the smooth, clean crescents at the end of my fingers. It's not reassuring if a lawyer bites her fingernails down to the quick. It's unthinkable in a judge.

'I don't need to,' I answer.

'You used to make the skin bleed. You remember how I tried to stop you? What was that stuff I bought for you in the drugstore?'

'Bitter aloes.'

'Yeah, that was it.'

'We'd better go. I should be home already.'

'I thought you were going to show me that boat.'

'The ship. It's another mile or so down the coast.'

'Let's go now. I really want to see it.'

Of course he wants to see it. I remember the hours he'd spend in the yard, working on that catamaran for nothing, while I bit my nails and brought to mind all those things the magazines used to tell you about how not to lose your man. Michael wants to see a boat, not black ribs and spars sticking out of the bog. They rise and fall to the swell of something that isn't either land or sea. You wouldn't know it was a ship, unless you'd been told. You might think it was the wreck of a house.

That's a lonely place. No pill-box, no graffiti, no steps down to the beach. It's not safe to swim because there's a bank of quicksand that shifts each winter. There's only land petering out into marsh, and the sea-wall rearing up over it, and the pallor of sea meeting the pallor of sky. It's beautiful. A beautiful, naked country. Not a tree, not even a thorn bush. Just cotton grass, and reeds, and bright spongy patches of green where the bog is deepest. And the light moving in wet bright splashes, with nothing to cast a shadow on it. Like the light on naked flesh, the beautiful shivering shadows. I look at Michael. He seems oblivious of me, staring into the sky, his flesh slack, as if there is no life left in it.

Michael pulls on his clothes, rolling the wet jacket into a bundle to carry. Suddenly he stops, and tenses.

'What's that?'

I listen too. 'It's nothing. Only a sheep.'

'Sounds distressed.'

'It might be caught somewhere. Once they're trapped they panic.'

The sheep cries again across the marsh.

'Every year sheep get caught in the marsh, where it turns to bog. They're supposed to be fenced off, but they get through the fencing.'

We listen, but there are no more cries.

'I thought you were a city girl,' says Michael.

'I am. I know this place, that's all. I used to stay a few miles away, in the summers when I was a child.'

'On vacation?'

'Not really. It was a kind of camp my mother found, for the summers, when she had to work after my father died. We used to sleep in old army tents. They didn't do much with us, just let us out all day long. I spent the whole of one summer building a hide out of driftwood.'

'That was why you came back here?'

'No. It was the job.'

'It's a great place for kids.'

'My children don't think so. They want to get back to London.'

My legs ache as I climb the steep concrete steps up the sea-wall. They ache from gripping round Michael's body. I had to spread myself wide to hold him between my thighs. It's the sort of pain you carry with you all day, secretly, like news nobody else has heard.

'See where the wall curves round? That's where it is. You can't see the bog yet.'

'It doesn't look far.'

It doesn't look far, because the air has cleared to a startling clarity that says more bad weather is on the way. That tanker out on the horizon looks as if it could turn and steam into land in minutes. But it's miles out. The green of the marshes has the metallic tinge it gets before rain. We'll have to hurry. More weather's coming, building up quickly, clouds chasing a small pocket of light and warmth.

Twenty-two

'There it is.'

On our left there's the liquid, deceptive spill of the bog, a darker pocket in the surrounding marsh. When I come back here it always looks smaller. It expands in my mind between visits. I start believing in it again, the way I did when I was a city child filling up empty days out on the marshes. We'd have to make our camp-beds by seven-thirty, and tie up the flaps of the big green tents so the air could blow through them all day. Then we lined up for porridge and bread-and-marmalade, which we ate outside, at long tables full of splinters, unless it was raining. After that we lined up again to wash our porridge bowls, dipping them in soapy water, then in clear. We lived outdoors, tucking our bare, scratched legs under us for warmth when the mornings were cool. Sometimes we ate breakfast in a flood of sun, with bees floating high above our tables and the tents throwing shadows so sharp they seemed like cut-outs on the grass. We washed outside too, girls on one side of a canvas screen, boys on the other. The water was so soft that it turned blue at a drip of soap. There was one girl who always took off her vest to wash. We stared at the pink rosettes of her nipples, the white, blue-veined skin that swelled around them. She had red hair. When the sun touched it, it blazed out, extinguishing her.

My father was dead. Each morning I folded up my bread-and-marmalade and put it in the pocket of my shorts. There was a hut where we played table tennis when it rained, and a rough field for football and rounders. None of us knew how to play cricket. There was solitaire and French skipping and a row of battered Bobbsey Twins stories in the corner of the hut.

Nobody ever saw me slip away, except Jenny. Every morning I'd make sure I was seen fetching a bat or ball, choosing a book or taking my turn on the cleaning rota. Then I took the path that led to the sea.

My father was dead and the bog was huge, with room enough in it to swallow the whole world. I would stand on the edge of the sea-wall, looking down at the shivering reeds, the cotton grass, the pink flowers which rattled when the seeds were ripe in the pods. I touched my pocket where I could feel the bread-and-marmalade. I'd eat it corner by corner, making it last. I leaned out, hoping I'd be able to see my face in the surface of the bog. I wanted it to give something back to me.

It was all right when I was alone, but sometimes Jenny followed me, and she didn't like me standing right on the edge. She always thought I was going to fall. She gripped my hand and tugged me back:

'Come away from the edge, Simone! It's dangerous. What are you doing?'

'I'm only looking at the bog.'

'It's not a bog, anyway. It's just part of the marsh. They don't have real bogs here, only in Scotland and Ireland. I asked Mr Hilbert.'

But I knew what it was. It was hard to get away without Jenny, but sometimes I managed it. Nobody else seemed to notice. As long as you came back at meal-times, and ate everything that was given to you, you could do what you wanted. A mouthful of gristly stew equalled an hour of freedom. We had our hair checked for nits once a week, when we had our baths. I never had nits or wet my bed.

I think the concrete edge of the sea-wall was sharper then. Perhaps it had been rebuilt not long before. I think there'd been flooding and the sea defences all along the coast had been repaired. When I stood there in my bare feet I curled my toes over the edge and rocked to and fro with my eyes shut, as far out as I dared. Then back. Rocking myself faster and faster in my own darkness, as if I was in my own womb. If the wind wanted to blow harder, it could take me. Every sound was clear, but I could never tell which direction it was coming from. When I was dizzy I'd open my eyes and the bog would swing towards me, bigger than the sky. And then I'd sit down on the edge of the wall and rub my wrists gently on the raw concrete, over and over, for a long time until there were red grooves in my flesh. No one ever saw them, not even Jenny.

The bog is not so big now. Jenny was right: it's marsh really, but I still can't call it that. It is a smooth, breathing bowl, a soup of water and vegetable slime. I point out the blackened, smooth spars of wood sticking up between tufts of cotton grass.

'Is that it?' asked Michael. 'That's the ship you were talking about?'

He is disappointed. It's dinky, like the English sea, so grey and small. People from big countries run the risk of believing that they're big, too. Big and inviolable. But they can drown in a puddle, just like everybody else.

'Yes,' I say. 'That's the ship. That's all you can see.'

'How do we get down there?'

'You climb down the wall. There are plenty of footholds. You just have to watch out for the barbed wire.'

'Is it bog, right there where you step down?'

'No. That ground's soft, but you won't sink. There, where it's bright green, that's where you have to be careful. It looks solid, but it isn't.'

'It's not so big. How deep is it?'

'I don't know. I don't think anyone's ever been to the bottom. Or if they have, they haven't come back to tell.'

'People have drowned in there, right?'

'That's what they say.'

'Let's go down and take a closer look, since we're here,' says Michael. But I put my hand on his arm.

'Michael, why did you come back?'

'I don't know.'

'You do. It was you who did it. I would never have written to you.'

'I can't tell you.'

There's complete silence between us, with a hundred sounds behind it. The hiss of the wind, a sheep's docile cry, the sea, the tang of metal striking metal somewhere far off. A landscape of sounds, knit together.

After a while he says, quietly, 'Why should you live like this as if I'm nothing?' I wait it out. He goes on. 'People respect you. But you should have stayed with me.'

I don't reply, and he looks out to sea, at the bruise-coloured clouds.

'Doesn't the sun ever shine here?'

'It'll blow away. The weather changes quickly.'

'I don't like to be closed in,' he goes on. 'I can't live with a locked door.'

I watch the sky, vast, loaded with weather, bearing it in from the west.

'The first night I was in the hospital, I heard the ward door shut and the sound it made. Muffled, like all the sounds in there. You know how a fire-door never slams. It squeezes shut like it's taking all the air with it. I didn't even know it was a door closing. I was going crazy. I had a lot of cuts and bruising on my hands and they'd been bandaged. I hit them on the bed-frame so I'd get some feeling out of them. But they'd given me a shot of sedative and I could have broken my hands and not felt it.

'There was a nurse who kept coming by my cot. I could hear him singing out loud even though it was night-time and the ward was quiet. It was one of those songs that works its way into your head and digs in deeper every time you try to pull it out. I couldn't make myself stop listening. Then I got frightened because he went away down the ward and I could still hear him singing, just as clear as if he was sitting on my bed. I breathed and counted and did all the relaxation stuff I knew. There was a clock on the wall and after a long time the hand jumped and I saw that only a minute had gone by. I began to think how many minutes there were in an hour. Then I started to count how many minutes there were until morning. I knew I was going to go crazy. I was too weak to get off the cot so I started to roll side to side, banging my head on the pillow to make it quiet. The nurse came by and he didn't say anything, he just looked at me and made a note on my chart. I wanted to scream out to make him talk to me but I knew if I did they'd take me away. I thought of all those minutes of the night and the minutes of the day to come and more days and more days, a whole long reel of days spinning out with no one able to find the end.'

'What was the song?'

'You don't ask stuff like that. You don't draw attention to yourself in there. Every word you spoke, you found you got a bigger pile of pills to swallow. Even if he'd told me I wouldn't remember now. My memory's fucked. I'm like one of those old guys who can tell you what kind of candy bar they stole from the store seventy years ago, but they don't know their way home.'

We climb down, Michael first and me after him. The spikes of barbed wire have rusted up since I was here last. The sea gets rid of everything so quickly. It just shrugs off wire and concrete with a relish that's almost joyful. I remember the sandbags there used to be, stained and heavy with the stitching split on the seams. Jenny and I wanted to build a house from them, but we couldn't lift them.

It's easy to climb down, and then suddenly the sea disappears, and most of the sky, and we're in the shadow of the wall, on the sucking, marshy ground beside the bog. There's a spar of wood sticking up, temptingly close. *Just reach out and you can touch me.*

'They find bodies in the bog sometimes, hundreds of years old,' I say.

'In here?'

'No, I read about it. They even found food in the stomach of one man. Grains of barley clogged together. I believe they planted them as an experiment and they sprouted. There was the body of a man who'd been hanged, with the noose still around his neck. They made a TV programme about him, and said it was probably a ritual killing. Listen – you know the song.

> *'Lavender's blue, dilly dilly,*
> *Lavender's green,*
> *When you are king, dilly dilly,*
> *I shall be queen,*
>
> *Call up your men, dilly dilly,*
> *Set them to work,*
> *Some to the plough, dilly dilly,*
> *Some to the cart,*
>
> *Some to make hay, dilly dilly,*
> *Some to cut corn,*
> *While you and I, dilly dilly,*
> *Keep ourselves warm.'*

'That's nice. I never heard it before.'

'You must have done. It's very old. They had it on the programme and they said it comes from a matriarchal era when the Queen used to choose a Corn King every year. All year he feasted and slept with the Queen. Then after the harvest he was killed and they spread his blood in the furrows so the crop would grow next year. If they didn't do it, the harvest would fail and everyone would die.'

'Wasn't the Corn King ever smart enough to remember what happened to the other guy the year before?'

'He must have done. He must have known.'

'You'll have to teach me the words.' Michael hums the tune, perfectly.

'You knew it.'

'No. So how come they were able to take the corn out of his stomach after all that time?'

'The bog preserved him. He shrunk a little and he was dark-brown from the peat. He looked like leather. They only found him by accident, when they were cutting peat. There must be plenty more, but they don't often find one.'

'Why would they want to? Let the poor guys stay where they are.'

'I know. It didn't seem right, the way they were filming his body on a slab. It was too close up. But I think they buried him afterwards. I don't believe they put him in a museum.'

'Jesus, in a museum, Simone? You can't be serious. This is a dead body we're talking about.'

'A very old dead body. It's *history*, Michael.'

He laughs and I laugh too. It's strange to think that the people who condemned him to death have disappeared. But you can reconstruct the face of the victim. If victim is the right word, and I don't think it is.

'You couldn't call him a victim, could you? Because he must have known. He could have chosen not to be the King.'

'I don't think you choose about a thing like that.'

He was killed, but he's survived when everyone else he knew has melted into air. I remember the forensic expert who built

209

a model to show how the flesh must have hugged his bones when it was warm and living.

'Were they thrown in the bog after they died?' asks Michael.

'I don't know. And then they found another, or two more, I can't remember. When the food in their stomachs was analysed, it showed they had all eaten the same thing. They must have been fed a ritual meal before the killing.'

'It's hard to believe that. That they would feed them.'

'No, think about it, Michael. People get bacon and waffles and syrup before they're put in the electric chair. I think we still do it nowadays for the same reason they did. It's not a favour, it's a ritual. If you feed someone everything they want for their last meal, then they won't trouble you after they're dead. They won't come back.'

'So what did they get to eat?'

'Grains and berries, and alcohol. The forensic evidence showed that they were killed immediately after eating. But you can't know what really happened. I mean, what they thought was happening.'

'No,' says Michael. 'You can't know that. Once you're out of the situation, you can't judge it. You don't know what the pressures were.'

We are right on the edge of the bog now. A small, cold rain has begun to fall, pocking the surface.

'You say there's a whole ship down there?'

'I think so. The bog pushes it up a bit, then it sucks it back again.'

'Is it safe to go across?'

I glance at him. 'That depends.'

'How d'you mean?'

'On your weight. On how much rain there's been. All kinds of factors. Do you want to try it?'

But he has hold of my arm, gripping it as tightly as Jenny did, thirty years ago. 'I'll go if you go,' he says.

'No, I don't want to.'

His touch prickles at my arm. With Michael you always know there's a body inside the envelope of clothes. He makes you know it. I take calm, slow breaths, and look away, along the empty marshes which are hooded by coming cloud.

'Don't you want to try?' asks Michael.

'No, I don't want to try.'

'OK. Here I go.' Still gripping me, he moves forward, his trainers squelching onto softer ground. 'I better take these off.' He bends down and pulls off the trainers, throws them onto the ground behind us, holding onto me all the while. I stare at his long white naked feet, and the dark hairs sprouting on the soft flesh of his toes. I watch as the feet begin to move. I brace myself.

The bog takes him casually. One minute it is him feeling the bog, the next the bog is feeling him. His foot goes down, astonished, through a surface that suddenly isn't there. He loses balance and jolts forward, pulling me with him. But the instinct to fling out his arms and save himself is stronger than the will to hold me. I step back.

The bog doesn't catch him. He doesn't fall face down. The jerk of my arm brings him backward so he falls on his knees, his hands deep in slime. But not too deep. He struggles out, though the bog pulls at him like a host with a visitor who wants to leave too soon.

'Shit,' he says. 'This stuff's worse than I thought.' He tears off a tuft of grass and scrubs at his hands. I watch a troop of bubbles roll up to the surface of the bog. From deep down, the bog knows something's going on. It sends up a little spasm of regret for what's escaped it, burps a few more bubbles, then settles back to digest what it's already caught. We sit on the damp ground, not touching.

He's fine. There was never any danger. The bog is shallow, like a bad dream that evaporates in daylight. But my clothes are wet with sweat. I look up and the bog is quiet and smooth again. There's even a butterfly on the reeds, its wings blowing about like sweet-papers. It ought to get out of the rain before they are torn and it can't fly any more.

'I'm so hungry,' I say.

'I think I have a chocolate bar in my pocket.'

'Chocolate!'

'Yeah.'

He picks out a half-eaten bar from his inside jacket pocket. The silver paper has melted into the chocolate. He picks this off, gently, dexterously. The chocolate has been soft but now it's hard again. He breaks it in half and offers me my share. Four squares of Cadbury's Dairy Milk. I lick it first, then scrape off a few crumbs with my teeth. The pleasure is so intense that I shut my eyes. I suck and swallow, and the sugar rushes into my blood. And then it's gone. Michael has two pieces left.

'You were really hungry.'

'I'm all right. I swam too far, I got tired.'

'Jesus, I forgot about that. You were swimming so far out I thought you'd never come back. Here, you have this.' And he holds out the rest of his chocolate to me.

'Don't you want it?'

Michael slaps his stomach. 'I may want it, but I surely don't need it the way you do.'

I eat his chocolate, gnawing the fat of it, the sweet calories that are light and heat. Blood warms the ends of my fingers.

'And now we'll go back,' says Michael.

'Back where?'

'Don't you want to go home?' He looks at the bog, the quivering reeds, the flat black skin that looks innocent as water. 'Strange place. Is it really as deep as you told me?'

'What do you think?'

'It's a duckpond.'

And now there's nothing left of what happened or didn't

happen. The spars of wood stick out, exactly as they did, and the rain falls lightly. I think of the body of the ship down there, its ribs arched in the bog like a cradle. I think there was a judgment here once, and an execution. I can't identify the judge or the executioner or the victim. Their faces are like leather, and anyway they're turned from me. But I can watch the gestures they make. They are familiar. I know how the judge withdraws as he gives judgment, making himself all words. Otherwise you couldn't carry on. The executioner looks like any one of the crowd until he steps forward, not importantly but casually, as if this has been agreed for a long time. Between victim and executioner there's always a start of recognition.

The victim stands there carrying his narrowed choice in his hands. A week ago he could have run. If he'd done that he might never have been caught. Perhaps he believed he would be safe, or else he trusted someone he shouldn't have trusted. Or perhaps he didn't, but he assented. He moved towards all this with the glide that we would call sleepwalking, and he might have called belief. A day ago he still had the freedom of twenty-four hours ahead of him. It seems so much when you look back and haven't got it any more. You could have stretched, or yawned, or slept. You could have had all those dreams you never had, packed into less than five seconds.

There's no time left now. An hour ago he ate, and felt the weight of the food descend his gullet in painful swallows, then lie in his belly. He knew he would not be able to digest it, but he had to eat it. His throat feels raw. No sound would come out even if he tried to speak. And he doesn't try to speak. He's beyond panic now, in a place where the trembling of his own legs doesn't disturb him. And that stain of piss on the front of his tunic has nothing to do with him either. The same wind flutters past them all, judge and executioner and condemned man. The same promise of rain or sun in the quiet marsh light. They are all three together in the equality of flesh, needing food and shelter. Then the judge opens his mouth and they begin to separate.

I remember how hard and cold my father felt when I touched him. I went forward to touch him. No. I went forward for him to touch me. For him to put his arms out and hug me. For me to smell the smell of him, and feel his body heat which was always alight, like a steady fire, and be grazed by the stubble on his cheek. But he didn't touch me. He lay there and felled me with a cheek of stone. I didn't move back. I didn't even wince. There was someone in the room with me, watching closely. My mother, maybe. I didn't cry out. I let the blow sink into me silently, and I'm still reeling from it.

Twenty-three

'Yeah, we'd better head back,' says Michael, as if it's already been decided where we're heading.

'You've really checked out of the motel?'

'Like I said, I left my bag at the station.'

'So where are you going now? The airport?'

He shrugs. We've climbed back up the wall and are fastening our jackets against the rain. 'I don't think so.'

'Then where?'

'Back home with you.' But it sounds like a question, not a statement.

'All right. Come back to the house and have breakfast.'

'Do you mean that?'

'I met you on my walk. You got caught in the bog. There was never any danger, but your clothes got wet and dirty, and you're a long way from where you're staying. I asked you back to the house. I thought you could borrow some of Donald's clothes.'

'You don't mean it.'

'You're right. I don't mean it. I can't have you in my house, Michael. I don't know what you'll do. I don't know what you'll say.'

'If you listen, I'll tell you.'

'Michael –'

'Please, Simone. Listen.' He turns to me. His hands, lightly clenched, stretch towards me as if they hold something which he is going to offer to me. 'Let's stop all this. Come back home with me, back to Annassett. You know it. I know you can still shut your eyes and see it. It's so beautiful. I'm not asking you to go somewhere you'll be a stranger. A place like Annassett doesn't change. You'll be at home there. How many people have something that's always been waiting for them? There isn't a day that I haven't thought of you there.'

'That's impossible,' I answer him in the kind of whisper I find on my lips in churches. 'That can't be true.'

'It's true. Listen, Simone, next month there'll be the fall colours and I'll take you up to Vermont again. We'll go to the apple orchards. You liked that, you remember? We'll take the boat out and fish before the storms come. You won't need to worry about a thing. I don't make a lot but we'll get by. I'll always have plenty of work. The summer people will be gone. That's when we have our summer. We'll go walking in the woods. One of those still days when the leaves are so thick on the ground they fly up every step you take. Yellow and red and all the burnt colours you can think of. And you still smell the ocean, even when you're deep in among the trees. You know there are Indian walls up in those woods? They find bones, when they're clearing. The guy who keeps the store now, you won't know him, he's new since your time. He reckons there was an Indian burial ground up there. It's all covered over now. I'll show you.

'The season's wound down, it's all quiet. You don't know what the place looks like in the winter, with the snow. It's so beautiful. That's the time I like it best, when the roads get bad and the whole town fills up with snow, so deep it takes you till noon to dig yourself out. You don't get strangers coming then. When the pond freezes up everybody skates there, and they put lanterns in the trees at night.

'You stay on late after everybody else has gone and there aren't lanterns any more, only stars and the moon. Big hard stars that give plenty of light. When you listen all you hear is the hiss of your own skates going round. You don't feel the cold. You'll be sitting on the edge of the pond, lacing up your skates, and I'll be turning circles on the ice and waiting for you. All I'll see of you is the cloud of your breath but I'll know where you are. I always know where you are, wherever I go. You're here in me, Simone. You're the best part of me now. All those letters I wrote to you from the hospital. I know you never got them. I tore them up, every one, because I was ashamed for you to get mail from that place.

'It won't be like that any more, Simone. All those bad times are finished now. You won't have to be afraid of anything.

'You're going to love the woods in winter. When the leaves come off the dogwoods the stems turn red, so red you'd think someone just came along and stained them that colour. Red as rubies. And when it freezes you hear those stems rattling in the wind like they were talking to one another. And the ice on the pond creaks before it bears your weight. Well you know, Simone, sometimes you could almost believe if you stood there long enough you'd begin to figure out all those sounds and understand what they were saying to one another. You know where I mean. The pond at Silvermine, where I took you to fish for bass.

'The winter goes by really quickly. There's plenty of work, getting the boats ready for the next season. I'm in the yard most days, but you can do what you want. Or you can work with me. People come by in the evenings. Maybe we'll do some travelling. Get in the van and go down South.'

'Michael –'

'You know, Simone, I always had this picture of you, right from the day you left. You remember the way you used to put those flowers on the table? Black-eyed Susans or daisies or whatever. It used to kill me the way you did that, with the place full of cigarette butts and beer cans and grass. When I walked back to the cabin I'd see those flowers in the jar by the window. You were always changing the water, and you'd cut the stems back because you said it made them live longer, you remember that? You wouldn't have a dead flower in the house.'

'I don't think so much about flowers now, Michael. I have two children.'

'That's no problem. That's fine. The boys can come too. It'll be a great life for them there. I'll build them a room. Hey, I could build them a boat.'

This is what he's come for. His face is shining. I never believed a face could really shine, like a candle that had waited a long time in a cold place and then felt the taper touch it and its own flame dip and then stream up into the air. All the flesh on his face is waxen and beautiful. He makes me feel heavy beside him.

'We have wild cherry in the woods in the springtime,' he says. 'You could bring in branches of it. You should see those woods then. You never saw anything so beautiful. Maybe it's even better than the snow. It was the first thing I saw when I came back, the trees lighting up one after the next, as far as I could see. And the twigs black as soot. They always bear the flowers towards the top of the tree as if they're pushing them up into the light. Jesus, you could die looking at it. But I didn't touch any of it. I didn't feel like I was entitled to do that.

'Simone, I can't believe this is really me, talking to you after all this time. Do you know what I mean? Do you feel the same? It feels like everything's rolling on top of me. Jesus, Simone.'

His hands hang down at his sides, and his eyes are wet. His face is transfigured by something I can't see. And I know that when the moment passes it will roll away and sorrow will step back into its old home. It has emptied him away. It's been emptying him for years. The war started it, and even by the time I met him he must have known he was never going to get himself back again. God knows what the years were like that led to hospital.

And for the first time I really see how big he is, how his

218

hands hang down and how strong he is. He's talking about a dream he's built for himself over long years when he counted the minutes, the hours and then the days. And you can't argue with people's dreams.

'I bought you a ticket,' he says.

'You bought me a ticket?'

'It's right here in my pocket.'

He reaches into his inside jacket pocket and brings out a cardboard airline wallet, flips out the tickets and plants his finger on one, then the other.

'See here. This is mine, this one here is yours. It's an open ticket, so you can use it any time.'

'You shouldn't have done that, Michael.'

'What do you mean?' he asks, fast, his face clenching.

'I mean – it's expensive. Those tickets cost a lot of money.'

'That's O K,' he says, relaxing. 'I have money. I know I don't look it, but I have money. Besides, what else would I want to spend it on?'

'Oh Michael.'

A flurry of rain spatters the tickets. 'Put them away quick, they'll be spoilt.' And he does. He puts his future, and mine, back into his inside pocket.

'We've got to move on, Michael. We can't stay here.'

'Then you'll come?'

The bliss has burned away. He can't see the white cherries any more, or the pond with one figure endlessly turning on the ice in a smoke of breath. There's still an afterlight of hope in his face, but I don't know how much he really believes in it. My eyes sting as they do when my son comes out of school bracing his thin shoulders against the disappointments of the day that's past. I can hardly bear them for him. I have to stand back because I am not the one who can comfort him. I'm not the one who can comfort Michael. I'm the past into which he's pouring everything, hoping that it'll stand up and walk.

But he has caught me too. Shut my eyes and I'll see them as he sees them. Flowers at the window, and ruby-red stems of dogwood against falling snow. The music of masts in the harbour, the weight of the Atlantic rolling grey.

'You can watch the whales passing, in winter,' says Michael. 'If you go up to the Point, some days in winter you'll see them for sure.'

I watch them now. Michael could always do that. The grey sleek backs travelling so low in the water that you would think it was the turn of the Atlantic rollers fooling your eyes. Until the whales blew. They showed us their backs above the water and then they went on out of sight into a life we can't touch. We can kill them but we can't touch that life. And the older I get the farther it flows away, until I'm not even listening for it any more.

Michael still stands on the Point to watch the waves becoming whales. I still cut back the stems on flowers. Donald bought me a bunch of anemones in spring, the first flowers he'd given me since we came here. They were blood-red, and purple, with black soot spilling off their stamens onto the table. They opened wide, like paper hearts, yawning their colour.

Michael stands, with his face fading and his hands hanging down.

On the seaward side, just here, the edge of the wall is sharp. It looks as if it was finished yesterday. And then there's the long drop to the beach. You mustn't swim from here because of the sandbanks and the tides.

'Michael,' I say, 'we must go back.' I touch his hand. He starts slightly, like a sleeper coming awake.

'OK,' he says.

He pulls up his hood, hunches into it and begins to walk. He's too close to me, and because I'm on the seaward side that means I'm walking right at the edge of the wall. I don't think he means to crowd me, but I don't like it. The rain has made the top of the wall slippery. I walk a little faster, to get ahead of him and put more space between me and the edge of the wall. He lengthens his stride and keeps alongside me.

'Michael.'

He turns his face to me. The life of his eyes has sunk right back now, into the place where prisoners hide their thoughts. His lips move. He looks as if he's counting.

'It's all right, Michael. We'll get back easily. It's not too far.'

It's raining hard again, and the rain cuts straight into our faces now we've turned back to the west. The top of the wall is slick with water. I struggle forward, my feet so heavy they seem scarcely to move. The air has turned sticky as nightmare. We will never get home. We're off the path and I'm still right on the edge, but by now we're past the sandbanks so it feels a little safer. There's a pebble beach underneath us again, and the beginning of breakwaters. The wind's starting to lift the sea, chopping it into short, uneasy waves. I wouldn't want to swim in it now.

And then suddenly Michael's much too close, bulking on my right side.

'Michael.' I don't know if he even touches me but one of my feet slips. I lurch and grab out and there is a long second where I hear myself whisper, not cry out his name: *'Michael.'* My breath catches, the concrete edge rocks under my feet, sea and sky juggle round me.

'Michael!'

I catch at him. He catches me. I feel him slip too but as his body jolts he pulls me in, across the front of his body, and I fall onto the sea-wall.

He is behind me and I don't see him fall. I am on my knees on the sea-wall, clutching the concrete. I hear a grunt, a thud.

Muffled sound. A room with the air squeezed out. I look round and there is nothing behind me but air. I look down and there are my fingers in front of me, gripping tight onto nothing.

Twenty-four

Michael lies on his back, on the beach at the bottom of the wall, looking up at me. He does not look away. I see the pebbles under his head, and the splay of his legs, and the way his head has been flung back. A gull peels out of a circling crowd, lights onto the beach and begins to walk towards him. I flap my arms and scream out and the gull flaps its wings back derisively, climbs up into the air, and hangs there, its eye on Michael. The nearest steps are about two hundred yards down the wall. I begin to run.

There is very little blood. I can see where he struck the side of his head against the wall, as he fell. I lift his head cautiously, and feel under his hair. It is wet and warm with blood. More blood seeps down onto the pebbles, but it doesn't fall fast. His head flops back.

Michael's eyes are open and now they are pale as clouds. They don't see me and they've got nothing to do with where we are any more. There is a thread of blood coming out of his right ear. Slow, seeping. He is absent and he doesn't feel it. There's no impulse in me to wipe it away.

I kneel down and put my face against his. It is warm, but it's not his warmth any more, only borrowed time. I am afraid of the time to come when his flesh will fight me off, hard as stone. I put my hand on the side of his neck, then I place my fingers on his wrist to hear the tick of nothing. No time passes. He needn't be frightened of the minute hand now. Then I sit back on my heels. The rain falls steadily on Michael's face, on his forehead where the hair is already wet, and onto his open eyes. It makes runnels as if the face is a pane of a substance I

223

have never seen before. I've never seen a dead face like this, accepting the rain on it without a quiver.

I unzip his jacket, and reach into his inside pocket. There is the cardboard ticket wallet, with the two tickets in it. He has only just put them back in there. If he could speak he'd say, '*I just put the tickets back in my pocket.*' But he doesn't speak. His lips are full and secret. I take out the tickets, then I feel through the rest of his pockets. There's a black leather wallet with a wad of notes in it, English and American. No credit card. No driving licence or photographs. A bit of paper with a telephone number on it. In another pocket there's a little bottle, an airline miniature of Johnny Walker. I put the tickets and the wallet in my own pocket. The rain falls harder and the song comes back into my mind.

> Some to make hay, dilly dilly,
> Some to cut corn,
> While you and I, dilly dilly,
> Keep ourselves warm.

It's the deepest dream there is. Two people folded away against the world. No matter if the song means death.

At the horizon there's another tanker. It looks rusty, but that's probably the colour of the paint. I hear the sound of Michael planing at a plank of wood, and I smell the pale shavings as they curl and fall. Down in the harbour the masts chink together, lightly. It's autumn. Soon the woods will be full of falling leaves. The life of the trees will sink down into their stems. The sap will thicken, and even if you cut the bark it won't bleed. The dogwoods burn all winter like rubies in the snow. I unscrew the top of the whisky bottle and put its mouth to mine. The taste makes me feel as if I'm about to throw up, but I don't. I've got to have the kick of the whisky in my stomach. I keep swallowing, tiny swallow by swallow until the bottle is empty, then I screw the top back on and put it in my own pocket. The beach swings round me as I lift my head.

I can't leave you lying like this. As soon as I'm gone those gulls will come down and walk up to you, closer and closer. It's won't take them long to realize they don't need to be afraid of you. Being human's a good protection, but it only lasts while you're alive. They'll tear at you. They know death when they see it. I'm afraid they will peck out your eyes. I should shut them but I don't know how. I'm afraid of shutting them and seeing them open again, emptily, not in greeting.

I get my arms under you and heave you over onto your face, using the slope of the beach to help me. As you roll, pain spurts in my back. I am sweating. I smell the stink of myself, sharp. When you are lying flat I pull the jacket off you, then wrap it over the back of your head and wind it around so it protects your face. It still doesn't seem enough. I pick up handfuls of the small pebbles and bury the edges of the jacket so that the birds won't be able to pluck them out with their beaks. I cover the cloth with pebbles, just as you buried the condom deep in the wet gravel. But my hands tremble, remembering your hands.

Twenty-five

My thoughts jump about as if electricity is shooting through them. They're fast and sharp, but they don't seem to join up.

I could go home. Get Donald, tell him what's happened and he'll help me.

I'm not going to do that. Donald will never be able to get it out of his mind. If he knows, this will never be finished. It will play over and over, whatever else we do. I'll see it in Donald's eyes and I won't be able to get away from it. Everywhere we turn we'll jump at the same shadow. And for himself, too, why should he know? He's innocent.

Michael cartwheels before my eyes. I hear a thud, like blasting in a quarry miles away. A dull sound that lifts the air and shakes it. I don't know what it is. His head strikes the concrete. I shut my eyes and he pulls me sideways, safe on top of the wall. He might have kept his balance if he hadn't done that.

I can't leave him here. It's raining hard and no walkers are likely to come down here now, so far off the coast path. If only I could run and scream and bang on someone's door and get them to phone the ambulance, phone the police, and set in motion everything you would do for a stranger. They'd wrap a coat round me and ask me what had happened and I'd tell them.

But here we are, out in the rain. There's no one to come who can take this out of my hands, because Michael is not a stranger. No one is less strange to me than him. I see us in the mirror again. The lipstick on his lips, the mascara I'd stroked onto his eyes. The skin of his newly-shaven cheeks glowing with unearthly cosmetic colour. *The only time a man wears make-up is when he's in his coffin.* You said that. I never realized that undertakers used cosmetics until you said that, and it fascinated me. You talked about the guys you knew who went home stitched into body-bags. But we were too young then to know what being young was. We couldn't believe we'd ever have to learn anything else, about having lines and sagging and finding everything funnier than we'd done when we were young. Like my children, who look at me and Donald, offended, when we roar with laughter at something they think is serious. All that youth, smooth as the skin of a plum. I think of your lost voice spooling out its endless confession in sleep. And in the morning I didn't have the sense to keep quiet.

'I don't want you to understand me, Simone. It's better that you don't.' Well, all right. I'm grown-up now and I've listened to it all. I absolve you. Is that what you wanted?

The boat. You would like the boat. You wouldn't want to be here on the pebbles with the gulls around. Even the rain is the wrong rain. You don't belong here.

You said this sea wasn't like your ocean, but all the seas join on to one another in the end. There aren't lines drawn on the sea like there are on maps. If you set off from here, sailing, you'd come to America. That's the way you have to think of it. It would take a long time, but you'd get home.

The boat is there, under its tarpaulin, and the oars are there too. I could take it out and no one would ever know. It hasn't been touched for months, you can tell that. It's only a little rowing-boat. I can easily handle it. The sea's not rough. But could I lift you? If I drag the boat up on the beach and use the slope as I did to turn you over, I could lift you. The other part would be more difficult. Don't think of that now. Think of it later.

If only I could go back along the shore. Nobody would see me then. But it would take too long, with all the breakwater and the shingle that makes it hard to run. I'll have to go back along the sea-wall then drop down to the beach again, and hope that no one sees me.

It's too risky to run. You can see the top of the sea-wall miles off. You don't know who might be watching, down on the marsh. A bird-watcher in a hide, or a man with the sheep. Or just a child. Even in this rain they'd see me. People remember someone running.

'Michael,' I say, starting to explain. But you seem to be slumping deeper into the pebbles as the minutes pass. I am afraid. I don't know how long it takes for a man's body to stiffen. If you were stiff and hard I'd never be able to move you.

I turn my back on you. I run clumsily along the beach to the steps, then climb to the top of the wall. The whisky is still in me but I wish I had more. It would be better to be drunk. At the top of the wall the wind catches me. It's beginning to blow up now. I put my head down and walk into it, fast, as if my legs are pistons. But I don't run. My heart bangs in my chest and hurts me, but that's just fear and the whisky. *I can do this.*

The Indian bones. I wonder if they bury them again, once they've been unearthed and cleaned and sorted. I wonder if they know the right way of burying them. Better to grind the earth back over them with the earthmovers.

'I left my bag at the station. I checked out of the motel.'

There aren't any photographs in your bag. You promised me that. I see your hands picking up jeans and sweaters and underpants and putting them carefully into the bag, one by one.

I'm running now. It doesn't matter. There's no one here and the rain falls like a blind between me and the country inland. Nobody will see me. My breath is harsh and loud and my feet thump on the wall as if someone's coming after me.

*

The tarpaulin glistens in the rain. It is carefully tied down, and at first I'm too shaky to undo the knots. They baffle my fingers until I'm whimpering with frustration. I make myself stop, put my hands on my knees, take in deep breaths. *This is my little shingle beach where I've swum a hundred times.* All I have to do is take it slowly, then I'll be able to untie the tarpaulin, drag the boat down the beach, and push it out onto the water.

When my hands stop trembling I untie the knots, one by one, and pull the thin cord through the eyelets. Water swooshes off the tarpaulin onto my clothes as I roll it off and fold it as small as I can, dry side inside. It's a small boat, old and in need of varnish, but it looks all right. Not too heavy. Big enough for two. The oars look newer than the boat. But though it's a small boat, it's heavy, and at first I can't get the leverage right to tip it over. It's stuck to the shingle like a snail glued to concrete. I rock it and wrench it and then one side is loose and I heave it up. A burst of daylight hits the inside of the boat as it rolls over and there it is. A crab winces sideways out of the shelter and buries itself back in the wet shingle.

By the edge of the water I tuck the tarpaulin under the seat, then I take off my boots and socks, and roll up my jeans. It's easy to push the boat into the water, but once it's there it rocks so I can't control it, and each time I push it round so it faces outward, the bow is shoved round by the wind. I throw my boots into the bottom of the boat, and wade out, holding the bow, steering it into deeper water. Then I lunge in, using my weight to shove the boat farther out. It's like trying to clamber onto a bike which is already moving. I hit my hip on the seat as I fall into the boat. But it's veering round already, trying to lodge itself back on the beach. I push off with an oar again, then quickly fit the oars into the rowlocks and pull. The first time I scoop too deep. The boat rocks violently but doesn't move. With the next stroke I get it, and the boat hits out over the choppy waves that are crowding back to shore. I dig the blades back in, again, again. I'm pulling away, fifteen feet from the shore and out of the turbulence of broken waves snatching at the pebble-bank.

My back hurts from where I lifted you. I don't want to be too far out. If I hug the shore now I won't be visible from inland. The sea-wall will hide me. Later on, though, I'll have to row out.

Lucky I'm rowing east. The wind is with me, blowing me on. The boat is light, too, and easy to handle. And I'm getting into a rhythm, bending to the oars, making a long, smooth cut through the water, heading out to clear the breakwaters. The sea is lumpy. If the sea got any heavier I wouldn't be able to manage the boat. *But I can do this.*

Watch the oars. Keep the boat straight. Don't look at the shore. There's no need yet.

I nearly row right past you. Maybe I'm not thinking properly, though everything looks so clear. Time keeps jumping. And there you are, just as I left you. From the sea your body could be anything. A sack someone's left there. But the gulls are still whipping round in the air above you.

I don't draw the boat up too far. I run it onto the shingle and drag it up so it can't drift. I search the beach, picking up the biggest stones. When I have enough, I take them back to the boat and put them under the seat, next to the tarpaulin. Then I go up the beach and kneel beside you again. I pick away the little stones I used to keep the edges of the jacket tight around your head. And you are there, just as you were before. I think you're paler now. You look more asleep than you did, even though your eyes are still open. I should have closed them. That's what you should do. I am afraid I'm going to damage you. The thought of hurting your dead face makes the whisky come up in my throat. Your eyes are open. I lift your head again and lay the jacket under you, then wrap it tightly around your head. You won't feel the stones now.

I need to lift you a little so I can get my arms through yours and lift you by the armpits enough so I can drag you down the beach. But I can't do it. Your head lolls, wrapped in the jacket. You are not so warm now but your joints still flex. The whisky comes up in my throat again and I turn aside and vomit it onto the pebbles, along with the chocolate you gave me.

There's sweat all over me. I've gone too far to go back now. It's too late to do the other thing and run back along the sea-wall and phone the police and the ambulance. It is much too late for all this to be turned back into an accident.

Do it.

I have to roll you down the beach. I put my hands under your sides and lever and haul until you roll awkwardly, flopping onto your other side. The pebbles crunch underneath you. Then I do it again. *You don't feel it.* I wipe the sweat off my face, kneel, lift, and you roll. Now you are by the boat, raised on the bank of shingle. I left the boat half in the water, half out, but the tide is rising fast and a wave rushes beyond the boat and slaps at you. I manhandle one leg over the side, then the other. Your torso hangs as I grapple to support it. And then you are in, just as the tide lifts and swings the boat. I stand in swirling water and the side of the boat thuds against my legs. For a second it rides above me, then I get my hands on the side, push down and scramble over the side. One of my bare feet touches your bare hand. You have pitched forward, doubled over and face-down in the water that slops in the bottom of the boat.

I can't row without touching you. I grab at the oars and steady the boat, then pull hard. Each time I pull on the oars my thigh rubs against your shoulder. Your weight is over one side, but I can balance it. I ship the oars, then unfold the tarpaulin and cover you, tucking you in. The boat swings round, out of control and low in the water. I sit down again, and begin to row outwards, facing the land and the sea-wall. The waves hit the boat, shock after shock. More water slops over the side. I lick my lips and they taste of salt.

Do it. Don't get frightened now. I'm in too deep. The sea isn't really rough. It's just choppy. And the rain's easing again. I can see the length of the sea-wall, just as I could when I was swimming. I blink and something seems to duck down on the wall. A figure. I blink again and there's nothing. Only the empty wall, the white-grey sky, the grey-green waves and the gulls which glide a hundred yards on one flick of their wings. They make wider and wider circles and I think they are keeping me in their sights.

The boat wallows on. Once I have to stop rowing and scoop up the water that is sliding about round my feet and throw it back into the sea. I am four hundred yards out, six hundred, half a mile. More. It's hard to tell distance over the water. The shore still looks much too close but the waves are getting bigger, and I'm afraid they'll swamp me once I get beyond the protection of land. But I keep on rowing anyway, shifting my hands to ease the pressure which burns my palms. I've got to row fast. I look at your foot where the tarpaulin has come loose. I ought to stop and tuck it back. Your face is down in the water at the bottom of the boat, but I can't see it because the jacket is tied tight. You would be drowned by now, in that water, if you'd been still alive. You would be dead twice over. I've never understood why killers keep on striking the bodies of their victims long after they're dead. But now I understand it. Once they're dead, that's not enough. You want them to be dead and gone too, but they won't go. I don't want you to go. I just want you to smile at me in the mirror and crack the perfect surface of the red I've painted onto you.

'Michael,' I say, 'Michael. Listen.' I stop rowing, and pull the oars up out of the water. The boat twists and then shudders as it takes the waves broadside. 'Michael.' I sit forward, and pull away the tarpaulin, then untie the jacket from around your head. Your face has gone dark, as if a stain has seeped into it. Each time the boat rocks, water bubbles round your nostrils.

One of those still days when the leaves are so thick on the ground they fly up every step you take. Yellow and red and all the burnt colours you can think of. And you still smell the ocean, even when you're deep in among the trees. You know there are Indian walls up in those woods? They still find bones, when they're clearing. The guy who keeps the store now, you won't know him, he's new since your time. He reckons there was an Indian burial ground up there. It's all covered over now. I'll show you.

Twenty-six

I lift your hand. It is cold, but your wrist still bends. I have to move you now. I brace myself against the pitching of the boat, and struggle to get your jacket back onto you, but it's impossible. Anyway I wouldn't be able to zip it up, with you lying face down. I reach under the seat for the stones, to cram them into your jeans pockets. But the pressure of your flesh won't make room.

It's late afternoon, slipping into evening. The kids are out of the water and changing under the supervision of Jim and MaryBeth. I have the next two hours off, until camp-fire. I have just finished slathering insect-repellent cream onto my arms and legs. The pool is blue and still, the diving boards empty. The paving stones around the pool are already dry. You'd think the long day of splashing and screams had never happened. The grass behind me is full of crickets.

Everything is bigger, sharper, more violent than I am used to. There is poison ivy in the woods, and snakes. A plague of caterpillars has eaten into a belt of trees behind the poolhouse so that their leaves are lace. Last night when we were driving, the car hit a skunk and its stink poured in through the air-conditioning. Every morning the sun comes up burning hot. My plane landed after a hurricane and when we came out into the air it was like being slapped with hot wet towels.

The kids I look after are tanned and rich. They have the sheen of a lifetime's steak and vitamins on their skin. I am supposed to be their counsellor, but they know everything there is to know about going to camp. They are nice kids, no problems here. Their teeth are shiny and white and perfect, or else they are still in tractor braces, waiting to become perfect. When I smile I am conscious of the NHS fillings in the back of my mouth. But they like the way I speak. I don't shout at them, so that may be why. The other counsellors bawl them out all the time. In the distance I can hear MaryBeth yelling at someone now, for getting dressed without taking a shower first.

My arms are deliciously warm, stinging a little from the day's sun. I lift my watch-strap to check the deepening of my tan. In a while I'll swim. I'm waiting for Julie, who is bringing some friends over. They have a car, and we're going to go for a ride later and have a beer. I can't believe how strict the bars are about underage drinking here. At home I've been going into pubs since I was thirteen.

The early evening light is as warm and sleek as melted butter. I stretch out on my towel and shut my eyes so the last of the sun can spill onto my face. I raise my arms over my head, and stretch luxuriously. I would never have thought silence could be as solid as a gift. I've changed into a white cotton bikini, now it's evening and the kids are gone. In the day I wear a swimsuit, because I'm teaching a diving group. I think they were surprised the first day to find that I could dive better than any of them, with my pale English body. Swallow dive, plain dive, pike and racing start. These kids know nothing about rainy Saturdays in the public baths, in the stink of chlorine, and coming up from a dive to find someone else's Elastoplast bobbing by your nose.

Shadows cut across me. I feel them without opening my eyes. It's Julie, with three guys and a girl called Anne who is due to start as a counsellor at another camp next week. I squint up at them through the sideways-falling bars of sun. Their tanned legs are huge columns, some smooth, some hairy. They swoop down on me. Anne seizes my left leg, Julie my right. Someone else grabs me from behind as I sit up. They all smell of beer already and they're jostling, fooling around, excited from the crush of riding up here in the car together. I let myself go limp as they lift me and rush me to the edge of the pool, then swing me out. As they let go I twist and the water slams up at me. I go down, down, letting out my breath in the way that makes you sink deep, sculling up water with my hands so I won't rise too soon. I send up a flight of bubbles to the surface.

*

I take off my waterproof, tie the sleeves at the top, pack stones inside the sleeves, tie the wrists. I twist the waterproof around your left leg and tie it, drawing the knot as tight as I can. Then I twist it again. But the tide is strong. What is heavy enough to take you down may not keep you there.

I want you to let out your breath now. I want you to do it, not me.

I kick off from the floor of the pool. I burst through the skin of the water and there you are, looking at me. Not right at the edge of the pool like the others, but standing back, smiling a little. You knew I was OK. I feel your eyes on my breasts as I climb out of the water. I stand at the poolside, gripping the edge with my toes. I poise myself, swing my weight forward and dive. It's a beautiful dive, I know it as my body slices into the water. I come up and turn on my back and float. The sky above me is a rich evening blue, with the white loop of an aeroplane's trail in it, high up. I think how far I am from home and I am completely happy. When I climb out of the pool and sit at the top of the steps squeezing water out of my hair, you are still looking at me. In a minute, I know, you'll walk over to me. But I look down, prolonging the moment before it happens, the best moment, while I squeeze runnels of water onto the pale cream paving-stones.

The boat rocks violently. I'm afraid we will both go over, my feet tangled in yours. If you fall out of a boat you only have about five minutes to catch up. Even in calm weather the boat goes faster than you can swim. You taught me that. I lift your left leg, with the weight on it, and rest it on the side of the boat. I kneel down and brace myself against the floor of the boat, pushing you up. You don't move. I shove and heave. I get hold of an oar and wedge it under you, then lever it down over the seat to lift you. The boat pitches and more water flops over the side. And then you move. It's so slow that at first I

236

don't realize that this is enough. This is going to do it. You've begun to lose your balance and once that happens nothing in the world can put it right. I feel your weight shift at the beginning of your fall. You're going over, but I don't know it, and I'm still grunting and pushing when you slide away like a baby. The boat heaves and I almost fall after you, then it smacks back and rights itself. There's no splash as you go in, sliding face-down on the water, your clothes belling out with trapped air. Then your left leg swings down as the weight of the stones begins to pull. Suddenly you are upright, standing in the water. And I see that the water is gaining, pouring back over you as you go down upright, your head bowed like a man in prayer. I see you quite clearly, first your whole body and a moment later just the top of your head, dark, with your body squat beneath it. Then going down. Then the grain of the water thick like darkness and you are gone.

You squat behind me and hold up the weight of my wet hair. 'Let me help you with that,' you say. I smell beer and cigarette smoke. Your body, your skin, your hair.

Twenty-seven

'You won't be seeing much more of me after the end of the month.' The usher appears from nowhere with such alacrity that I suspect he has been hanging about in the hope of catching me. I've come in early to do some reading; I'm in open court at ten. A wave of fear flashes over me. Does he know something I don't know? What is he trying to tell me? *You're not safe yet, don't think it. A few more weeks and that's your lot.*

But he wouldn't know. He's only the usher. I've got to stop jumping at shadows. He stands in front of me, blocking my way, washing his big, meaty hands one over the other.

'Yes,' he goes on, 'that's it. I've done my time.'

'You mean you're retiring?'

'Retiring on a full pension.'

'Well . . . that's very nice.'

'And I can tell you now, I shall be glad to get out of it. I never thought I'd say that, but then I never thought things would change as much as they have. There's no dignity in it any more. Hurry-scurry, head-down, a mound of paperwork every time someone goes to the toilet, if you'll pardon the expression. And the judges we get aren't what they used to be, present company excepted, of course. No style. Civil servants, the lot of them.' He spits it out, grinning. He's been waiting to say this for a long time, this excessively punctilious servant of the courts.

'No, you used to get some real characters, but that's all been done away with. My mistake was going over to the civil courts. I could have been in the Old Bailey by now if I'd played my cards right and stuck with the criminal.'

'You're moving then, are you, when you retire?' It's alarming how much I want him to say yes. I want him out of the way, in some big anonymous city where I'll never have to think of him again. *He knows too much.* It leaps into my mind. It almost leaps onto my tongue. *Leave me alone. You know too much.* But he doesn't; of course he doesn't. He knows nothing. To him, I am what I appear. A district judge with no style, who probably only got the job because she's a woman. Eating her sandwiches in her chambers. No character to speak of. A sign of the times, and of the way the law's going. He's glad to be getting out of it.

'Oh no, it suits me here. I've got a little place down on the coast, about five miles from Wrerne Bay, I expect you know it.'

'Yes.'

'Beautiful bit of coastline. Takes a bit of getting used to, no good if you're looking for sandy beaches and funfairs. But it grows on you. I go walking miles along the marshes.'

'I know where you mean.'

'And you're what? About six miles the other way?'

'Yes.'

'*You'll* feel the difference, after London. I daresay it came as a bit of a shock at first.'

'No,' I say coolly, 'I know this area well. I used to spend every summer here when I was a child.'

He reassesses me, immediately absorbing this new piece of information into his picture. 'Well, of course,' he says, 'London's no place to bring up children these days, is it?'

I think of the teenage posse, out of their minds on boredom and cider, hanging round the War Memorial in the village on rainy Saturday nights. Too young for the pub, too old for home, their evening building to its climax of throwing up over the pavements.

'We were happy there,' I say, looking him straight in the eye. 'In London.'

'Oh well, it's horses for courses, isn't it?' he says, consigning me where I belong. 'Give me the marshes on a summer's evening any day. Somewhere between nine and ten, when the light's going. There's some places they can't change.'

And there he goes, stick in hand, his big, square body facing the light of the sea and the strange midsummer light that seems to shine out of the marsh. He's got a dog with him. A collie that races ahead with the flag of its tail waving. He lets it run wild on the beach, calling it off fiercely when it unearths a dead crab or –

'No,' he says. 'This month is the last I'll be opening and shutting these doors.'

'I wish you luck.'

He nods, baring his teeth again in that grin which I used to think deferential.

'Likewise,' he says. 'Likewise, I'm sure. Madam.'

I go on past him, my wig box and case heavy in one hand, the bag with my gown and tabs in the other. My heart is knocking in my chest again, too hard. I went to the doctor last week, after nights of lying awake trying to slow it down. I can't be ill. He examined me, and then he said he thought I needed a holiday. Or some relaxation classes. There was a counsellor attached to the surgery now who ran a course of relaxation classes. They'd been a great help to several of his patients.

'That's no good to me,' I said, picking up my bag, 'I can't afford to relax. I've got to keep going.' I smiled, to make it into a joke.

'Well, I can't give you a prescription for that,' he said, smiling too.

Now I put my fists on the windowsill and lean on them, looking out. It is a perfect autumn day, clear and crisp. The sky looks like something you could drink. There's a very faint trail, high up, and the shining point of a plane, going westward.

No sound comes in through the double-glazed window. I find I have raised my hands and spread them on the glass.

I remember once, when I had my own practice and still did some criminal work, I had to go and see a client who'd been remanded in a new high-security wing of the local prison. At the entrance the outer door opened, but not the inner. You stood between inner and outer doors, sealed by glass, a sandwich of flesh held in transparence, while the time switch took effect. I don't know how long I stood there. Thirty seconds perhaps. A guard, watching me. He had the sullen grin on his face some of them get when they see a female solicitor coming in to a prisoner they consider dangerous. *You'd soon find out, if it wasn't for us*, that grin says.

My room is warm and stuffy. I should have done some reading but all I've done is stare out of the window and feel my heart beating steadily, much faster than it ought to beat. I put on my gown, my tabs, arrange my wig, look at my watch. It is ten to ten. For some reason, I find I am thinking of Mr Rossiter. I wonder if he is seeing his children every Sunday between 2 p.m. and 5 p.m. I wonder whether he is still keeping a diary of the times he went to fetch them and found they were ill, or helping at the school fair, or suddenly invited to a birthday party. I think of how he waited for me outside the car-park. I can't remember everything I said. I hope I said the right things.

'All rise,' orders the usher, and I come into court. I bow, they bow, I sit, they sit. I spread out my papers on the desk, shuffling statements. In a moment the clerk will ask me if I'm ready to begin. I'm not ready. I look out at the barristers, the solicitors and their clients behind them, the witnesses. It's a road traffic case.

'Are you ready to begin, Madam?' asks the clerk, and I nod.
'Yes, please.'

The clerks reads out the case of Islett v. Conrad.

Mrs Islett is thirty-four years old, and has two children who attend Cabot Lodge Primary School in Slatter Road. She shares the school run with two friends, each of whom has a child who attends the same school. On this occasion Mrs Islett had four children in her car, one in the front and three in the back. The child in the front was secured by a seatbelt, the children in the back were not, although seatbelts were fitted. Mrs Islett was unaware that the children in the rear were not wearing their seatbelts. According to her statement she had ensured that all the belts were fastened before she started the car.

Mr Conrad is twenty-eight years old, a salesman for Glaston Glazing. On the morning in question he was proceeding along Ellesleigh Road in an easterly direction, at a speed of between 25 and 30 m.p.h. Mrs Islett was stationary at the junction of Ellesleigh Road and Clare Avenue, waiting to turn right. Mr Conrad had precedence. As he came up to the junction he was indicating left. Mrs Islett, assuming that he meant to turn left onto Clare Avenue, checked that the road was clear in the other direction and then pulled out onto Ellesleigh Road. But Mr Conrad did not turn left; instead, he carried straight on and his vehicle struck Mrs Islett's. As a result of the collision eight-year-old Kylie Barrett, a passenger in the rear of Mrs Islett's vehicle, sustained a fractured elbow. Mrs Islett suffered from shock, bruising and minor whiplash. Since the accident she has been unable to drive and is now receiving treatment for depression.

Witness statements confirm that Mr Conrad indicated to turn left. One witness states that he may have also slowed slightly. Whether he slowed or maintained his speed, all three witnesses confirm that he drove straight on, colliding with Mrs Islett's vehicle. They also confirm Mrs Islett's statement that Mr Conrad jumped out of his car after the accident and abused her verbally.

I look at Mrs Islett. She is thin and tense, wearing a smart lime-green suit which drains any remaining scrap of colour from her face. She walks stiffly, staring straight ahead. As she comes forward to give her statement from the witness box she trips, striking her leg on the edge of a wooden bench. She gives a mouse-like shriek of fear and pain. Mr Conrad watches her with his arms folded. His face is impassive. Well-shaven, dark-suited, his shirt electric white. He leans forward to say something to his solicitor, catches my eye, thinks better of it and sits back again.

Mr Conrad gives evidence that he had turned left into Ellesleigh Road from Sheraton Hill, a quarter of a mile back. He did not notice it at the time, but he must have left his indicator on. No, he does not think he slowed down. He was travelling at between twenty-five and thirty miles per hour, too fast to take the sharp corner of Ellesleigh Road and Clare Avenue safely. If he had intended to turn left, he would have slowed down to about ten miles per hour. In answer to cross-examination by Mrs Islett's barrister, he repeats the evidence in his statement. No, there was no question of him changing his mind about turning at the last minute. He gives his evidence well, and doesn't get flurried by the barrister's waiting silence into saying more than he means to say. He makes an effective contrast to Mrs Islett, who sounds as if she can barely remember what happened.

Perhaps she can barely remember what happened. The witnesses remember, and Mr Conrad remembers. He even happened to have glanced at his speedometer just before the crash. Everybody remembers that the children in the rear seat weren't wearing their safety belts.

As the evidence continues I glance behind, onto the public benches. There's a woman who looks like an older, wispier version of Mrs Islett, sitting next to a gingery man who is bolt upright, as if he's waiting outside the headteacher's study. There

243

are two other youngish women. I wonder if these are the mothers whose children Mrs Islett was taking to school?

I think they are. I think that is what this case is all about. Mrs Islett cannot bear the thought of what happened, and what might have happened, to those children in the back of her car, who were not wearing seatbelts and were not her own children. She finds it so unbearable that she has almost managed to blot the accident from her mind, and cannot even retrieve it convincingly when she finds herself in the witness box. Instead of memory, she has depression. But if it can be proved that the accident was Mr Conrad's fault, then she will be able to hold up her head with the other mothers. She will be able to remember.

The picture of the accident emerges slowly through the witness statements and cross-examinations. A woman in a hurry, four children packed into the car, squabbling and shouting. One of the school-run children arriving late at Mrs Islett's house, so that they were in heavy traffic all the way, making them even later. Seatbelts which may have been fastened, as Mrs Islett states, when the car left the drive. Children bobbing and jumping all over the back seat, as attested by another witness in the car travelling behind Mrs Islett. And the same witness states that the driver of the car, whom he identifies as Mrs Islett, turned right round in her seat at a set of traffic lights and shouted at the children. He remembered because he felt sorry for her. All those kids.

Mrs Islett was late for work again, for the third time in the past fortnight. Mrs Islett was heading for a formal warning, which she had been told by her employer she would receive if she were late again.

I listen to Mr Conrad's barrister winding up his case. He's good: a young barrister getting his first cases, and putting them well. There's not a trace of nervousness in him, any more than there is in his client. I put a question to him and he answers with just the right blend of courtesy and firmness. Mr Conrad and Mrs Islett are rungs on a ladder he's going to climb fast.

I look at Mrs Islett. She is very pale now. I think she realizes that the evidence is not going her way. The courtroom is stifling, as it often is just before a judgment. I beckon to the clerk.

'I'm going to retire for a few minutes before giving judgment.'

Back in chambers I put my hand over my chest and press in hard. I walk up and down the room, clearing my mind.

I know Mrs Islett's life. I know it as if it's my own, though she's nothing like me. She has children. And she'd do anything for them. And now look what she's done. A small case, heard by a small judge, and it's going to destroy her. She's the type who will always believe that a judgment given against her means she's been publicly branded as a liar. And why shouldn't she believe that? She'll think that no one will ever trust her again. They've trusted her with their children, and she has failed to protect them. She's let the kids run riot in the back of her car, without their seatbelts. She's pulled out onto a main road without checking the oncoming traffic as she should have done. All the time she'll have quick little pangs of thought running into her like needles. *How can I ever face Kylie Barrett's mother again? He swore at me. He opened the car door and swore at me. He said I was a stupid bitch. He said I shouldn't be on the road if I couldn't look where I was going.*

I want to take her hands and lead her away, in her lime-green suit, and sit her down somewhere and say, 'It's not so bad, what you did.'

Michael was right. I can't do this any more. There's sweat on my forehead so I turn to the mirror to wipe it away. My face looks out at me, strange under its wig. I take off the wig and my face appears as I know it, soft and surprised, the hair springing up where the wig has crushed it. I lean into the mirror and look into my own eyes. I don't know if I'd trust this person, or believe a word she said. I comb my hair, put back the wig. As it settles it turns me into monochrome, black and white. My hands are sweating. Even though the blisters from rowing have faded, they still burn. I ought to wash my hands, but I seem to have been in here a long time already. Probably it's only a few minutes. I didn't look at my watch when I retired. I should have done that. I'm forgetting things.

Once one habit peels away the others follow it. You have to hold on, or the next thing you'll find yourself parading down the street in your nightdress. Habit is everything.

I wouldn't give good odds on Mrs Islett. She looks desperate. She's been clinging to this case, but if she loses she'll let go, and sink down. I remember a client I had, a woman who lost her children after a long dispute over custody. That was in the old days. She held on for a while, living in a bedsit and holding down a job while the kids lived with her former husband and his new wife in the house which had been her home. I know because she came in to see me once. She only wanted to talk to someone. After that I lost sight of her.

Then one day I met her when I was rushing to the baker's at lunchtime. She was sitting on the pavement with her feet in the gutter. She had a bottle of British wine and she was cuddling a sheepskin hot-water-bottle cover. She didn't recognize me, but I'd said hello before I knew it. I wished I hadn't. She remembered who I was, and the remains of her former self came floating up like bubbles from a wreck. And then she started stroking the sheepskin again and her eyes went off somewhere, and I hurried to get the bread. I made sure I came back the other way. That was a woman who had a house on the Glebe estate, a job in Tesco, two children, fitted carpets. She left them all, because she fell in love.

*

I go back into court, and again they rise. Again we go through the little dance which precedes everything in this world. I look at Mrs Islett, and Mr Conrad, and gather the papers together in a pile in front of me. I clear my throat.

The door opens. It's the usher, holding the door wide in a pantomime of willing service. Some member of the public coming in when the case is all but over. The law students are the worst.

The usher enters, and the door swings to behind him. But as it swings someone else comes in. I spread my hands on the papers in front of me. I feel myself rise, but I force myself down.

He slips into the public bench and sits there, watching me. It's an open, friendly, curious look, as if he's just waiting to see what I'll do next. I've never seen such a look on Michael's face before. It comes from long before I knew him, when he was a child. Long ago, before he learned to play basketball. He sits heavily and comfortably, his thighs planted broad on the bench. He wears jeans and a short-sleeved shirt. There is no mark on him, no blood. He settles himself as easily as if he has just come in from the next room. He waits. I clear my throat and fumble for the glass of water on my desk. All the faces in court are looking in my direction, but that's normal. It doesn't mean anything. The usher is watching me from the door. His face is intent, as if he's watching his dog with something it's caught. Unease ripples through the courtroom. I see the two barristers glance behind them, then back at me. The clerk leans towards me, confidentially. 'Madam – '

'It's all right.'

He continues to sit there. He is beautiful. I can see beneath the flesh of Michael at forty-eight the shadow of Michael as I first knew him. As if nothing ever goes away. It is just packed somewhere we can't see it. I see the fall of the thick dark hair I used to run over my lips, and the short grey hair that the sea combed upwards as it took him down.

I look at him, feasting my eyes until they hurt. Then I look away, down at the papers. Mrs Islett is waiting. I could divide the blame in half, like a baby, but that would be unjust. This is a trial of evidence.

I can hear the babble of the children in the back seat, and the back of my neck prickles with irritation. They are giggling over some joke no adult could ever share. They tell it over and over again. Their giggles rise to shrieks, they roll and drum their heels on the back of the seat. I pull in and stop the car. I turn and lash them with my anger. Now they are my children, Matt and Joe.

I see their faces shrink as my rage throws them back against their seats. I see their fingers fumble slowly at their seatbelts. These are my children. I would do anything for them. I have done everything for them. *You don't understand,* I say. *I did it for you. It was all for you. I had to protect you.* But they look away. Their hands creep towards one another and hold on tight, as if something about me frightens them. I drive on. When I catch their eyes in the mirror they duck their heads down.

My face is soft, but you have to be hard to get where I am.

I face the court where Michael sits, and I begin to deliver my judgment.

Twenty-eight

I don't believe in ghosts. I could walk through a graveyard at midnight and I wouldn't be afraid. When the children were frightened of the dark I'd take their hands and walk them from room to room without putting on the lights, feeling our way. *Look, there's nothing to be frightened of.* But in the dark I can feel the print you leave on me.

I'm in my house, in the dark. Donald is sleeping, and the children, all sleeping the confident sleep that doesn't come to me any more. Donald says he's going to stop drinking. He says we'll just make a pot of coffee in the evenings. I look at him as if he is mad. He has got the woodshed packed with wood now, enough to last through the whole winter. Matt's teacher has given us a box of apples from her garden, and Matt has wrapped each apple in newspaper and laid them on a shelf which Donald put up in the woodshed. The shed breathes out the scents of wood and apple.

'I feel as if we're starting to belong here,' Donald says.

They sleep their confident sleep. I want to cover them up so the wind doesn't blow on them. But when I reach to hug the boys now they wriggle out of my touch. They run to Donald to show him things, not to me.

I don't know why you stay here. My hands hurt. I hold them up to the light to see if there are still blisters under the surface of the skin, but if there are I can't see them. Why do you stay here?

I think you want my company. You are pulling me towards you and I feel myself going. It's like an arm around my waist, firm and warm. Not ghost-like at all.

Do you remember those Indian bones? You said to me once: 'This whole country is built on Indian bones.' And I said, 'Maybe, but you can't live thinking like that. That's the way the world is.' I'd been in America for two months when I said that. And you said, 'Oh, so that's the way the world is, Simone?' And you smiled in a way I always put down as teasing, mocking; but now I don't think it was. I think you may have loved what embarrassed me in myself. And you saw my hardness, which I didn't dare show to anyone else. Later that day you cooked steak for us. You beat it out on a wooden board, slapping it over when one side was finished. I'd never seen that done before.

'You have to break the fibres to make the meat tender,' you said, as you pounded the meat until the steak spread out flat. You chopped up a bunch of parsley and scattered it over the surface of the meat, then turned it again. You crushed peppercorns and spread them over the steak as well. The pan smoked blue on the fire, and when you tossed the steaks in there was a hiss and a leap of steam. You let the steaks char on one side, then flipped them over. You had two plates ready, but no potatoes, no mushroom or quarter tomatoes. You saw me looking and said, 'You don't need any of that other stuff when the meat's as good as this.'

It was the biggest steak I'd ever eaten, and it covered my whole plate. You poured out some pepper vodka you'd got from Calvin, and I ate the whole steak, a mouthful of the charred, tender flesh, then a mouthful of burning spirit. Afterwards we lay back, gorged and sweating. A bit later you put your hands behind your head and at first I thought you were talking to me, then I realized you were quoting something. A poem or the lyrics of a song, about Buffalo Bill:

Buffalo Bill's
defunct
           who used to
           ride a watersmooth-silver
                          stallion
and break onetwothreefourfive pigeonsjustlikethat
                                    Jesus

he was a handsome man
                      and what i want to know is
how do you like your blueeyed boy
Mister Death

I nearly said that I never knew you liked poetry, but I shut my mouth. Later on I found the poem in an anthology in the town library, and I copied it out. It looked different on the page, and more difficult than it sounded when you said it. When you said it the words flowed out of your mouth as if they were part of you. I never heard you say any other poem, or talk about one either. You'd learned it a long time ago, and kept it with you. You told me that you used to say it over and over when things were bad, like a charm. It was beautiful and insouciant and you understood every cadence, because it was your history.

how do you like your blueeyed boy
Mister Death

The distant barking of a farm dog hammers the silence. I get up noiselessly and go to the window, and look out. I keep very still. I can see a long way, as far as the faint rise of sea-wall. Beyond that there's the sea, moving inwards, feeling into the crevices of the land, bearing all its burdens with it. Wind moves, and the shadows of branches poke and rummage on the ground, as if they are coming towards the house.

I think I can see you. Just there, by the gatepost, where the dark is thickest. You are standing very still, so that the moon won't catch you and light you as you move. You are standing still, and looking towards me. You count the windows, white with reflected moon.

I have shut all the windows on the ground floor of the house. But maybe, without knowing it, I have left one open.